fearless
little
WEREW🐾LF

KATIE SALIDAS

ISBN-13 978-1-7321014-2-5
Cover Art by
https://www.wegotyoucoveredbookdesign.com/

Published by:
Rising Sign Books
http://www.KatieSalidas.com

For more information about my books email:
katiesalidas@gmail.com

Autographed Editions of all Katie Salidas books may be purchased at
www.KatieSalidas.com

Titles by Katie Salidas

Chronicles of the Uprising
Dissension
Complication
Revolution
Transition
Retribution
Annihilation

Little Werewolf
Pretty Little Werewolf
Curious Little Werewolf
Fearless Little Werewolf

Immortalis
Carpe Noctem
Hunters & Prey
Pandora's Box
Soustone
Dark Salvation

Olde Town Pack
Moonlight
Mated

Be sure to stop by KatieSalidas.com and sign up to the
Paranormal Posse Newsletter.
All new subscribers will be sent a FREE ebook.

Autographed Editions of all Katie Salidas books may be
purchased at
www.KatieSalidas.com

1

"Remind me again why I agreed to this." Giselle stared blankly, hardly recognizing her own reflection in the mirror.

The same eyes she'd known for the last seventeen years gazed back at her. Beautiful. Youthful. And notorious for scrutinizing everything. Her curse and the reason she'd been set upon this path. Of that she had no doubt. But in a world where everything hid behind a cloak of deception, allowing herself to blindly accept what lay before her solved nothing. Had she chosen that path, an innocent woman would surely have been put to death. And she'd never have known about her father or the magic that brought her into this world.

Her lips might now be coated in a luxurious shade of plum, but their purpose had not changed – still speaking the truth and unabashedly calling to question anything that did not add up. Truth came with its fair share of turmoil. But that too had wrought good.

Still spunky. Still Giselle. Her reflection revealed no physical alteration, unless you counted the makeup and the sophisticated outfit. That gave her a small out-of-body experience, but nothing physically had changed since the last time she'd taken a good long look at herself. And yet within, the difference was unmistakable.

Could anyone else see it? Or was it now that she was finally witnessing the reflection of what others recognized when they looked at her? A leader. Someone to be proud of. Someone worth looking up to.

The sudden weight on her shoulders that came with the title of Alpha had settled, and she wasn't yet up to the task of bearing that heavy mantle.

Di rolled her eyes and tipped Giselle's head back to apply another quick brush of mascara. "And you call me the drama queen." Clearly unimpressed with her sister's lack of enthusiasm, Di put the tiny brush back into the bottle and spun the chair around, making Giselle face her. "No matter if you act the part or not, I will not have you going out there looking like you just rolled out of bed, Miss Alpha."

"Really? That's what we're doing now?" She wondered how much of Di's attitude was jealousy and how much was pride in how well she'd made sure Giselle was living up to the new honor.

"What? It's your title. You're the new Grand High Muckety Muck."

Giselle snorted. "I prefer Poobah, if you don't mind. Emphasis on the *grand* part."

Di made a show of bowing low with a flourish of her hand. "As you wish, your Grand High Poohbahness." Both girls erupted into giggles as Di recovered from the bow and immediately grabbed a tissue to wipe the tears from the corner of her eye before she could smudge her makeup.

"Well done." Giselle praised her sister with her best impression of a British monarch.

Even with the weight of the world falling on her shoulders, she knew she could count on her sisters to keep the mood light.

Titles had never meant much to someone used to being a lone wolf. *That* she connected with – the simplicity of existing and relying on your instincts and senses; making decisions through cunning and attention to detail, rather than following the order and judgment of others. Those decisions only affected one person. This was basis of how she lived. Down to her very core, she could follow no order if it did not meet with what her heart told her to do. Yet despite that, everyone claimed Giselle had been born to lead a pack.

Especially now that she'd learned of her bloodline and who her father had been, she couldn't deny the blood claim to the title of Alpha. Maybe in a few years' time, she'd grow into it.

But that wasn't in her stars.

"You're dwelling again." Di's tone had toughened, and when Giselle looked up, her sister was brandishing a fresh tube of lipstick. "Stop overthinking this. Try to be happy. Okay?" Before Giselle could answer, Di attacked with a quick swipe of creamy color.

Alpha was more than she had been prepared to handle. After all, she'd only just learned that being a werewolf was okay. Most of her seventeen years had been spent feeling like a lost little girl and a freak of nature. No less than a year after finding a pack, she was to be crowned queen of the freaks, so to speak. Life, at least for her, was moving at breakneck speed, and she'd never had the benefits of training wheels.

"Well, I've done all I can. The rest will be up to you." Di spun Giselle back around to face the mirror. "And you will do fantastic. No more stressing out. It's giving you crow's feet. You were born to this. You will rock this. Now go out there and wow those Silverman boys and make sure they go home and tell everyone in their pack how amazing you're going to be as the next Alpha."

Not usually the one to give pep talks, Di was more brute than inspiration, but her words helped, as did her skill with blush brush. Giselle's makeup was impeccable, a skill she'd never mastered herself. She counted her lucky stars for her two sisters. Thanks to Di and Taylor, she'd never have to worry about leaving the house disheveled. They always had her covered.

"I'm saying goodbye to the guys, not meeting with heads of state, but thanks for the touch up."

"Um, hello? Those *guys*… They're from the big pack up north. I'm not letting my sister and the future Alpha be seen by them looking anything less than stellar! I don't care what you think, boys gossip just as much as girls. You will send them off with a story of your spectacular beauty and smarts."

"You're putting way too much emphasis on this two-second goodbye. Besides… they're my cousins. Family. And they've already seen me at my worst. Remember?"

"Stop downplaying this!" Di huffed.

"You dare order your Alpha around?" Giselle narrowed her eyes playfully.

"You're damn right I do. Especially when she's being a big crybaby. You're an Alpha. You have to look the part. Always! And it's my job to make sure you do. Well, mine and Taylor's, of course, but you're already dressed appropriately, so … hair and makeup are my domain."

Di scrutinized the lines on her face. "Though I need to get you a better foundation. You're losing your summer tan already."

"Okay, that's enough. Let me go down and say my goodbyes before they die of old age waiting on me."

"As if. We wolves live forever," Di retorted. "They can wait."

If she hadn't been in a hurry to get downstairs, she'd have been tempted to ask about that. Rumor had it that wolves lived a long time; some longer than others. And she'd heard the phrase *immortal* thrown around once or twice in passing. Mental note for later: she'd need to learn the truth of that in due course, as well as all things wolf, if she planned on really doing the Alpha thing right. More reasons to stress out. She knew so little as it was.

Giselle stood and waved Di away before she could do any more. "I'm fine. Great work. You can tell me all about foundations later."

"You're welcome." Di put her hands on her hips, glaring at Giselle as if her lack of appreciation for proper makeup application was an insult.

"Thank you." Giselle tried to sound as gracious as she could while scooting out of the bedroom door to avoid another lecture on looking one's best.

Outside her room, the house felt different. She'd taken forever to get ready, no thanks to her sister, but she hadn't expected to anger anyone with her tardiness. But it was there: anger, or perhaps disappointment. The negativity traveled all the way up the stairs to smack her in her perfectly made up face the moment she stepped out into the hall.

Something had to be up. No way was this negative a vibe coming from a couple of teenage guys. Giselle took a peek over the stair rail before heading down, and spotted the solemn faces of her cousins along with a matched set of frowns on Gavin and Martina.

"Sorry, guys. I didn't mean to take so long," she started to say as she came down the stairs.

Ace and Jay were waiting by the door as if eager to leave. Rather than sporting the happy-go-lucky flirtatious vibe she'd come to expect of them, they looked as if their father's death had taken all the wind from their sails and wanted nothing more than to be rid of this place.

"Thank you for the hospitality you and your family have shown us, especially in this difficult time," Ace began to say, pausing respectfully to look each person in the eye. His hesitation seemed more frightened than sad, and Giselle looked instinctively toward Martina to see if she'd caught the same feeling too.

If she had, she gave no indication. Martina stood hand in hand with her husband, both wearing the traditional funeral black they'd worn since David's death. Both of them carried grave expressions to match.

Ace took a breath and cleared his throat before continuing. "Mother has been in contact with us, and there have been some developments that I'm afraid I have to make you aware of before we leave."

His all-business tone contrasted sharply to the playboy image he'd carried only days before, and it broke Giselle's heart to see how much his father's death had altered him. Jay too stood like a man who was holding back a dam of emotions. Men saw it as a sign of weakness to cry, it seemed. And these were wolf men.

She wouldn't fault either of them if they broke down in tears. She'd only just learned of her own father, and if anything happened to him before she had the chance to get to him, there was no doubt she'd be a blubbering mess. No point in bringing that situation up, though. It was clear by the way both guys were standing at a perfect parade rest that they were all wolf and only here to state their business before moving on.

"Thank you for sticking around these last few days while we sorted out the bad business of cleaning things up. I hope you found our hospitality up to your standards." Giselle had memorized what Martina had instructed her to say and hoped she was coming across as natural, though she felt as if she were standing in front of a class giving a speech.

Ace's lip quivered for a second before he gained control. There it was – that show of emotion. Poor guy. She just wanted to reach out and hug him; but that wasn't how wolves acted, and cousin or no, she still barely knew him. Had he been Di or Taylor, she'd have wrapped her arms around him and squeezed as tight as she could.

Standing perfectly still and looking dead on, Jay had complete mastery over his body and emotions. The perfect soldier.

"Your hospitality was more than adequate. And we thank you," Ace said, his tone flat.

Awkward was an understatement, and short on more pre-designated speeches, Giselle broke the silence with her usual brand of brash curiosity. "Okay. So, what's up with your mom?"

Jay sighed heavily breaking his eyes-forward stare to give her a sympathetic nod. "There has been some contestation of your claim as Alpha." He held his hands

7

up as if in surrender. "Not by me. Or my brother." He glanced quickly at Ace, who nodded in agreement. "A council of Alphas has been called in to decide on the validity of your claim."

Her world came to a crashing halt in the span of a moment, and all eyes landed on her, as if she had suddenly been brought under a spotlight.

Gavin released Martina's hand and took a step closer to Giselle, coming up right behind her as though he expected her to faint and need to be caught.

Martina sucked in a breath, perhaps waiting for Giselle to take the news badly and react physically.

Behind her, Giselle felt two others come close: Di and Taylor, no doubt.

They all towered around her, making her feel as if the walls themselves were closing in, but despite the way they all reacted to the news, Giselle felt nothing. Numbness, perhaps, rather than nothingness. She'd been unsure of the title already, so part of her took this news with relief that she might not need to take up that heavy mantle. And yet another growing part within her wanted it. Either way, she was paralyzed to react, and after the silence in the room had gone stale, she still couldn't muster a response.

Ace jumped in. "Your presence is requested immediately, to go before the council of Alphas, so you'll need to head up north with us."

That, more than anything else they'd said, hit her with the blunt force of a bat to the head. She'd been led to believe it would be a simple dog-and-pony show, and she'd be given the title and could return home to lead her life as it was. Now she'd have to actually fight for a title she had never wanted. In front of all the Alphas.

"And if I don't go?" Giselle asked.

"Then you forfeit, obviously," Ace said. He met her eyes with sincerity, and he reached out to hold her hand. "Don't do that. It would not only hurt you in the future, it would do damage to our family and pack. We are joined by blood – you and us. Cousins. Family. And the actions of some members create a ripple effect to others."

Her first impression of him had been that of a playboy and a young, carefree guy. He could easily have laid a claim to the title of Alpha if he'd wanted it, and she knew he'd been groomed for it as the elder of the two sons, if only by minutes. And yet, here he was telling her not to let go of her own claim.

"Could I simply pass it to another family member, then?" she asked, hoping *yes* would be the answer.

"I wish it were that simple. But no. It is yours to claim first. If the Council judges you unworthy, then the title succession will be decided by the Council," Ace said.

"Couldn't be simple, could it?" Giselle mumbled under her breath, before remembering everyone in the room had supernatural hearing too. Embarrassment set in. What a fine job she was doing at the moment acting Alpha-like. The Council would see through her in a second and brand her with the scarlet letter F straight across her forehead for all eternity. *Failure.* "I need to think about this." Being let off the hook sounded tempting. But not at the cost of bringing shame to her newfound family.

Ace remained hopeful, at least in look. "You have until the end of the week. That's when the Council will convene and decide. Even if you don't want to be Alpha, this will be an event you won't want to miss. Regional

Alphas from all across North America have been called in for this."

"Of course she's is going." Di spoke for Giselle. "She's going to be Regional Alpha. It was what she was born to do, and we will make sure she is there and looking her best."

"I guess my decision has been made, then," Giselle said nervously. Adding the pressure of having to plead her case in front of every major player in the wolf world was not exactly her idea of a good time, but if she was going to try to be one of them, she'd have to deal with them eventually.

Ace's smile returned, and she was glad to see it. His face didn't suit a frown at all. "You'll do fine. I'm sure this is just a formality, since you were lost to us for so long. It sounds all scary, I'm sure, but really, it's just an excuse to gather the Alphas for a party."

"Well, when you put it like that, okay." Giselle chuckled politely, while reminding herself to breathe slowly to avoid passing out.

"Got it. Next time I will lead with the party angle," Ace said, but there was no laughter there. He was holding back for sure, and she couldn't blame him, after losing his dad less than a week prior. She hadn't known him long enough to truly understand his actions, but anyone who'd suffered a loss like that would be off.

Jay, on the other hand, had remained suspiciously tight-lipped and avoided eye contact with her, choosing to let his eyes roam everywhere else in the room but to Giselle. That made her nervous.

"We'll make our travel plans, then," Martina said, bringing the room back on point. "And we'll see you in Washington by the end of this week."

Ace extended a hand and shook with Gavin and Martina before pulling Giselle into a big bear hug. "You'll do great." He winked as he released her from his crushing grip.

Jay finally acknowledged her and reached out to give her a hug as well, but his was much lighter and less personal than his brother's had been. "Keep your friends close, little wolf, and watch your back," he whispered, before backing up and turning his attention to Taylor and Di for their good-bye hug.

Had he meant that as a warning to her or as a cautionary note as they entered into new territory? she wondered, but before she could raise a voice of question, the guys walked out the front door to the car where Richard, her newly appointed bodyguard, was already waiting to drive them to the airport.

"I don't like this," Giselle said, as the door closed, leaving her with her pack. She walked over to her favorite spot on the couch, from where she had a commanding view of the rest of the living room, and sat, grabbing a decorative pillow to squeeze her frustration out on as she sank into the cushion.

"What's bothering you?" Martina took a seat next to her and tugged away the fancy pillow before Giselle could split a seam and send stuffing all over the room. "Are you mad that we have to go so soon?"

"I'm not mad. Stressed out, maybe. But definitely not mad," Giselle replied.

"Then why are you trying to kill the couch cushions? Maybe retract the claws a little bit and tell me what's got you so riled up."

Breathing always helped. She'd tried yoga and hated it, but the breathing they'd taught had the best calming effect, so she went with that. A deep breath in through the mouth and then slowly push it out. When she'd taken a moment to compose herself, she found Martina and Gavin both patiently waiting for her to speak.

Di had already zoned out with a magazine she'd found on the coffee table. Taylor had wandered into the kitchen, and it sounded as if she were grabbing a soda.

Despite her attempt to calm down, when Giselle opened her mouth, the words poured out with all the control of a firehose. "Ace and Jay were acting strange. This whole Council thing. And why the sudden push to do it quickly? I thought we had time to transition power."

Martina's features tightened as she sat thoughtfully for a moment before responding. "Power must always be established among our kind. We thrive on leadership and routine, despite how it may seem. The Regional Alpha is an important title, so it would only make sense that they have some due diligence in this process."

"I get that. I do." Giselle sighed, knowing she hadn't been clear with her barrage of thoughts turned into words. She tried to focus on a single thread of the issue bothering her; maybe they could work it out into the bigger picture. "But Ace and Jay. They were acting very... odd."

"Honey, they just lost their father." Martina sounded shocked that she would even mention the way they were acting.

"No. I know that." Frustration forced a small growl up Giselle's throat. She was speaking English, right? Why wasn't anyone understanding her? Of course they would act weird after losing their father. But not *that* kind of weird. "I expect them to be sad, but Jay told me to watch my back. Like a warning. Like *he* was warning *me*."

"You're heading into unfamiliar territory, dear," Martina said matter-of-factly.

How was this not a huge red flag to Martina or Gavin? Neither of them seemed the slightest bothered by what had just happened. Business as usual. Even her sisters were milling around like it was any old day, instead of the day they learned Giselle was going to have to put up or shut up about her birthright.

Martina was right, of course, about going into new territory and needing to be careful. And that would be a business as usual werewolfy thing. No one could fault anyone in her family for shrugging their shoulders at that; but Giselle's gut was telling her there was more to this than Martina's simple explanation.

This meeting of the Grand High Poobahs of the Alphas had deadly intent. And the consequences would go so much further than simply making her family look bad. That had to be what Ace and Jay were worried about. And the warning… who would be out to get her? Who had raised the red flag that made the Alphas decide to call this meeting? So many questions. Things that should be bothering her family, and yet there they sat acting as if she were the drama queen, overplaying her hand. A lesser wolf would let this go. Enjoy the ride and see where it took them. But Giselle could never do that. She had to get to the bottom of things. And seeing as she was on her own again, with fears and concerns, she decided to play their game.

"Whatever. I'm not going to stress it. Let's talk travel. Who's going with us?" Giselle asked.

"I am." Di's hand flew up as if she were answering a question in class.

"Of course you girls will all go," Martina said. "My sister will be back by the end of the week – she and Jeffrey can watch the house, and we'll all go together. It can be a little family vacation."

Giselle laughed out loud. *Vacation*. Hardly. This was going to be super-stressful.

"Try to relax, Giselle," Martina said soothingly. "The worst that can happen is you come home the same girl you've been since we knew you. Remember that. If they deny your claim, you're still our Little Werewolf."

2

Martina's words carried so much truth, and yet they couldn't soothe the tension knotting her stomach. There was no shame in being their little werewolf, and she'd have happily remained that if it were allowed. All she'd ever wanted was a family to accept her for what she was. She'd only ever dreamed of her fur-ever home. And she'd found it with them. The irony was because of family – blood – she was no allowed to simply be a little werewolf any longer.

Be careful what you wish for. She was Murphy's Law's bitch.

The night crawled on its belly like a snail in no particular rush to move as Giselle tossed and turned, praying for sleep to take her away from her troubled thoughts. Her mind churned out scenarios of doom surrounding her upcoming trip north to Washington. Jay's warning left so much to question, and as her family was already shrugging it off, she didn't want to beat a dead horse with them. They were as stubborn as she when it came to the way they saw the world, and in her exhaustion, Giselle just couldn't muster the energy it would require to open their eyes to the potential truth.

Everywhere she looked, wolf politics threatened to destroy the happiness she'd found with her new family. What was the point of being supernatural if you couldn't even enjoy it? Perhaps that was the grand *screw you* of the cosmos. You could be human and boring; or supernatural and deal with endless amounts of unwanted drama.

Exhaustion only amplified her bad mood, and as the sun peeked through the edges of the window, it became painfully obvious that sleep had turned its back on her.

Giselle rose from her bed as quietly as she could, not wanting to wake her sisters. In her current frame of mind, conversation would be little more than Neanderthal-like grunts and snarls, which would only serve to add more confusion and anger to her agitated state. No. That sort of thing was best left for a time after she'd been properly caffeinated. She dressed and headed downstairs for the one thing that might help snap her out of the funk she was in and put a little pep into her preparations for travel.

Gavin, always the early riser, was already in the kitchen brewing the first pot of coffee for the day. Again her plans for a quiet start to the morning had been thwarted. Was it that much to ask for a little time alone to clear her thoughts? Apparently so. But unlike her sisters, whom she could easily brush aside, her adoptive father and co-pack leader was not so easy to ignore, and his position demanded a teensy bit more respect.

Giselle slowed her descent down the stairs, taking deep cleansing breaths so she might appear fresh when she hit the kitchen.

Busy with a pan of what smelled like bacon, Gavin's back was to her as she stepped foot onto the tile floor, but quick as any wolf, he'd already prepared for her company and set out an extra mug on the counter.

"You're up early." He slapped a few more strips down on to the hot pan.

Tantalizing even in her sleep-deprived state, the smell of bacon just beginning to sizzle awoke her inner wolf and she sat begging. The whole house would be up soon with the call of that salty siren as an alarm. What wolf could resist? Hell, she knew more than a few humans who'd be roused from a coma if tempted with fresh, hot bacon. And as good as that sounded, she was still not ready to deal with people who expected her to do the words and talking thing.

Second only to the smell of delicious cooking meat, the pot of fresh coffee begged for her attention. Caffeine was most certainly what she needed. And then maybe a slice or two of bacon, slathered in maple syrup.

Gavin spun around to fetch his mug and began to pour his own cup of wake-up juice. "Late night or early morning?" he asked with a knowing glare.

As Alphas went, Gavin broke the mold. He had never been the hard-line type of father or wolf. He often allowed mistakes to be the teacher, and let Giselle have a long leash. Had Martina asked the same question, Giselle might have been tempted to be evasive, knowing that they'd already talked the night before, but with Gavin she felt she could just speak her mind.

"Couldn't sleep. Might need something stronger than that." She pointed to the mug he was pouring coffee into.

"Still angling to get that espresso machine, are ya?" Gavin laughed, as he nudged the empty mug her way down the counter.

"It's a triple shot kind of morning." Giselle yawned loudly, then realized she might have just woken the house.

"That bad? Still feeling the pressure?" Gavin's tone carried no tone of impatience, thankfully.

The last thing she wanted was to hear more about her overactive imagination. Not that she expected that from Gavin.

"No point in rehashing it." Giselle brushed away the words with a wave of her hand, swatting them like flies.

Gavin nodded. "No point in refuting it, either." He tipped his mug and winked. "Go with my blessing, but bring back something for Martina, or she'll be angry."

"She'd never know if you hadn't set the bacon alarm. I'm surprised people aren't lining up already for a taste."

Gavin turned on his heels. "Thanks for reminding me." He flipped the bacon, and its wafting smell put her under a spell. She almost considered forgoing coffee to be first in line. "You can stop drooling already. I'll send you off with a few slices."

Above them both, the ceiling rumbled. Too late. The house was awake. "We've got incoming. I'll have to get some for the girls too."

"Price of doing business." Gavin pulled a few glistening ribbons of bacon still sizzling at the edges from the pan and set them down on a plate he'd previously prepared with a paper towel. "Do you have enough cash to cover their drinks?"

"Yeah. I can cover it." Giselle swiped a handful of bacon and turned before he could stop her. She ravenously shoved the hot strips in her face as she headed for the key rack to pick up the car keys. "I'm taking your car, okay?" Giselle ducked into the garage and hit the door opener to muffle any sound in case Gavin tried to protest. His jeep was always more fun to drive than the car she shared with the girls. Any chance to drive it was worth the lecture she'd get later.

Early as it was, traffic was non-existent and the coffee shop blissfully empty. Giselle gave in to the temptation to stay and enjoy the non-wolfy silence as she sipped her favorite caramel-laden triple shot beverage. No doubt with the siren's call of bacon, the entire house was awake, so she couldn't stay long, but a few stolen moments of peace wouldn't hurt. And the second they saw her with coffee, all would be forgiven.

Tasting of pure sugar and caffeine heaven, the moment the liquid touched her lips it revitalized her spirit. Things didn't look so foreboding. She'd find a way to wow the Council. And there was the underlying bonus she'd almost forgotten about with this trip – she'd finally be able to meet her long-lost father.

Sure, he'd be comatose, but she'd see him. More than just a thought, more than just a picture in Cassandra's wallet, he'd be a real, tangible presence in her life. A connection to who she was and could become. That alone would be worth the trip up north and the snooty wolves she'd have to woo.

Laughing at her own thoughts about wooing strange old wolves, she failed to recognize the scent of the wolf who'd just walked into the coffee shop.

She was mid-sip when he strolled up behind her. "May I beg an audience with your highness?" Asher asked.

She swallowed the singeing liquid quickly and turned in time to see him recovering from a low bow. The royalty jokes were beginning to grate on her nerves, and Asher was the primary reason for it. She punched him in the arm as he rose to meet her eyes. "Seriously, man... This is getting old."

"This will never get old." Asher flashed her his award-winning smile, and his teeth sparkled in the early light. No guy should have weapons that powerful. Though she alone seemed immune. At least, this morning she was. "You're like our own personal princess now. And I'm kissing ass as hard as I can to ensure my place in your court."

"Seriously, dude. Enough!" Giselle rolled her eyes and returned to sipping her drink.

Asher scooted into the seat across the small table. His face scrunched in confusion. "You're supposed to be happy about this."

"I am. Just... it's a lot to take in."

"Yeah, and it will only get better. You're about to have a list of suiters a mile long. Everyone will want to be the mate..." He waved a hand as if to show her the line already forming behind him.

She glared at him as if trying to will his mouth to stop moving. She'd already tuned out his words, but those lips of his kept flapping. "I'm going to stop you right there. I've got a boyfriend. Remember?"

"A witch." Asher laughed. "You saw how well that worked out for your family in the past."

"That's a low blow," she growled. Her level of caffeine had not yet risen enough to deal with his wolfy elitism.

"I didn't mean it like that," Asher said cautiously.

"Yeah, you did," Giselle snarled at him. Caffeine was starting to take effect, and before she opened her mouth again, she paused and took a moment to breathe. Asher was a dick sometimes, but not intentionally so. His family was the upper class of wolves in that area, and they often forgot their manners in mixed company. "I know you aren't trying to piss me off. Wolf laws and such. Whatever. I get it."

"Yeah, babe, you're in the spotlight now." Asher's famous smiled returned. "At some point, though, you'll have to make a choice. The wolfy way…"

"At some point. But not today." Giselle gulped the last bit of her drink and stood, hoping Ash would get the hint that she was done with the conversation.

Asher stood as well and waited for her to walk before he followed. "Sooner than you might think. Maybe even before you officially take the title."

"You think they'll push that hard right off the bat?" She'd wanted to end the conversation, and leaving would surely do that, but as she took a step toward the door, she remembered she was supposed to grab drinks for the rest of the family. With a silent curse, she changed course and headed for the counter to order.

Asher kept time with her like a shadow. "Wolves are not known for allowing gray areas. Pretty black and white about things."

"And you wonder why I'm not chomping at the bit to take the roll. I live in the gray areas." Giselle pulled a twenty-dollar bill from her wallet and ordered five more coffees to go.

Asher placed his order as well and again followed her to a table to wait out their drinks. "Hey. Maybe you'll usher in a new age for wolfdom."

"I'm not even going to justify that with a response." Giselle tried to hide her laugh, though the image of her face on a campaign poster was amusing.

"I believe in you." Ash scooted up close and nudged her shoulder with his. "Giselle. Making Wolves Great Again!"

She couldn't hide the full-blown laugh that bubbled up from her chest this time. "Are you my PR person now? Is this the official Giselle for Alpha slogan?"

"Anything to earn brownie points with my liege." Asher puffed his chest and saluted.

He was a jerk sometimes, and then others... Giselle sighed. He could be so damn adorable. "I sense much brown-nosing in you."

"We all have to be good at something." Asher flashed his signature smile-and-wink combo at her.

Giselle rolled her eyes, feigning annoyance. "Yeah, because kissing ass at a college level is something to aspire to."

The barista called out Giselle's name, and she was quick on her feet to go retrieve the drinks.

"At least I know who to turn to when I'm feeling low."

"Happy to bolster your spirits." Asher winked as she walked out the door drinks in hand. "Now, knock 'em dead and come back an Alpha!"

3

"Who needs caffeine?" Giselle arrived home like the conquering hero with treasures from a far off land. Her offering to Gavin seemed to appease him enough to let her off the hook for taking his car.

The smell of bacon still lingered in the air, though Giselle couldn't spot a single slice left. At least she'd managed to snag those precious first few off the pan slices before she'd run. Her stomach growled in protest.

"Giselle, honey. Just in time. I have our itinerary booked. We leave in the morning." Martina came up behind her and snatched one of the coffees. She sniffed the top of the lid. "Caramel latte?"

"What else would I order?" Giselle followed along as Martina walked to the kitchen table.

"Too much sugar, dear." Martina gave the obligatory speech about eating healthy, but drank the coffee nonetheless.

Giselle set the tray of drinks on the table and backed away quickly as the other wolves descended on their prey.

"I want you to pack enough clothes for a week. One of those days will be a special event, so dress to impress." Martina had a pad of paper in front of her, and between sips of her drink she scrawled down notes. "Richard will be here later this afternoon. He'll act as our liaison for the entire Council event. Giselle, you will sit with him tonight for training. And I have you sitting next to him on the airplane. We have a few days to cram as much knowledge into you about wolves as we can. You will listen; you will learn. Are we clear?"

And so it begins. Giselle nodded and sipped her drink, knowing that she was in for a long few days.

Martina continued to check things off on her list. "Di, I need you and Taylor to help with wardrobe. Giselle has to look and act her best, and it will be up to us to make her shine."

"That's what we do best." Taylor smiled way too happily for as early as it still was in the morning.

Di at least had the decency to look exhausted, but despite the light circles under her eyes, she still managed to look runway-ready with a perfect messy bun and lip gloss. "Whatever you say. We'll work some magic on her."

Giselle almost took that as an insult, but she knew the girls' skills and had witnessed the transformations they could work. If anyone could make her look her best, they'd do it. "So all I need to do is sit here and look pretty?" She snickered. "Ash was right. This is sounding more and more like a political campaign. When do I get my banner?"

"Are you taking this seriously, Giselle?" Martina had clearly missed the joke.

"Just trying to lighten the mood. Last night you said—"

"You have one chance to prove yourself. One. That's it." Martina cut her off. "If you fail, that's it. You don't get a do over. So if you want to avoid embarrassment, then you will do your best with this one chance."

So much for being her little werewolf. Giselle pursed her lips. "I will do my best. I'm trying not to stress out about it. Like you told me. Remember?"

Martina's face softened. "I just want you to put your best face forward. We get one shot at this."

"And if I fail?" Giselle asked.

Martina sighed. "Then you return to normal life."

"I don't want to fail. Honestly. But if I don't laugh about it, don't try to see some humor in it, I'll give myself an anxiety attack."

Taylor threw an arm around Giselle. "I can whip you up a campaign poster if that's what you want."

Giselle laughed. "Making Wolves Great Again."

Martina cracked a smile. "Oh, good lord. You're ridiculous. Both of you."

"But at least we're laughing now," Giselle said.

"Let's make a deal, then." Martina tapped her pencil on the edge of her paper. "Be present and willing to do what you are called to do, and I will not bog you down with lists and schedules."

"So, I go with the flow?" Giselle asked. "While you make lists behind my back?"

Martina winked. "What you can't see, can't stress you out."

"And that's why you're the Alpha." Giselle laughed.

Martina slugged down the rest of her drink and returned to her paper.

Di strolled into the kitchen and by the sounds of it was making a plate of food.

Giselle's stomach growled, reminding her that she couldn't live on coffee alone, no matter how much sugar it had in it. She stood ready to follow Di towards breakfast, but Taylor grabbed hold of her instead.

"Got a minute?" her sister asked.

Giselle whimpered as Taylor lead her away from the kitchen toward the stairs. "But breakfast…"

"Won't be long. I promise. I just want to talk with you in private for a minute. Please." Taylor tugged at Giselle's arm.

With a defeated sigh, Giselle allowed herself to be taken up the stairs toward their bedroom.

"So, you talked to Ash today?" Taylor asked, busying herself with her suitcase to avoid eye contact with her sister.

"And you're bringing this up because?" Giselle asked, feeling angry that she had been pulled away from food to talk about a boy. And not just any boy… Ash.

Taylor folded a shirt and shoved it into her suitcase with a loud sigh. "Because it's time I let it go, and I wanted you to know… I'm totally cool with any…" Taylor snatched up another shirt from her bed and rolled it up. "Relationship…" She slammed that shirt into her suitcase as well. "Whatever the two of you have."

If Taylor thought she was convincing anyone with that act, she was sorely mistaken. It was plain as day that she was not truly over the hurt Ash had caused with his rejection. But Giselle understood the gesture. Girl code and all, she would never entertain the idea of a relationship with anyone her sisters had eyes on.

"I do have a boyfriend already. You remember that, right?" Giselle hoped that reminder would soothe the tension she could see in her sister.

Taylor barely glanced at Giselle as she stepped past her into the closet to grab more clothes. "Yep. And I love Damien. He's a great guy. But you know how it goes with our kind, and you're going to have a suitor list a mile long once you're made all official and stuff." She walked out of the closet with a pile of clothes conveniently covering her face. "So I want you to know that I will not stand in the way."

"Yet your tone and body language tell me otherwise," Giselle said.

"Me and Ash were not a great couple. We are going to be awesome friends. And that's cool. I just have a lingering sense of jealousy, that's all."

"Because of me being Alpha?" Giselle asked.

"No, silly. I'm totally psyched about that. But you've had both Ash and Damien at your beck and call since you joined our pack." Taylor stopped mid-fold. Her fingers dug into the fabric of the pair of jeans she was prepping to go into her suitcase. "It's hard not to be jealous of that when you don't seem to try at all."

Giselle reached out and pulled the jeans away from Taylor's hands, and finally her sister looked up. It wasn't pain she saw behind Taylor's eyes; it was longing. Her sister was such a beautiful person, and as long as they'd known each other, Taylor had been single. Odd, since she was the outgoing one. The girl who belonged to all the social circles and was uniquely gifted in the art of fashion. She deserved someone fawning all over her. Someone who appreciated all she could bring to a relationship. Ash was an idiot for letting her go.

"Taylor, you're the best, sweetest, and prettiest girl I know. Don't tell Di I said that. You're in for one hell of a wolf when the time comes. Trust me. Ash was stupid to walk away from you."

"Thanks. He is an idiot. But not my problem any-more." Taylor laughed, but it was empty. Giselle's words might have comforted her some, but Taylor was clearly not completely happy.

"Well, I never said I was taking him on. But I'm glad your blessing is there on our friendship. That means a lot to me," Giselle said.

"Just do me a favor." Taylor resumed packing her bag, but she did look up when she spoke.

"What's that?"

"When the time comes? Let Damien down easy."

Giselle sighed.

Taylor met her eyes with determination this time. "You know it has to happen eventually."

Everyone, it seemed, felt she and Damien were a bad idea. And Giselle hated to admit that she understood why. However, the more people told her not to do something, the more her defiant nature began to surface. "I hate having my hand forced."

"I've learned that about you." Taylor laughed genu-inely this time. "But in our world, an Alpha has to be able to produce heirs."

She nearly stuck her fingers in her ears at that point. "Puppies? Hell, no! That's years down the line."

Taylor sighed loudly and set down her clothes. "Da-mien is not like other high school boys. He's the type who'd stick around for the long haul." She took hold of Giselle's hands, holding them lightly in hers. Before, when she talked of Ash, she wouldn't make eye contact, but now, she looked deeply into Giselle's, silently pleading for her to listen and understand. "It would be unfair to drag him along for that long, only to have to cut him loose because of your duty." Having said her piece, Taylor let go of Giselle's hands and returned to her suitcase.

The thought had weighed heavily on Giselle's mind since learning the truth of her mother and father. She'd already tried once to let Damien off the hook, but he'd held on tight, proving yet again his loyalty to their relationship even in the face of his family's disapproval.

"Seems my relationship is the topic on everyone's mind," Giselle grumbled. "Ash warned me in much the same fashion."

"It's unfair. That's for sure. And another reason I'm not jealous of what you are to become." Taylor smirked and began to roll socks to stuff into her suitcase.

"Thanks," Giselle grouched.

"Just being honest," Taylor said. "You can't have it all."

Truer words had never been spoken. But it wasn't a question in her mind of Damien over Asher. If she were forced to drop her boyfriend for her role as Alpha, then she'd remain single for as long as possible. No one would dictate to her whom she could be mated to.

4

Hours flew by as packing took the focus of the day. Matching proper outfits and shoes kept Taylor and Di occupied. Tasked with making Giselle look her best, they took extra care in selecting just the right outfits, littering the floor of their bedroom with castoffs. By the time Richard arrived, Giselle was more than happy to trade fashion for fighting tips. At least it would be more interesting.

She met him in the dining room. Standing with his arms crossed and his eyes narrow and focused directly on her, he was an intimidating sight, leaving her feeling like prey in the predator's deadly gaze. It was only when he opened his mouth to speak that she felt at ease.

"A lot can be said for giving off a menacing appearance." Richard relaxed his stance, allowing his arms to fall to his sides.

"Reading my mind again?" Giselle asked.

"Don't need to. Your body language gives everything away. The moment you walked into the room, you lost the courage you naturally carry."

"That obvious, huh?"

"If I can see it, I guarantee you all the rest of the Council will. At all times, remember to hold your head high. Appearance is everything." Richard held out a hand, indicating she should take a seat, and then shoved a notebook and pencil down the table.

So much for this being that kind of training. She'd hoped for a sparring match to work off the tension, but it looked like the only muscles she'd be working were in her fingers. Giselle sighed and flipped open the notepad.

"You don't have to know everything to be an Alpha. Some of the best Alphas out there surround themselves with knowledgeable wolves who assist in decision-making. But you must have complete certainty when you speak. Just like appearing weak can make you look bad, sounding weak has the same effect. If you are wrong, you can admit it later; but when you do say something, you must believe it with all your heart."

"And if I know I'm wrong?"

"Then keep your mouth shut." Richard pulled a chair out and sat heavily on it. "When you are Alpha, you will be the pillar upon which others will build their trust. Don't give them reasons to waiver in that trust. Play the game."

"This isn't me," Giselle said, more to herself than to Richard. Lone wolves were not leaders.

"Being an Alpha has more to do with others than it does yourself," he replied.

Giselle groaned, feeling a longwinded speech about to come her way. "Why don't you take the role, then? You're much better suited for it than me."

"I'm old enough to know what the job entails, but not young enough to want the position." Richard laughed and relaxed back into his chair.

"You don't look that old. What, like forty or something?"

"Or something," Richard replied, but the fact he had not confirmed his actual age had her wondering. Wolves and age was an ambiguous subject.

"Whatever. I'm a kid. I'm still in my selfish years. I'm too young to have such responsibility."

"You don't appreciate the position... yet. " Richard jabbed a finger in her direction. "Drop the petulant child act, sweetheart. I've known you long enough to see through it."

Giselle was mid eyeroll just as he said it, angry he'd seen through her façade.

"Your age is a factor, yes." Richard relaxed, letting his hands fall back to the kitchen table. "That is why you would have a Regent in your place. But make no mistake, you were born for this."

The more people told her she was born for this, the more she wanted to run screaming from it. Maybe if just one person would say something like, *You'll be total crap at this, just give up*, she'd feel the need to step up and prove them wrong. But no. Everyone and their brother just had to big her up and pile on the pressure with their praise.

"You think just because my dad was an Alpha that I somehow belong in the role? That's the kind of backwards thinking that killed off the monarchies."

Impatience darkened Richard's eyes. "Not all monarchies are dead, little werewolf. And yes, Alpha blood runs in your veins, whether you want to believe it or not. It's apparent in the way you inspire others to take up your causes and follow you into certain danger."

"No one follows me anywhere," Giselle muttered.

Richard let out a sigh that sounded almost like a growl. "When you finally learn to harness that power and have the wisdom of age to back up your decisions, I have no doubt you'll make one of the finest Alphas in North America."

Giselle was at a loss as to what to say. The snarky teen in her wanted to throw in something condescending and cliché. His speech had all the hallmarks of a wizened old mentor from a comic book schooling the reluctant superhero. But her wolf reacted differently, as if wanting to rise to the occasion and take its rightful position on top and usher in a new era for her kind. Both sides of that coin felt at war with each other, and she was just the battleground waiting to host the victor.

"Try not to put too much pressure on yourself just yet. Yes, you are meant to do this, but as with all things, you must learn and grow into your role. You need to first educate yourself on what it is to be a wolf. To live in a pack. Understand the dynamics. The rules. How we live both with and apart from human society. This is the primary reason for regency, anyway. To give you this time."

"Then why must this decision be made now?" Giselle asked, looking around to see if her sisters or maybe Martina might decide to crash the party and give them something else to discuss. Then again, the only topic any of them wanted to discuss was her becoming Alpha.

"Our territories are held by power. They are not merely assigned lines on a map. A long time ago, the North American continent had nearly as many High Alphas as there were states, each one warring with the next for control of land and resources. Much as the humans settled and organized into regions and later states, we too narrowed down the field of governing Alphas into smaller and smaller numbers, until we have what you see today. That, however, can change just as quickly as it came about if another territory senses weakness and decides to move in and envelop more lands."

"So if other Alphas want to take over our territory, why am I being brought in to be judged by them?"

"Because we have to show them you are strong enough to hold your territory, and maintain the guise of a unified Council. Regional Alphas meet two times a year to discuss matters of state and settle border disputes. So anyone who will rise to power will quickly get to know these other Alphas."

"Sounds like there's a lot of playacting involved." Giselle rolled her eyes.

"All politics is playacting of some form. Some politicians do it better than others. Sometimes looking like the biggest and baddest wolf in the pack is all it takes to bully the other wolves into doing the right thing, and other times a true show of strength is needed. You'll have to master the former and employ others to do the latter in your reign."

"Because I'm a girl?" Giselle grumped, feeling the conversation had taken a slightly sexist tone.

"Because you're a pup. You are not of age, so you cannot fight right now. But yes, when you do come of age, you had better be able to fight your battles yourself with that attitude."

Giselle was no fighter; not in the physical sense. And Richard was right, understanding her limitations meant picking battles correctly. All the more reason she shouldn't be a leader. Her mouth ran away with her more often than not. She'd surely piss off the wrong person eventually, and then where would she be? "Playacting, then. Got it! I'm the biggest, baddest wolf out there, as far as anyone knows."

"You're a Silverman," Richard corrected.

"And that means?" Giselle asked.

"You come from a powerful family. That by itself carries weight. Remember that. Both your father and David were very powerful Alphas and held the territory in peace for a very long time."

"Then shouldn't the role pass to David's sons, Ace and Jay?" Giselle wondered why she'd been chosen so quickly as replacement when it was their father who'd died.

"The true claim belongs to the eldest living Silverman… your father." Richard's words sounded carefully selected. Her father was a topic she'd yet to really dive into. This visit north would bring her face to face with the man who'd traded his life for hers. Emotions ran deep where he was concerned. All her life she'd wanted a family. She'd felt as if she'd been unwanted. With the recent encounter she'd had with Cassandra, she'd learned that not only had she been wanted more than anything in this world, but that her birth had been a key reason her father had been rendered unconscious. *Not dead*, as Richard had so poignantly put it. And though she'd never met him, or even been raised by wolves, by rights of his lineage she'd suddenly been awarded the title of Regional Alpha.

"I still don't understand this whole line of succession thing. Those boys were probably bred for this, so why not just pretend I'm not involved?"

"Because we are creatures of habit, who are ruled by the most rigid of laws."

"Clearly," Giselle scoffed, earning her a scornful look from her instructor.

"Even if the role will be superficial at first, it is important that order is established for the rest of the packs." Richard's tone had long since passed the point of impatience. "And that the other Alphas see a Silverman still has control."

Giselle sighed. Fighting just meant prolonging the lecture. "Okay. Fine. What important wolfy knowledge are you going to impart to me today?"

"You're going to have to do a little better than that if you want to convince the other Alphas that you're truly interested in taking up the position."

"I am. Interested, that is." *Playacting*, she reminded herself. *Now or never*. If she couldn't convince Richard, she'd never convince the Council. "I want to know more. I grew up in the human world, so this all seems a bit tedious to me."

"It is. And will always be." A smile broke through the stony mask Richard wore, as if he finally felt he was getting somewhere with her obstinacy. He stood and took a lap around the kitchen table as he spoke. "There are essentially five primary packs in North America, who control all the smaller packs in their region. All will send representatives to this Grand Council. Those representatives will be the ones to judge whether or not you are worthy to take up the Pacific Territories. The Olde Town pack controls the New England portion of the east coast. The Rufus Reds control the southeast and parts of Louisiana. The Loups are situated in the heart of the United States and extend as far west as Colorado. The

Lobos come from northern Mexico and in through Arizona, with some reach into Utah. And then you have us Long Teeth from the Pacific coast. Up in Canada, we have dealings with the Lycans, but I don't know if they will send a representative or not. Best to be prepared, though."

"And I am supposed to remember all this how?"

"By paying attention and taking it seriously." Richard jabbed a finger down at the pencil and paper in front of Giselle.

Feeling slightly embarrassed, she picked up the pencil. "How do you spell Lobos?"

Richard growled behind her.

"Sorry. I'll figure it out." Giselle quickly jotted down what she could remember about the packs.

Richard continued walking circles around the dining room as he started again. "Now each territory has a different system of cooperation to ensure all supernatural creatures play nice. For example, Aiden Whelan and his mate Fallon manage the Olde Town Pack. They are friendly with the witches in their territory and are the judge and jury for all supernatural activity happening within their borders. Their wolves are more militarized and trained than any other pack in the country. They tend to see more action as well, being on the upper coast in more densely populated areas. The Reds to the south are more laid back. They don't actively monitor for supernatural infractions, and allow the vampires to be the ones to handle the control and registration of supernatural activity."

"Wait. Vampires? How have I not met one yet?" The more she learned, the more she understood just how little she knew of the supernatural world. Sure, she'd heard rumors of vampires. However, he'd not only confirmed it but alluded to the fact that she'd have to deal with them directly in days to come. At least some parts of being an Alpha could be interesting. Did they have long fangs like in the movies, or did they retract? Maybe they really did sparkle. The possibilities were endless, as far as she could imagine. Meeting them would be a treat.

Richard seemed more annoyed by the mention of them; his lip twitched slightly as he droned on. "Vampires are a secretive bunch by nature. Their aversion to light makes them scarce when the majority of our kind are active, though we have dealings with them on occasion."

"If there are vampires, I want to meet them. Who manages them? Do we?"

"Your city here was ripe with them a few years back, but they attracted unwanted attention and were scattered."

Now things were getting interesting. Why hadn't anyone mentioned this before? "Really? By who?"

"That is another level of politics you'll have to learn in a future lesson. Today, let's just make sure we cover who you'll be meeting."

Giselle tossed down her pencil. Of course the minute they hit upon a topic she was interested in, they had to drop the subject. One thing was for certain: when she was Alpha, she was going to find out all she could about vampires. And any other supernatural creatures they'd been hiding away from her.

"In our territory we have a *don't ask don't tell* policy. As long as they aren't actively killing in our territory, we don't require them to reveal themselves."

"So they do kill?" She gulped back a tiny kernel of fear. Vampires were still interesting, for sure. But she'd rather not be on the menu.

"Can we save vampires for another discussion? I'd like to move on to the Loups. The heartland of America is so large that they often delegate management of the region…"

Richard kept talking, but Giselle lost track of the conversation, wondering how much of the supernatural world had lain right under her nose. In a way, it made her feel better to know that there were so many others. More than just wolves. More than witches. A whole ecosystem of magical creatures was out there waiting to be found. And as Alpha, she'd have to know all about them, of course.

"Are you listening?" Richard's tone yanked her sharply from her thoughts.

"Yep. I'm listening," she lied.

"At least you remembered to sound confident with that lie." Richard's eyes were like spotlights, bringing into focus the fact she hadn't written a single note. "If you wish to look like a fool, by all means, ignore what I'm telling you."

"Okay, I zoned out when you mentioned vampires."

"That I believe – but they are not the topic for tonight. We fly out tomorrow. You'll begin to meet delegates immediately. You need to know who you'll be meeting because I can guarantee they will know all about you."

"What's to know?" Giselle tried to shrug off her life story.

Richard wasn't playing her game. "In Nebraska, Misha Noels and her mate Brianna control the Loups, which consist of four major packs below them, each with their own wheel and spoke level of pack hierarchy. They're sticklers for the rules of law and will probably act as mediators for this meeting. They have no tolerance for emotional outbursts. They do not negotiate. Their word is law, and in their territory they are judges of all infractions, but..." Richard held his hand out, finger pointing to the page for her to write this down. "They leave sentencing to be decided and carried out by the individual Alphas underneath them."

No more screwing around. Giselle scrawled out exactly what Richard had said, commenting, "So they like to lay down the law but don't get their hands dirty?"

"Yes. They prefer not to see the ugly side of things."

"Good to know." She added a few more exclamation points to the sentence she'd just written to make sure she remembered that fact.

"Precisely." Richard nodded and continued to pace. "You'll do well to remember that about them."

Giselle added a few exclamation points to the end of that sentence, her own short hand for noting important things.

"Now... the Lobos are a widespread bunch. Overlapping two countries, they live on the fringe of society and are probably the most lenient of all the North American packs. They are, however, a deadly bunch to deal with. They play nice until you cross them, and then it's no holds barred. Tito Valdez and his mate Yanira will probably be sent in as representatives. Best to win them over first, as they can be excellent allies to have, especially if you bring the Regency here to Vegas. You'll be neighbors."

"Is that it?" Giselle looked up from her paper.

"One more. The Long Teeth – that's us. We've been in Washington for a long time. You're going to have to play nice with Vivian, the former Regent's wife and current interim Alpha, while you're there. There will be some dissension among her group because they're losing the power and prestige of commanding the Regional Alphas pack."

"So basically, a bunch of people who have always been in power are going to look at me and judge whether or not I'm worthy?"

"Precisely."

"Me? A lone wolf who just barely found a pack to live with?"

Richard Sighed. "A wolf who united two warring packs. A wolf who has allied herself with the local witch coven and proven her leadership skills. A wolf who has the backing of two wolf packs to her claim. Yes. They will judge you worthy. You've done more in the last year than many of the Regional Alphas have done in the last decade. Have some faith in yourself."

"This is ludicrous," Giselle whispered under her breath.

"Confidence," Richard droned.

Giselle puffed out her chest and met him dead in the eyes. "This is ludicrous!" she said proudly.

Richard cracked a real smile and a light chuckle tumbled from his mouth. "Better."

"Joking aside, do you think I have even half a chance?" Giselle asked.

Richard stepped close to her placing a hand on her shoulder. "I see your potential. But you must make *them* see. If you can do that, then yes."

Honesty, bluntly as he offered it, was appreciated, and Giselle hoped she could live up to his evaluation of her. The next few days would prove quite interesting either way.

5

Sleep came from the helping hand of more than the recommended dose of sleeping aids. It was either that or spend another night tossing and turning, leaving her useless to the family when they went to meet with the Washington wolves.

The sound of her alarm failed to rouse her from the medicated slumber, though in her dreams she heard the echoes of its shrill call.

How long it had been allowed to go off was anyone's guess, but when she did wake to the rough shaking from Di, she could tell the hour was late.

Already dressed, hair and makeup done, and with overpowering scent of flowers assaulting Giselle's senses, Di appeared as if she'd been up and at it for hours.

"How many pills did you take last night?" her sister asked.

Giselle groaned. Her eyes refused to stay open. Each time they fell shut, it was like the weight of the world was holding them down while a tiny voice whispered for her to come back into the darkness.

"Time?" Her voice refused to cooperate, cracking as she tried to push the word out.

"Nearly ten, lady. The alarm has been going off every ten minutes for the last hour." Di sounded annoyed, but Giselle couldn't keep her eyes open long enough to see if she looked the part. "Taylor should be done in the bathroom soon. Go splash some water on your face and wake up. We're leaving in a couple hours." Di's voice trailed away.

Giselle fought against the pull back to sleep and sat up on the bed. With her vision as cloudy as her head, she took a moment to wipe away the fog before standing. Sleep had been good. She'd needed it more than she could say. For those blissful moments, she had let go of the stress and anxiety. But, as her mind rebooted and the tasks of the day became real, she could feel the tension returning.

Taylor wandered in wrapped in towels, fresh from the shower. Giselle barely grunted at her as she walked past to throw herself into the shower and wash away the last remnants of that blissful night of sleep.

If ever there was a question if true magic existed, the only proof needed would be hot running water. Better than any enchantment she'd known, the power of a simple act of taking a shower was mystical. It cleansed the soul as well as body, washing away stress and anxiety as easily as it melted away the grime of daily life. No matter how bad she felt, taking a shower, at least for that moment, helped make things better.

Washed, dressed, and ready for the trials the day would bring, Giselle headed downstairs for some much-needed caffeine. The doorbell rang as she hit the last step.

Damien was standing on the other side – she could smell his cologne before she even opened the door.

"Come to see me off?" she asked as she pulled the door open.

There was a reason she liked that boy, and right at that moment it was the offering of coffee and donuts he'd arrived with. "When do you leave?" Damien asked, as he stepped over the threshold and handed her the loot.

"Couple of hours." Giselle stole a quick sip of coffee as she led him down into the living room. "We were supposed to take a few days, but I guess Martina found a last minute deal. The whole family is heading out to be my support because apparently I am going to need it." As soon as she sat on the couch, Giselle dove into the bag of donuts. Boston Crème. Her favorite. He'd brought two, so she snagged one and handed the bag back to him.

"You don't sound so excited." Damien dug into the bag and pulled out his own donut.

"More nerves than anything else." Hungrier than she'd thought, Giselle inhaled the donut in just a couple of bites, hardly enjoying the sweet cream center in her haste. "I'm not used to the spotlight, and this is going to put me right on center stage." She wiped her mouth clean and picked the coffee up, tipping it toward Damien in silent thanks before guzzling it down.

"You'll do fine." Damien took his time, slowly eating his donut, making Giselle wish she hadn't been so ravenous.

"I really wish people would stop telling me that."

Damien looked confused. "Would you rather someone tell you that you'll fall flat on your face and make a huge fool of yourself?"

"Kind of. At least then I wouldn't feel like people were blowing smoke up my ass," Giselle said, watching as Damien popped the last bite of donut into his mouth.

"Do you always have to be so negative?"

"I'm not being negative. I'm being real. Why would anyone in their right mind give me the leadership of the entire Pacific Coast region? I'm a kid, and more than that, I'm barely a wolf as it is."

"You're wrong there. You are all wolf." Damien whistled while he sent his eyes wandering. They lingered for a moment on the deep v of the shirt she'd chosen – or rather, that Di had chosen for her to wear. She could see why now, as Damien's eyes hadn't budged since landing there.

But Giselle wasn't in the mood for flirting. "Thanks," she muttered. "But my assets aren't what make me a wolf."

"Okay." Damien held his hands up in surrender. "In all seriousness. You are definitely wolf, no matter what you think. And an Alpha straight to your core. So stop acting like you don't belong, and allow yourself to take a place in the wolf world."

Even the witch was giving her Alpha advice. The absurdity of that had her laughing out loud. "Okay, fine. I'm all wolf, baby!" She winked.

"That's the right attitude. And you're going to wow them. They'll be begging for you to lead them."

"Well, now you're just laying it on thick."

"You want me to stop?"

"Nah. I could use a little confidence boosting right now. Go on. Tell me more about how awesome I am."

Damien snorted. "I've created a monster."

"Pretty much. Now you have to deal with the consequences. I'll be completely insufferable to deal with. Power hungry. Narcissistic. The works."

Damien hissed and scooted backwards. "Yeah. About that. We might have to call it off…"

He was joking, and she knew it, but the moment the words crossed his lips, she was reminded of both Taylor's and Asher's warnings to her. She would have to end things with him if she becomes the Alpha.

"I said something wrong, didn't I?" Damien's tone shifted. "I was just joking, you know. You can be as big-headed as you like."

"You didn't say anything wrong at all. You're one hundred percent right about us." Giselle set her coffee down and took Damien's hand. "You know what that means for us when I take over as Alpha, right?" Giselle gazed into his puppy-dog eyes – those gorgeous and insanely sweet eyes that had captured her attention from the first moment she'd looked into them.

Damien sighed and turned away, hiding himself from the scrutiny of her gaze. "Yeah." The humor in his voice faded.

"And you're still pushing me towards this fate?" Giselle asked, almost hoping he'd say otherwise.

Damien looked everywhere but in her eyes, as if he couldn't sum up the strength to face her response to his words. "You act like things have to happen all at once. That everything is a black and white issue. Can you not just let things unfold over time?"

"Haven't you learned yet? Everything with the wolves is black and white. And at some point our relationship will be affected." Giselle sighed, letting go of his hand, and then stood and began to pace around the coffee table. "And when it happens, it will be before either of us is ready."

Damien stood and blocked her path. He avoided her eyes and pulled her into a tight hug. "I'll take what I can for as long as I can. And even if we're pulled apart by duty, I will always have your back."

She didn't need to see his face to know those words hurt him to speak. Her heart was already breaking, and she hadn't yet been given confirmation by the Council on whether or not she would be Alpha.

The future was clear either way. She was wolf. He was witch. History had already shown them what happened when the two tried to mix.

Still, she hugged him back, determined to hold on as tightly as she could, for as long as she'd be allowed to.

6

Despite the game of musical homes she'd played growing up, Giselle's experience with travel had been limited, and flying was a rare treat. The whole circus act of trying to check in and make it through security, scuttling about carrying shoes and purses in large plastic bins while bored attendants verified your gender and sent you for a pat down, was pure comedy.

Had she been in any rush through the process, Giselle might not have kept such an even temper. For her, the longer it took for them to get to their final destination, the more time she had to enjoy just being herself. Because as soon as she stepped off that plane she'd cease to be Giselle the newly-adopted wolf, and she'd instantly transform into the future Alpha of the Long Tooth region.

At least that was what Richard had implied when they boarded the plane. However, when she stepped off it, there was no mysterious feeling that came over her. Unless the overwhelming need to sneeze counted.

Time spent in the dry heat of the desert had changed her, and the moist cloying air clogged up her nose within minutes.

She'd take a few sneezes though if it meant being around so much green. The desert was a monochromatic palate of browns, but now they were no longer confined to that portion of the color wheel. Here, where rain was more than a rare sighting, the ground was covered with grass, trees bloomed with flowers and fruits, and all manner of plants it seemed grew naturally without the aid of sprinkler timers and miracle feed to keep them alive. And even better, as they drove toward their first destination, Giselle noticed the complete lack of cacti.

"Holly crap, it's so green." Taylor took the words straight out of Giselle's mouth.

"And smell that air!" Giselle said with a chuckle. There were wolves here – that was obvious – but the natural smells of earth, grass, and flowering trees masked them so well, it was a reminder of their place in nature. Here they were home. This was where their kind belonged. This was where her kind lived. And that sobering reminder brought her back to task.

"Don't be nervous," Martina whispered in her ear, as if saying the words could somehow remove the knot tightening in her stomach.

Giselle kept her eyes locked on the road as their rented minivan cruised down the highway. "I wasn't until you'd reminded me," Giselle lied. Her Worry in all shapes and sizes consumed her thoughts, and no amount of empty platitudes was going to remove them. She stared out the minivan's back window, marveling at the way the trees created a barrier between them and the neighborhoods nearby.

"You can't lie to a wolf."

"Just taking it all in," Giselle said absently, as she continued to look around and take in all the greenery. She'd missed that most of all. Growing up she'd loved it; taken it for granted. Two years in the desert had stolen that beauty from her, and being back here in the thick of it, where grass grew unchecked and trees were wildly green and lush, gave her a slight pang of homesickness. A little voice in the back of her mind begged her to rethink her determination to stay in the desert.

"It's quite beautiful here." Martina glanced out, as if trying to see what Giselle was looking at, and then shook her head. "Vivian has asked us to stop in as soon as we're in town. I'm sure it'll be a quick greeting; just an ice breaker. And your first opportunity to meet your father. Then we can all go out and have a nice meal together. Okay?"

She'd said it so nonchalantly. *Meet your father*. Like it was as simple as meeting an old friend.

Chief among the thoughts clogging her mind was wondering what it would be like. Meeting someone important was always hard to do, but her father, Alpha that he was, had been left in a state of nothingness. She would see him more than meet him. And there was no way for her to truly prepare for the feelings it would stir.

Given that Martina had made the comment so easily, she couldn't have known how those words would affect Giselle. She smiled back at her adoptive mother, appreciating that in her own way she was trying to lighten the mood.

"Food solves everything." Giselle's stomach growled in agreement. "Can we order steak?"

"If you play nice, yes." Martina winked.

Gavin and Richard in the front of the van mumbled something that sounded like they'd arrived, and the nerves that had not bothered Giselle for the majority of the day came rushing back. She reminded herself to breathe. *In through the nose, and out. Slow and steady.*

7

The seat of power for the Pacific Coast had been in the pack home in Olympia, Washington. She'd seen the wealth that her friend Ash's pack had amassed and the beautiful home the Thrace family lived in, but nothing had prepared her for the lavish estate of the Silverman pack home. *Hotel* would have been more apt. Stepping out of the car, her feet landed on a gorgeous cobblestone driveway. Under the porte-cochère they were shaded from the sun, though there was really no need with the overcast day. But still, the lavishness of the home she'd yet to step into had made its mark on her. This was a pack that had wealth, one she could have belonged to under better circumstances; and yet... she did. Though she did not feel it.

"Hold your head high. Don't let them see you nervous," Richard whispered in Giselle's ear.

"I'm not nervous," she lied. Her nerves were teetering on the edge of a breakdown, but not for the reason Richard was thinking. Meeting other wolves, especially Ace and Jay's mother, aroused her curiosity, especially now that she saw the mansion – no, palace – they lived in. And years spent as a lone wolf had given her a natural curiosity regarding others of her kind. Excitement more than nerves gave her the strength to head toward the house of Vivian Silverman.

"We're to meet with your family first. There will be a formal reception." Richard spoke as if he expected her to hang on his every word, but Giselle's train of thought had derailed the moment she'd laid eyes on the towering home.

She reminded herself to breathe again. Slow her heart. Rein in her excitement and nerves before they overwhelmed her.

Thank the gods for Di and Taylor. They took her by the hand, offering their support, and that show of solidarity gave her the strength she needed to proceed up the stone steps toward the large set of stained glass French doors.

Richard's voice droned on in the background, a faint whisper overpowered by the roar of Giselle's thundering heartbeat. Try as she might, she could neither slow it nor will her nerves to ease up. Despite there being no enemy at the gates, the fight or flight instinct had taken hold. Giselle reached the front door but couldn't muster the strength to ring the bell.

She wasn't just meeting other wolves; this was to be her first encounter with her father. Orion Silverman. Once proud and strong, now laid low by Fate. The unknown sent a chill of fear through her, freezing her legs where she stood and halting her progress. What would she see when she was brought face to face with him? Could she handle it?

"Lovely. Just beautiful." Martina's voice was filled with joy. "I can see why they chose this as home." She joined Giselle and gave her a reassuring hug. "You ready for this?" she whispered.

"Sure." Giselle put on her bravest face.

Before they could ring the bell, the doors parted, and a man greeted them.

Neither particularly tall nor short, he failed to stand out as an impressive wolf of the north. Perhaps that was why he'd chosen to be a butler and work for the Alpha family.

Giselle looked at him with curiosity because he was an unknown wolf; however, the feeling was clearly not mutual. The butler hardly gave her or the family a second glance, speaking over them rather than directly to them. "Welcome, Hernandez pack. We have been expecting you. Nancy here will take any coats and hats." He raised his hand briefly to indicate a small woman waiting with arms held out, and then continued to drone on as if he'd rehearsed not only his speech but the actions as well. "You will please follow me to the solarium for tea and coffee." He didn't bother to wait for them as he turned on his heel and began walking away.

"Well, okay, then," Giselle whispered under her breath, unimpressed with the snooty way they'd been greeted. By the smell of them, both the butler and the maid were wolves, but neither of them showed any respect in her presence, merely formality. Noteworthy, but not something she'd bring up just yet. If they had been informed she was the new Alpha to be, there should have been quite a bit more bowing and scraping.

Jay's earlier warning haunted her, a subtle reminder that there would be enemies all around her.

Eyes and ears open, she reminded herself, as the pack walked after the butler.

Down the hallways and through a set of lovely wooden double doors sat a room bathed in light. Windows from floor to ceiling, and above, a glass roof, allowed every last drop of sunlight into the room. She could imagine on a truly sunny day this room would be brilliant. Today, however, overcast as it was, the natural light felt cozy. Cushy, oversized couches in a paisley pattern of cream and tan were situated in a large u-shape facing the back lawn. A table sat on the back wall, covered with carafes of tea and coffee and another tray with little cakes and finger sandwiches.

The flight over had been long, and the bag of peanuts she'd been offered had done nothing to take the edge off her hunger. She could easily devour all they'd offered and still not sate her wolf's growling belly. She hoped the meeting would be short, remembering that Martina had promised steak. That had her wolf sitting up and begging.

Seated on the couches were two people she had yet to meet: an older woman, about Martina's age, and another who was maybe a year or two older than she herself. These must be David's wife and daughter. She'd hoped to see Ace or Jay, but they were nowhere to be found.

Neither the woman nor the girl stood to greet them. Richard stepped ahead of Giselle and her family.

"Madame Silverman, may I present the Hernandez pack? Alphas Martina and Gavin." He paused for them to step forward. "And their daughters, Taylor, Diana..." He paused again as the girls stepped forward in turn. "And finally, Giselle Richards, daughter to Orion Silverman."

The butler stood still, as if waiting for more orders. Giselle had never had a butler before, but she'd seen actors play them on TV. None, however, looked as miserable at their job as this one did. Rather than keeping a stiff upper lip, he appeared to be looking down his long nose at her and her family, as if having to announce them was not worthy of his position.

"Thank you, Derek, you may go." Mrs. Silverman waved her hand in dismissal "You'll have to excuse him. He's new. A gift from our friends in the central territories for hosting such an important event. He needs quite a bit of training still," she finished, with a polite laugh.

Giselle wondered if she should too. Not knowing what was expected of her had her anxiety turned up to eleven. The weight of all eyes landing on her nearly stopped her in her tracks, but she knew she had to pay the part. Giselle stepped forward and nodded to the two women in turn. "It is a pleasure to meet you both," she said, keeping her voice still and calm.

A long pause had Giselle sensing more than just animosity between them. If her claim as Alpha was acknowledged, she'd unseat this family from their comfortable position as leaders of all the Pacific Coast, but even more than that, she could feel their hatred and blame for the death of David. Still, though, they were wolves, and held true to their respect for position. Breaking the silence, Madam Silverman forced a smile across her face.

"Welcome to my home. I'm Vivian Silverman and this is my daughter Leila. You've already met our boys. They are fetching Orion, and should be along shortly."

Giselle gulped back a knot of fear, still not emotionally ready to see her father.

Martina took the open invitation, hooking an arm through her husband's and pulling him with her to sit on the couch opposite Vivian.

Giselle turned to her sisters first, hoping to convey with eyes alone her desire to be as far away from that woman as humanly possible. There was no mistaking the vibes of hatred emanating from Vivian, though it hadn't been Giselle who'd ended her husband's life. When her sisters returned dumbfounded stares, Giselle looked to her escort for advice.

If Richard was bothered by the waves of unpleasantness Vivian was giving off, he didn't show it. He held a hand out toward the couch and turned his head ever so slightly in that direction. The signal was clear; she had to go sit.

So much for a pleasant meet and greet. Already she felt the fibers of a noose tightening around her neck. *Keep your enemies close* was an old adage she'd learned. This meeting already had all the hallmarks of that sentiment. And yet, decorum dictated she play along.

Releasing a heavy sigh, Giselle straightened her shoulders and stepped forward toward the couch. Mimicking Martina, she hooked an arm through each of her sisters' and pulled them along as her own personal entourage.

"You needn't be afraid." Vivian's tone said otherwise. And the slight curl to her lips was definitely not a smile. "You are guests here. And as I understand it, we might soon be calling you our Regional Alpha."

"I wish that it could be under better circumstances." She'd meant it to sound kind, but somehow Giselle managed to say it with a bit of teenage snark. "Sorry, I mean… for your loss." There was no saving herself from this conversation. She'd already addressed the elephant in the room, and Vivian couldn't have looked angrier.

Vivian cleared her throat. "Wolves are often taken before their time. Such is the way of this life as an Alpha. One never knows who's hungrier for power."

Giselle's jaw nearly hit the ground. Had she heard Vivian correctly? Was that a threat? She looked to Martina for confirmation and found her adoptive mother being held back by Gavin's firm grip. Yep. That bitch had threatened her. But this was neither the time nor the place to shift and accept that challenge.

"The problem with those who are too hungry" – Giselle locked eyes with Vivian – "is they often make dire mistakes. David did not…"

"Don't you dare speak his name." Vivian tossed her drink aside, letting it crash to the ground and shatter. She lunged at Giselle, but before she could reach the little werewolf, Richard inserted himself between the two.

"Not the time. Not the place. If you wish to make a formal challenge, you will do so at the appropriate time. And as she is underage, I have been appointed her warrior." His words were delivered with all the power and conviction of an Alpha, yet Richard had openly rejected the position.

Giselle wished he'd just take it. She wasn't cut out for this life. Bowing and scraping, ordering people around… The lavish home would be nice, but all the fine trappings of this life she could do without.

Vivian's features hardened. She stared down her slender nose, threatening death with her eyes, and then in a flash, straightened and smoothed her dress and called out for her butler. "Derek, please see to this mess."

Martina growled from where she sat, Gavin still holding her firm. "You will refrain from threatening my daughter again, is that clear?"

"She is no more your daughter than I am. You are simply her guardian."

"And her Regent until she comes of age. You would do well to remember that." Momma Wolf was out and ready for a fight. Martina had never looked so fierce. "A threat to her is a threat to me. And I do not need Richard to take my place. My teeth and claws are ready when you are."

Vivian chuckled and returned her attention to Giselle. "You do inspire quite a lot of loyalty, don't you, little werewolf?"

Giselle didn't bother to take Vivian's baited question.

"I've heard of all the trouble you've caused as well. I highly doubt the Council will accept *your* Regency at the meeting, but you can continue to delude yourself."

"She has the birthright lineage to the position. Daughter of the true Alpha. Not the second son," Richard said.

"The true Alpha abdicated…"

"You and I both know that's not how things work. In death alone can an Alpha leave their post."

Vivian brushed away Richard's words like a troublesome fly.

"And," Richard continued, "Giselle comes with the backing of both the Thrace and Hernandez packs in Las Vegas."

"Yes. So I've heard." Vivian turned her back on Richard and took a seat next to her daughter, who'd sat nearly stone-still the entire time.

Where Vivian was openly aggressive, her daughter appeared neutral; or perhaps she just didn't care about the fight. Giselle wondered how she was feeling, having just lost her father and forced to entertain the people who had killed him. That had to be hard, but neither a tear dropped nor a muscle in her face twitched to reveal anything she might have been feeling.

"Is this how it's going to be, then? Why were we asked to come here if there would be open hostility between our two packs?" Gavin asked, his calm tone a sharp contrast to the women in the room.

"As the former caretaker of Orion... done so out of duty to my husband," Vivian shot an angered glare at Giselle. "I am now relinquishing that task to his rightful family."

That Giselle hadn't been prepared for. To see her father, yes – but not to suddenly become his nurse.

"We had not been informed that this exchange was to happen so soon. But we'll make the appropriate alterations to our plans to accommodate him," Gavin said.

"See that you do. He requires special feeding and changing, as he cannot perform those tasks at all. I've had his care instructions drawn up by the nurse, so you'll know what to do. Take special care around the full moon. He does still shift at random." She finished with a cocky smile.

Giselle doubted Vivian had ever cared for her father at all. She'd paid a nurse to do it all, and now this exchange was simply a way for her to get back at them for what happened to David. Too bad she was underage; she'd love to accept the challenge Vivian had issued.

The sound of a chair being wheeled down a tile hallway caught Giselle's attention. She took a breath and mentally prepared for the worst.

Ace came through first, holding open one of the large French doors leading into the solarium. Behind him, Jay was pushing a wheelchair.

Giselle stood and turned fully to take in the sight of the man sitting limply in the chair.

He'd once been tall and proud, that was certain. Even emaciated and weak, his body filled the frame of the chair, nearly overflowing. Long waves of brown hair framed his face, and through his dead expression she saw the emerald green of his eyes.

He stared blankly forward, giving no indication that he actually saw what was in front of him. His mouth hung slack, allowing a tiny dribble to escape the corners of his lips.

A far cry from what she'd imagined her father to be; and yet seeing him now, she felt the connection to him.

Her heart sank, knowing what had happened and feeling guilty that it was her birth that had played a part in making him this way.

"Father," she said meekly, taking a step towards him. "We don't know each other. And maybe we never will. But I am your daughter. Giselle." She reached out a hand and allowed her fingertips to graze the tops of his hands resting neatly in his lap.

Maybe he heard her. Maybe he didn't. None of that really mattered. She needed to speak, if only to break the silence in the room, and talking to him was infinitely better than that.

She'd have thought him a corpse, given the chill that clung to him and the gray of his skin. His breath, so shallow it might not register to human ears, was barely audible even to hers. The rise and fall of his chest were millimeters of movement. And yet, despite all that, she knew he was alive, and she hoped he could hear her. Perhaps his consciousness was there somewhere, trapped in this frozen body.

There was hope there in that thought. Though it meant her father a prisoner of his own mind, if life remained within, there might be a way to help him. Fate was cruel, but she couldn't imagine that he'd have done something bad enough to deserve this. Even if he had broken magical laws, it was done so to bring new life into the world. A child to be loved. Only that child hadn't been loved for many years.

Giselle gazed into his glazed over eyes, trying to make a connection, trying to find that hint of life left in there.

"I am glad to finally meet you. And I promise we'll take good care of you." She squeezed his hand to emphasize her point, and at that moment, she could have sworn she felt a muscle twitch.

Giselle turned around toward Martina, needing someone to speak. And more than that, needing an adult to take the reins now. She would take care of her dad. But it was Martina and Gavin who took care of her at this point, and they too had to extend that same promise.

"We will make the necessary arrangements, of course," Martina said. "How soon will you need us to take him into our care?"

All eyes turned to Vivian, and at first, it appeared she would use her anger as a reason to abandon him immediately, but with her boys also looking on, she hesitated.

"He will need to leave my care when you return to your... home."

Giselle let out a sigh of relief. They hadn't prepared for this. They were no doubt staying in a small two-room suite nearby. It wouldn't have been fair to attempt to bring Orion there.

"Thank you for your generosity," Martina responded.

8

It wasn't proper Alpha-to-be behavior, nor was it even respectful of the people in the room, but the moment Ace was told to take Orion back to his room, Giselle jumped up and followed.

Murmurs of disappointment rose up in her wake, but she didn't give them time to catch her. Once she'd breeched the double doors and made it into the lonely hall, it was as if all the air rushed back into her lungs.

"Seriously?" she called after Ace, who was walking slowly ahead.

"Not the greeting you expected, I know." Ace sounded as if he were ready to accept the tongue lashing Giselle was about to give him.

Anger dug its claws into her, and like a wounded animal, Giselle wanted to lash out. He could have warned her it would be like this. He could have offered her tips on how to deal with his pack. Sending her in blind to be ridiculed and laughed at by Vivian was an act of hatred in and of itself.

The words nearly came out of her mouth, but then Jay's warning had been just that. Ace had not come out and said anything, but at least his brother had had the decency to try.

In her hesitation, she hadn't noticed that Ace stopped walking. He turned to her, and there was no animosity in his eyes. If anything, she saw pain. Here was a man hurting, and by the looks of him, doing all he could to hide it.

"Don't judge Mother too harshly." Ace offered a hand in friendship. "She's deeply troubled by the death of our father." Standing there, with all the outward resolve of someone ready for the gallows, Ace looked like someone who'd taken more than his share of abuse already. "Aim your anger at me. I can handle it."

Giselle opened her mouth, still wanting to lash out, but her venom had disappeared. "I am angry," she sighed, wishing she had better words for that moment.

"And you have every right to be. None of this is fair." Lines that she'd not noticed before etched his face. A weary sigh escaped his lips, and when she did not take his outstretched hand, he let it fall limply to his side."

"Why didn't you warn me about what was to come?"

"I should have known better. And for that I am sorry. This transition is more than just moving a seat of power. Our pack has…" He stopped short, biting his tongue.

More secrets. More lies. Honesty, it seemed, was too hard for her kind. Everything had to be shrouded in mystery, even when that could mean life or death for another.

Anger rumbled up her chest in a growl that revealed just how close to the surface her wolf was.

Rising to the challenge, Ace met her eyes, his own wolf peering out from behind them. An Alpha meeting another Alpha, ready to prove themselves. Ace shook away the haggard guise and stood at full height, reminding her just how tall and proud a wolf could look, even in their human form.

Impressive was an understatement. He radiated power that commanded attention. Youth gave vigor to that power, and if they had not been related, she most certainly would have felt an attraction to his animal magnetism. But despite the great show, Giselle refused to be intimidated.

She was an Alpha, despite admitting to others she didn't feel she deserved the title. When challenged, her wolf easily rose to the task, fearing nothing from the male standing toe to toe with her. Giselle held her ground as her wolf gave power to her words. "I am the daughter of Orion Silverman. I am your kin and *your* Alpha. I am here to claim my right, and I will not be lied to any longer."

The silent battle of wills between their wolves came to a standstill. Ace neither lowered his eyes nor blinked. His only acquiescence was being first to speak. "You are family. And you are Orion's daughter. But you are not *my* Alpha."

Though she would not admit it aloud, he spoke the truth. She was not his Alpha. Her wolf felt it too. They were equals as much as they were family. She kept her eyes locked with his, still carrying on the silent battle of wills. "Speak to me as family, then."

Those words earned her the win in this battle. With a heavy breath, Ace dropped his eyes, gazing down at the silent form of Orion, sitting unaware of the events around him. "My mother's place as Alpha's mate is now unstable. Our pack is in a state of transition, beyond just losing the regional title."

In her haste to be done with the formality of taking the title, Giselle had not considered the ripple effect the change of power would have.

"Because I will not remain here?" she asked, knowing the answer before he nodded to confirm it.

"Mom cannot remain the Alpha, as she only married into the role. So, the local packs want to select a new Alpha."

"And that entails?" Giselle had an idea already.

"A fight. Always a fight," Ace sighed, and turned to push Orion's chair down the hall again.

"Will she fight?" Giselle asked.

"If she can, yes. Or I will have to step in."

"And your mom blames me for putting her in this position, I'm sure."

Ace nodded again.

"And what about your sister? What's her deal?" Giselle said, remembering the stone-cold stare Leila had given her.

Ace shrugged. "She hasn't spoken since Dad died."

"I'm so sorry." Giselle could understand Vivian's issue, but Leila looked as if all the lights had been turned off and no one was home. Loss affected people in funny ways, though. Giselle felt bad for initially thinking poorly of Leila.

"She'll come around eventually. Just let her be until that time. Don't pick a fight." The warning of a big brother was there in his voice. Alpha or no, she'd definitely heed it. That poor girl. She couldn't even imagine what was going through her mind. Loss of a father; her family in turmoil.

Silence passed between them as they slowly walked down the hall. She hated it – all the stress and animosity, the pressure to perform according to laws she didn't understand. And worst yet, learning she had family – real blood relatives – and that fact being the reason for all the drama. Sometimes it was better not knowing who you were.

"So. Between you and me... How do you feel?" Giselle asked.

Ace let out a deep sigh. "Worried."

"You too, huh?" Giselle felt relief at his instant honesty. If they could only keep it up. All the half-truths and secrets served no one, least of all them. Especially if they were to work together in the future.

"Yeah. For me, this means new leadership. A new type of life."

"How so?" Giselle asked, realizing she was showing exactly how little she knew of wolf politics.

"I was raised believing I would be the next Regional." He stopped and turned to Giselle. "Not that I'm mad that you were offered the position. I'm fine. Really."

"Those who are truly fine don't have to repeat it over and over." Giselle winked at him.

He cracked a smile, and for that brief moment she saw the old Ace – the carefree guy who'd first showed up at their door in Vegas. The one who blatantly flirted with her sisters. "Okay. Truth." He stopped pushing Orion's chair and turned to face Giselle. "I'm disappointed and sad. But I have no anger toward you, cousin."

"I get it. And if we're being completely honest, I'm not sure what I'm doing here."

"Well, that makes two of us."

"Okay. So we're on the level." Now that he'd dropped his guard, Giselle felt no harm in speaking freely and revealing just how little she knew of pack hierarchy. "How does my being here and being Regional Alpha impact you?"

Ace continued his stroll down the hall. "I won't be Regional, but I might be pack Alpha. We'll still live here, and this territory needs an Alpha. If Mother doesn't want it."

"Does she?" Giselle asked. "Really?"

Ace shrugged. "She's used to being the Alpha's mate. She's used to Father's power, and the money that being Regional Alpha takes in. Tributes from the other territories."

"And that ends when you guys no longer hold the Regional spot?" Giselle asked.

"Right. So there will be a slight restructuring there. We have money, so that's not the issue. But we'll no longer have that added power. Mother might not handle that well."

"And you will?" Giselle lifted an eyebrow, waiting for the lie to follow her baited question.

"I'll try."

Giselle matched pace with Ace. "And if you have to listen to me? Would that be so bad?"

"Do you know how to manage the packs?" Ace's tone was pure snark.

"I'll learn."

"You'd have to. Packs are always quarreling. Father spent countless hours fielding complaints and settling disputes. He used much of the tributes paid to the Regency to fund the travel expenses of those who were sent out to physically re-establish order."

"Sounds like managing a bunch of bickering children."

"Worse." Ace laughed.

"What do they fight over?" Giselle asked.

"You name it. Vampires, witches, shifters, other packs, the Acta Sanctorum, human transformations, the list goes on."

"Human what, now?" Giselle asked, shocked at what she'd just heard.

"Oh, boy, you really have just cut your teeth, haven't you?" Disappointment darkened Ace's tone. "See, this is what worries me, and probably more of our kind. You grew up human. You're still learning what it is to be wolf. Makes anyone nervous. The changes you could bring."

"I get it. I have a ton to learn." More and more, she felt she was wrong for this job. But she saw no way to back out. She'd already been warned that embarrassing the family could have further implications that would affect Ace, Jay, and the rest of the Silverman family. And that would further ripple out to the local packs that she'd not even had the chance to meet yet. Yet if she were given the title after wowing the Council, all that responsibility would be heaped onto her shoulders. One look at Ace said he was feeling that same pressure, and more so now that he'd learned the truth of how unprepared she was. "I promise. I will do my best." Her words were meant to reassure Ace, but she needed that assurance herself, with no one to guarantee it.

"I will honor whoever is *my* Alpha. Without question." Ace spoke plainly. "I trust the judgment of the Council. But if I'm worried, others will be too."

"Can I be honest?" Giselle asked.

"I thought we were being honest."

"When I first met you, I took you for a playboy."

Ace puffed his chest proudly and the corner of his lip cocked upward in a grin to match. "Oh, that I am. Most certainly. Have the ladies lined up to be the next—"

"But seeing you alone," Giselle cut him off, "like this—"

"We're cousins… remember?" Ace finished her sentence before she could.

She shot him a shut-the-hell-up glare. "Not interested. And… Ewwww. We're family, dude. How could you even think that was where I was going?"

"You called me a playboy." Ace shrugged.

"Let's just get this clear now. No. Hell. No. But check with Taylor. Just saying."

"Good to know." Ace winked, completely unfazed by her outburst.

"As I was saying. I took you for a playboy, but now I see you have a head on your shoulders, too. I was wrong to misjudge you without knowing you."

"Easy to enjoy the freedom of youth when you know responsibility is years away. I expected father to reign for a century or more before he passed the title down. Plenty of time to make bad decisions. But now…" Ace sighed. "Time to do my part for my family."

Giselle nodded. "I know what you mean." The mantle of Alpha had only been sitting on her shoulders for a week, but already she'd felt the change within her. "What about Jay?"

"He's the lucky one. Second son, if only by minutes." Ace snorted. "Lucky bastard. He can enjoy his youth longer. If I'm granted the local Alpha title, his role will be the right hand… an enforcer."

"Ever wish you were the second son?" Giselle asked.

"Sometimes," Ace replied. He stopped at the end of the hall in front of a door that looked wider than normal. "This is where we've been having your father stay. All of his stuff will be packed up before you make the journey home. You might want to see it and have some time alone with him before you take off. The nurse comes in once every hour to check on him, but there's also a call button here if there's an emergency." He pushed Orion's chair in through the doorway and wheeled him around to the side of the bed where a TV was on, playing commercials. "I'll leave you two to get acquainted."

"Thanks." Giselle followed inside and sat down on the bed.

Ace walked to the door. "If I misjudged you, I'm sorry."

He left her contemplating the words without giving her a chance to form a response. Not that she had one, but she did wonder what his current judgment of her was.

9

The constant chatter on the television acted as white noise behind the screaming of her own anxiety. So much pressure to put on a good show, only to win a title even she knew she wasn't qualified for. And there was no way out of it without ruining her family's good name and making more enemies than she'd already racked up – enemies that that until recently had not known nor cared about her. Had she never been adopted, Giselle imagined herself as a happy lone wolf, living out her days without the pressures of pack life or blood.

Her eyes instinctively drew toward the figure seated alongside the bed. Orion's presence had barely registered while she had been dealing with Ace, but now she was alone, face to face with her father.

All she'd ever wanted was family. She'd gotten her wish, and all the drama that came with it.

In her mind, she'd built up Orion to be a man of such great stature and commanding presence. Even enfeebled as he was now, she expected to see the glory and might. And now that she did, Giselle was left with a strange sort of numbness.

He was clearly a broken man. Whatever he might have been in a former life had evaporated, leaving behind the shell as a reminder. And though she shouldn't, Giselle felt that part of it was her fault.

What was she supposed to do now? He sat deathly still, his chest barely rising and falling with each shallow breath and his eyes glazed over as if he were asleep, but the lids had not quite gotten the memo.

Giselle scooted over on the edge of the bed, her knees butting up against the chair Orion was sitting in, and the moment they connected she felt that strange spark.

No words could define the sensation, and the moment it was there, it vanished, leaving only the ghost of its presence in her mind. She was connected to him. Of that she was certain. But the depth and meaning behind it she could not fully grasp.

"I wish I knew what to say to you." Giselle looked at Orion's face, feeling awkward about making eye contact, although talking to him without at least trying to face him felt somehow disrespectful. He was there in the room. Whether or not he responded to her should make no difference.

"I always wondered where I came from. Spent a lot of time alone growing up. I didn't really fit in. Too tomboy for the girls. Too tomboy for the boys, too." She laughed awkwardly. "I made friends with the walls of my room, for the most part. When I had a room, that is. This one seems nice." She rambled on, trying desperately to make small talk to fill the void and decrease her own feeling of unease.

Reality often proved stranger than fantasy. Her fantasies had always played out with her parents reaching out with open arms to embrace her. They'd tell her fantastic stories to explain why they'd had to leave her, and promised never to do so again.

Knowing the truth now, she wished her fantasies had been real. Seeing the shattered remains of what had been done to those who'd brought her into this world made her childhood trauma seem so much less horrible.

At least she'd had a life. A roof over her head. Even now, she had a family that had taken her in, and a pack that loved her and wanted her with them. She had so much to be thankful for. Even amidst the awkwardness of this meeting, Giselle knew she had a father. And he deserved more than to be hidden away in this room.

"We don't have much back in Vegas. That's where my new pack is from. But I promise you, we'll do our best to care for you and make you part of the family. I won't leave you sitting in a room all day. I promise." Giselle placed a hand on her father's, wanting that strange sensation, their connection, to last more than just the brief moment of initial contact. Like the heartbeat of a hummingbird, there grew a vibration between them. Energy. Magic. Giselle still could not find the right word for it, but as she held on, she swore she heard the echo of her name being called out.

A tap on her shoulder pulled her snarling from within her own thoughts. She turned around with the ferocity of her angry wolf ready to strike out and found Taylor behind her.

She took a moment before she spoke. The sudden anger, that desperate need to protect – that wasn't her. Giselle pulled her hand away from her father's, and her heart immediately slowed. "I'm sorry. I don't know what came over me."

Fear, the like of which she had never seen in her sister's eyes, held Taylor speechless.

Giselle stood and faced her. "Are you okay?"

"You were like in a trance. I was calling your name. And then you... What the hell happened?"

"I don't know. It was so weird. He totally reacted when I touched him." Giselle whispered to Taylor as if saying it out loud would sound insane. "I felt something. Like... I just can't explain it."

Taylor closed her eyes and sighed.

Why was it that no one could ever take her at her word?

"I'm sure it was just one of those reflex motions. Nerves making his hand jump or something when you brushed against his arm hair or whatever." Taylor's sympathetic tones only sounded like mocking to Giselle. "He's been a vegetable for years now. But Vivian said he shifts occasionally. That might be it. We are near another cycle."

"It was more than that. I felt it. There was a connection there... like... magic."

"Awww, honey." Taylor pulled her into a big hug. "Of course there's a connection. He's your dad."

Hugging was the last thing she wanted from her patronizing sister. Giselle pushed away and turned to Orion, half hoping he would have moved or done something to prove she wasn't just making things up.

"Giselle, please," Taylor called after her. "I want you to be happy now that you have a dad, but don't expect miracles. It will just lead to heartbreak."

"I know you're trying to be all nice and sisterly. So I'm not going to get mad that you instantly assume I'm going to do something stupid. But really, for once, just indulge my crazy and pretend to be excited. I felt something. A real connection when I touched his hand."

"You're right. I'm sorry. You totally have the magic touch. I saw it all happen. It was amazing and unbelievable."

"And now you're patronizing me," Giselle groaned. Taylor's eyes rolled so hard they nearly popped out onto the floor. "Sorry, sister. You don't get it both ways. You can have down-to-earth me, with all my naysaying, or you can have super Yes Woman, at your service."

"Whatever."

"Look, I get it. I do. And I really want you to be happy. But I also want you to realize that you cannot fix every problem. Some things are unfixable."

She hadn't even gotten to the part about fixing him yet, and already her sister had proved she would be no help. Naysayer or no, Giselle had felt a connection. There was magic there – and she knew exactly who to talk to about magic.

"It's time for us to head to the hotel," Taylor said impatiently, when Giselle failed to respond to her.

"Fine. Let's go." Giselle looked back to her father. "See you soon. I promise." She squeezed his hand before letting go.

"You think he can hear you?" Taylor asked.

Giselle looked back again. Her father stared blankly, as he had been doing the entire time. Giselle looked back to Taylor. "I do. I really do." She couldn't explain the feeling, the connection when she touched him – not yet, at least. But it was there. And she knew he was too. Somewhere trapped inside his own body, Orion was there.

10

"Despite what you think, I am on your side." Taylor sounded as if she were trying to convince herself more than Giselle. "I just want to see you relax a little. You've been super stressed for a while now. Even before this whole Alpha business."

She led Giselle back down the long hallway. In the distance, raised voices and the sounds of a struggle suggested the meeting had not gone as civilly as originally planned. Giselle dreaded going back into the solarium to deal with that horrible woman Vivian.

"I'll relax when we're back home, living our normal lives again. I promise I'll never complain about sitting through another boring lecture in Mr. Harper's class again." Giselle laughed awkwardly.

From what she could glean from the muffled sounds behind the door, Martina and Vivian were disagreeing on costs owed for the care and transporting of Orion back to Vegas.

"You know that's not true." Before they hit the double doors, Taylor took a turn left, passing under a thin archway back into the grand foyer. "Alpha or no, you'll still have to sit through them and pass his class, all the while, managing these squabbling wolves." Taylor angled her head toward the doors as they passed them.

"From what Ace said... yeah. Nothing but bitching all the time. Why bother?" Giselle's annoyance revealed itself in the weary tone in her voice.

The entire house was a giant nerve waiting to be tweaked just so. At any moment, with the right words or actions the whole place could explode into violence. She remembered how hateful the Thrace and Hernandez packs had been when she'd first arrived. Coupled with the angry shouting from the other room, it formed an image of her future – playing mediator to people who refused to simply get along. More and more she realized this wasn't for her. But Giselle had no choice in the matter.

Anger wasn't her issue, though all outward appearances seemed to suggest it. She'd always had an even temperament. Always tried to feel a situation out. But with the extreme stress and pressure she was under now, Giselle felt ill-equipped to deal with the overwhelming amount of emotions it created.

If only she had time to digest what was happening – but no, the wolves demanded immediate action, and as a result, two families were poised to destroy each other over who got to be in charge of whom. Stupid, really; especially since Giselle would have never known or cared about it if they hadn't made her queen in their stupid game of chess.

"Ignore my grumpiness, Tay, I'm just exhausted right now," Giselle started to say as they cut a path across the large foyer to the front door.

Leila stood by the entrance, arms crossed, scowling as they approached.

If she hadn't known better, she'd have thought Leila was looking for a fight; but Giselle remembered what Ash said, and rather than go with her gut and assume the worst, she tried to approach with kindness. "Hey. Thanks for taking such good care of Orion. And I'm so sorry for how things turned out."

The look she received in return for her sympathetic words had more contempt than appreciation, but Leila did not verbally respond to Giselle.

Body language spoke volumes without the need for words. Leila might have been in mourning, but her lack of speech was not the root of the problem. Silently seething with rage, she looked as if at any moment she might lash out in anger.

Yet another person affected by Giselle's sudden acknowledgement as Alpha presumptive.

Making enemies for just being alive was the theme of the week, it seemed.

She ignored Leila as best she could as she walked past, ready to head to the van and be done with the Silverman pack for the day, but as she hit the first step, Leila broke her silence.

"Just a stupid mutt. Totally not the Alpha type. Don't even know why you would want the job." Leila's tone matched the rage Giselle had sensed, but her words had been far nastier than she would have expected.

A snarky comeback tiptoed to the edge of Giselle's tongue, but she held it back, despite the impulse to retaliate. Cooler heads were expected when one was supposed to be a leader. At least, that was what the voice of her subconscious was trying to convey. What would be the point? Leila's lifestyle proved she was nothing more than a pampered little princess, completely out of touch with the lives of regular girls. Her opinion barely registered on Giselle's scale of importance, though the insult stung a little.

"Bitch," Giselle mumbled under her breath, and continued down the stairs. A fight would only prolong their departure.

Taylor did not have the same level of restraint, and Giselle hadn't noticed until too late that her sister had not followed her down the steps.

"You're just pissed because you and your family are nothing special. Just one of us now." Taylor had turned on Leila and looked ready to go full wolf.

"I will never be one of you. Alpha or no, we will always be better than you."

"Keep thinking that, sweetie. Because once Giselle is your Alpha, snark like that can have you banished from her territory," Taylor responded.

Giselle was about to put an end to the conversation. Pleased as she was that her sister had gone to bat for her, the whole conversation was going nowhere. But before Giselle could pull her sister away, Leila responded, "That lone wolf will never be Alpha."

For the first time ever, Giselle didn't feel like a lone wolf, but hearing someone use it in such a way had her hackles up.

What was wrong with being a lone wolf? If anything, being a loner had taught her more life skills than being in a pack had. She was resourceful, inquisitive, and self-sufficient. When others relied on the judgment of leaders, Giselle had learned to rely on her intuition. When those in power were doing things wrong, even when their intentions were good, she made it a point to bring in the truth and see the right decisions were made. Being a loner was probably the reason she kept being told she was suited for this job. She'd never seen herself as a leader, but in the time she had known her pack, she'd taken that role, and she'd inspired loyalty and trust.

"Small minds should not try to comprehend large concepts." Giselle put all her annoyance into to the tone of her snarky response as she took hold of Taylor's arm and pulled her away from the little princess.

Behind her, with a whole lot of huffing and puffing, the pissed off wolf demanded that Giselle return and defend her words.

Giselle smiled inwardly, knowing her response had had the desired effect.

"Go mop the floor with her," Taylor said.

"Don't need to. She'll be fuming for hours over that comment. If I knocked her out, she'd spend the next bit sleeping it off." Giselle didn't have to look back to see Leila storming into the house; the fading sound of her crazed ranting was proof enough she'd hit her mark.

"But she'd have bruises to remember you by."

"She's got mental ones now, trust me," Giselle laughed.

"What are you going to do with her?" Taylor asked.

"Nothing. I don't have to do anything with her. She's so certain I won't be Alpha anyway. If I'm not, she can relish her victory, and who gives a damn? You know I don't care about power."

Taylor stopped dead in her tracks. "But it's your birthright."

"Um... hello?.... Orphan." Giselle pointed to herself, as if she needed to make sure her sister understood exactly who she was. "I lost my birthright the moment I was born."

Taylor had disbelief all over her face. "Only because you were lost. Now you're found, and wolfy royalty to boot!"

"Whatever." Giselle shrugged, as if hoping to shake loose the title and all the weight that came with it. "I'm just glad I found my family."

"And because of that, you're able to claim the title," Taylor reminded her.

"Great. If they want me to have it, I will. If not, that's cool too."

"I can't believe how nonchalant you are about this." Taylor still refused to accept that Giselle didn't yearn for power.

"That's because nothing has happened. I mean… aside from me finding Dad." He'd taken up the bulk of her excitement. That touch. The spark of life. She felt it. There was something still within that shell of a man. And she'd do whatever she could to bring him back to life. The rest of the trip was kind of annoying, if she was being completely honest with herself. The whole Alpha changing of the guard seemed just an excuse for a spectacle.

Even the Council meeting seemed a bit over the top. There would be a vote, and Vivian as Alpha of her family pack would be given a say. There was a real possibility that Giselle would not be allowed to take the title of Regional Alpha, birthright or not.

Giselle really didn't know her own mind about where she stood on the whole issue of taking the title.

On the one hand, it would be cool. But on another it meant the spotlight would be on her, and even going back to Vegas and living with her pack in their small family home, she'd never have the same simple life she'd grown accustomed to.

But, whatever the outcome, she'd face it head on. She just wanted to get it over with quickly, so she could focus on Dad and maybe bring him out of his shell.

"I think I lost her," Taylor said, and Giselle realized she'd let her train of thought derail mid conversation and hadn't even noticed Martina standing there in front of her.

"Honey, are you okay?" Martina asked.

"Just a lot on my mind," Giselle replied.

"That girl was talking trash. Don't let her get to you," Taylor replied.

"I couldn't care less what she said. What I want to know is, when is this part going to be over with, so we can go home and get back to normal life?"

"I know this is a lot to deal with. I promise once this weekend is over, we'll be back home. I've changed our flights and arranged for a special van to pick us up, so we can get your dad home with us and settle in."

Martina's care and attention to detail was part of what made her such a good head of the family. She was the kind of wolf who should be Alpha. One silver lining in the whole ordeal, if Giselle was made Alpha, was that Martina would get that opportunity.

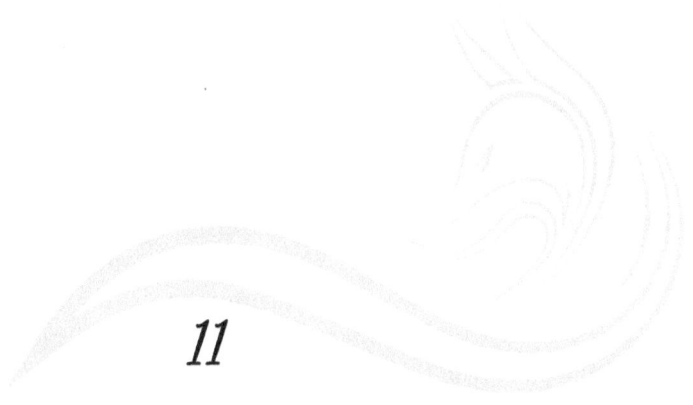

11

"We don't have long, so sit down and pay attention." Richard whipped his hand out, his finger an arrow pointing to the dinette set in the small living space of their two-room suite.

Tension had left everyone in the hotel room unable to sleep the previous night, and no amount of coffee had tempered their annoyance. That, coupled with the fact that there were only two showers, one each in their adjoining rooms, meant the queue had formed before Giselle had even risen for the day.

She grumbled, desperate for revitalizing spray of hot shower water, and resigned herself to sitting down for another lecture on wolf politics.

"You will be alone tonight." Richard's words slapped her in the face.

"What?"

"At least for the beginning. The – we'll call it a reception – before the dinner party."

Richard's tone might have been matter-of-fact, but his words sent Giselle's heart racing.

"Why? They can't do that!" She jumped to her feet, but an angry glare from her mentor had her quickly returning to her seat.

"It's a test. Obviously." He sighed in annoyance. "You'll need to show them you are worthy of the title without the leash of your parents guiding you."

Giselle huffed. News like this required more caffeine than she'd been allowed this morning, and the sludge they'd set out on the counter might as well have been decaf for all the effect it had waking her up. "I can't do this."

"You can and you will, little wolf." Richard scowled down his sharp nose at her. He had the kind of face that could intimidate you with a smile, and the way he glared now had her wanting to escape.

"I'm just not the girl for the job and yet you people keep pushing me to take it."

"If you act the way you are now, you'll certainly prove you're not up to the task, and the Council will be forced to open the position to challenge."

"And that means there will be a lot of people fighting. I get that."

"No, you don't. Alphas fight to the death. It's not just fighting. You playing your part will help keep lives from being lost."

"More pressure. That's exactly what I need," Giselle said in exasperation, with all the power of teenage angst to back it up.

"Suck it up little wolf, and listen." Richard might as well have smacked her in the face for all the gentleness of his words. "Yes, you save those lives. But beyond that, you prevent wars. The regional Alpha keeps all the packs in check. You're a neutral party, so if you come to power, you can maintain that balance. But let's say an Alpha from one pack that is warring with another pack becomes Regional Alpha. They then have the power to destroy the pack they were already at war with."

She couldn't believe in this day and age wolves would be so petty. "But they—"

"Yes. They would." Richard cut her off before she could finish. "No doubt you've already heard that the Regional is responsible for keeping the peace. That's a full-time job."

Giselle sighed, knowing there was no way out, but silently prayed for some miracle to save her.

Richard blew out a calming breath. Whether he'd seen the panic in her eyes or felt a change of tactic was needed, he took a moment and sat down next to her before continuing with a noticeable change in tone. "It's a lot to ask of you, but no more than you've already shown you're capable of. Remember it was you who brought the Thrace and Hernandez packs to peace."

Giselle nodded, unable to find the words to speak.

"I'm only asking for you to do your best tonight. Take this one day at a time. But know I have faith in you."

"As do I." Martina came in through the adjoining door, her hair wrapped up in a towel. "And we will be with you for the meeting. Richard and I both have made sure of that, as your Regent and enforcer. You only have to be alone for the reception, so they can get to know you."

At least she had that. Hobnob for a couple of hours, and then she would get backup. That she could manage.

"Okay. What do you need me to do?" Giselle asked.

Her words sent a collective sigh of relief through the room. Richard turned to Martina, and as if a silent conversation passed between them, she took her leave.

"Representatives from all the Regional Alpha packs will be there. Remember the people I told you about?" Richard asked.

Giselle had written it all down but couldn't remember where she'd put the paper. "Kinda."

"Doesn't matter. Let them introduce themselves. Makes them feel important. And along those lines, you should act impressed by them all."

"So I'm sucking up, then?" Giselle asked.

"Tone it down a bit." Amusement lit Richard's eyes, and if she wasn't mistaken, there was a slight chuckle hidden in his words. "General interest is all you need to show. If you are to take the position, you will be their equal, so do not set them too high above you at the start. But yes, you want them to like you, so make sure you acknowledge their importance."

"Will my sisters get to come at all?" Giselle prayed the answer would be yes. They'd make her look good physically, but having them near also helped bolster her confidence, too.

"No." The words came out with utter finality.

Damn. Giselle sighed, dropping her gaze to the small table as if interested in the grain of the wood. Until recently she'd survived on her own skills. Dealt with countless new families. Always having to play cute and sweet and hope for acceptance. How was this any different? Same play, just on a new stage. Once she realized that the people she'd be acting for held no more importance than in previous performances, she realized the strength she needed was already there. She could do this. And do it well. "Okay. What else?"

"Always make eye contact when speaking. Show them your own personal dominance, but speak with respect and interest."

Giselle practiced with Richard, meeting his eyes as she asked, "And what should I talk to them about?"

Approval softened the sharpness of Richard's gaze. "Very good. Ask them about their territory. What kind of issues they see affecting our kind. Business-like questions that show you have an interest in the politics of our people."

Be the leader. Think like a leader. "What if they ask about me?" Giselle wondered, knowing that her own personal story was the reason her birthright was being called into question.

"You will be grateful for the Hernandez pack taking you in. You will talk of how you brought the two packs together. Always play up the wolf side of your life."

"But if they ask?" It would come up. How could it not? How many wolves grew up as she had?

"Be brief, and don't lie. A wolf can smell it, you know."

More so than he probably understood. She laughed to herself. "Yes. I know."

"Then keep that in mind when you speak."

If she thought she'd hit her quota of nerves before, she was drowning in them now. Giselle's eyes found the pot of sludge still sitting on the counter and resigned herself to getting another cup. If she was going to be on her best, she would need plenty of energy, and maybe a bit of sugar to put some pep in her step.

Martina returned to the room, dressed for the day, and snatched up her purse. "Coffee run?" she asked.

"Oh, thank the gods for you!" Giselle nearly tripped over her feet to hug her adoptive mother.

"Oh, you are desperate, aren't you?" Martina laughed.

"I honestly don't know how I'm going to pull it off." She hesitated, knowing they were all counting on her. Even now she could see Martina's apprehension. "But I will. I promise. Best behavior."

"I know you will, dear." Martina's words were hopeful more than certain.

Giselle understood what was at stake. Pressure to perform had her stomach churning, but she would not let her family down over that. Martina had been so good to her – given her a home when no one else had. Despite her innate ability to cause trouble, Giselle would never do anything to directly harm her family.

"You'll see. A little caffeine and the fashion stylings of Taylor and Di, and I'll be a shoe-in for Alpha. They'll be begging me to take the position." Giselle overplayed her hand in the hopes that her false confidence would bring a real smile to Martina's face.

Nearly hitting the mark, her adoptive mother laughed. "Three shots of espresso?" She winked and left the hotel, purse in hand.

Giselle turned to see Richard still sitting at the table. More than anything, the old wolf looked tired.

"Any final advice before I begin the total makeover?" She didn't need to see her sisters standing in the doorway behind her, just waiting to get their claws on her and turn her into the Alpha she was meant to be.

"I'd say *be yourself*, but we all know how that would end." Richard winked.

"Did you just try to make a joke?" Giselle laughed.

"Time will tell." He nodded. "Your entourage is waiting."

12

Night's cool breeze gently kissed her face like a dot-ing mother sending her child off to school for the first time. It blew through her loosely curled hair, whispering encouragement as Giselle stood outside of the hotel. She'd needed a few moments to clear her head before going inside to the reception hall where the wolves were waiting.

Above, a clear sky showed the moon nearly full, and she wished nothing more than to shed her skin and call her wolf forward to bask in the silvery light. How long had it been since she'd run free, allowing the breeze to ruffle her fur? How much longer would it be before she could do so alone? Here especially, on unfamiliar ground, she'd not be allowed the privilege, though it was the one thing that was sure to center her and calm the anxiety she was feeling.

"No pressure. None whatsoever. Just another day." Giselle tried to relax, whispering the words like a mantra to steady her nerves. She'd made the promise. She would do this. But though her mind was set, she could not control the way her heart raced at the thought of what was riding on this evening.

It's do or die time. She started inside, walking as proudly as she could, head held high. Half the battle was acting, and she could do that, at least.

As she approached the doors to the reception hall, Derek, the butler from Vivian's home, stopped her.

"I'll announce your entry, miss." Still as snooty as ever, his presence added to her concern for the evening. If he was here, did that mean Vivian had weaseled her way in? And if so, why hadn't her adoptive mother or Richard been allowed in?

He opened the door and called out to the room, "Miss Giselle Silverman."

Giselle cleared her throat. "Richards."

Derek looked down his nose at her. "Are you not Orion Silverman's daughter?"

The question caught her off guard for a moment. She was, yes, but her name had been Richards for as long as she could remember. "Yes."

"Then you will be addressed by your father's name, or reject his lineage."

If she could slap the snark out of that man's mouth, she would; but seeing that all eyes in the banquet hall were now looking at her, she pursed her lips and walked away. He'd be taught a lesson in manners once she became Alpha. That thought bolstered her confidence as she stepped into the room. She held her head high, as Richard had instructed.

Eyes watched her from all around – old souls with deceptively youthful faces. Wolves had longevity that often masked as immortality, she'd been told. Her pack was relatively new, but she knew some of these wolves had been around for centuries. Richard had done his best to brief her on politics as well as manners, but nothing could have prepared her for the sudden rush she felt entering the large ballroom.

Like the baseline of a song, waves of power throbbed within the room.

Giselle stopped short as the doors closed behind her, and she took a breath, allowing her heart to calm while attempting to recognize the people Richard had warned her about as well as hunting for an exit should she need it.

For the amount of people it held, the room seemed overly large. The Alphas had spread themselves all around, leaving wide gaps like invisible territorial boundaries that she'd have to cross if she wished to speak to them all.

Centrally located, a seating area had been set up for a feast. Giselle reminded herself that once they got to that part, she'd have back up again – Martina and Richard would be there. All she had to do was get through this initial reception.

She'd been so caught up in her own thoughts while staring at the place settings that she hadn't noticed the person behind her.

"You look nervous, kid."

Giselle nearly jumped at the sound of those words. Was her nervousness really showing that badly? Not even five minutes in and she was failing. She had to do better than this.

With a calming breath, she turned and greeted the woman who'd spoken to her, remembering she was supposed to be sucking up.

She'd expected to find an older lady with a business suit, perhaps brandishing a glass of chardonnay. Not in a million years had she expected an Alpha to be a young blonde woman with a pixie cut sporting red-tipped ends. Definitely not the business suit type, either. This Alpha wore her power in her presence, not her outfit, which was way more casual than any other in the room. If Giselle had known she could get away with a leather shrug over a long maxi dress, she'd have totally gone for it.

"My nerves are that obvious, huh?" Giselle asked, trying to keep her tone light and not give away the shear terror she felt inside. This woman was an Alpha, despite her look. She was someone Giselle was supposed to be fearless around. Head held high, and all that.

"We girls are so much better at reading body language than the men." The woman smiled brightly, disarming Giselle with genuine good-natured ribbing. "But don't let them know I said that."

"I won't." Giselle's guard went back up after the momentary lapse. Richard had warned her to be wary of all the Alphas, but he hadn't told her to expect one so young-looking. Of course, age was ambiguous where wolves were concerned, but this Alpha not only had the youthful look, her style screamed it as well.

"It's okay. I don't bite," she said with a slight chuckle. "Okay, bad joke. I know. But you looked like you needed a laugh."

"Sorry. I'm being rude, aren't I?" Giselle scrambled for something respectful to say. That was what was expected of her. Respect. Class. Importance... no... interest. "You are...?"

"Not going to bite your head off for taking a breath. Seriously. You look like you're going to have a fit. Don't be so stressed." Her smile had turned to concern.

"Damn. And I was going for calm and collected. Failed again." Giselle chose to go with the flow rather than try and save the moment with sarcasm.

"I'll have to take off points for execution, but you still have a chance to impress me during the swimsuit competition."

Giselle snorted with laughter and tried to cover it with a cough. "You are not what I expected."

"Neither are you, but here we are." The wolf laughed too. "The others might care if you're trying to impress them. Don't do that with me. Just be yourself, and we'll get along great."

That was exactly the thing Giselle needed to hear. And despite what Richard had told her about being careful, she felt that this wolf at least was being honest. She was different, and not just because of her youthful appearance. There was something else there below the surface, almost as if she were a kindred spirit. Giselle smiled genuinely and extended a hand. "You, I think, are the first Alpha I'm glad to meet."

"We're not all that bad. I'm Fallon, by the way." She shook Giselle's hand lightly and let go, quickly grabbing a glass from a tray as a waiter walked past. "Take a chug of this before anyone sees. It will help." She offered the drink, and Giselle slugged it in one go.

"Thanks. I'm Giselle."

"Oh, I think we all know who you are." Fallon laughed and snatched the glass back from Giselle before anyone spotted it. "You've got quite the backstory, little werewolf." She winked. "And I hear if the vote goes well, you'll be bringing the leadership back to my home town."

Giselle thought for a second. She'd never seen this woman in Vegas. Richard had shown her a few photos of the main Alphas. But Blondie was from the Olde Town Pack. "Wait... I thought you were from Boston?" Giselle asked, hoping she had not confused the Alpha with someone else.

"Looks like you've been given the quick summary on us." Fallon giggled. "Yeah, I live in Boston now, but when I was human, I lived in Vegas."

"What do you mean, *was*?" Giselle kicked herself for not paying better attention now to Richard's talk. But he'd droned on for so long she'd hardly been able to keep her eyes open.

"I'm a turned wolf," Fallon said with a flippant wave of her hand through her two-toned blonde and red hair.

"Showing how much of a noob I really am, aren't I?" Giselle chuckled to hide her confusion. The term human transformation had been thrown at her once before but the reality of it left her dumbstruck.

If Fallon had any clue how utterly confused Giselle was, the blonde wolf was not letting on. If anything, she looked even more amused to be chatting with Giselle. "You've still got me beat. You grew up like this; I'm still working through the whole supernatural thing."

Hearing that solidified the reason she'd felt at ease with Fallon right from the start. They were kindred spirits, in a way – both having grown up human and apart from all the wolfy politics. And that settled it. Fallon was definitely someone to make an ally of.

"I grew up human. For what that's worth. And then right about the time I got boobs" – Giselle pointed to her chest – "I got the tail too." She wiggled her hips for effect. "So I'm thinking we're evenly matched."

True amusement sparkled in Fallon's eyes. "Well, good, then we can be buddies." She threw an arm around Giselle and led her away from the tables.

"I could use a few more of those." One vote in her favor. At least, if she were reading Fallon's offer of friendship the right way. Having the backing of the Olde Town pack was definitely a step in the right direction. And beyond that, Fallon was more than interesting. She had no need to pretend as Richard had instructed. Giselle leaned in and whispered, "I hope you don't take this the wrong way, but I have to know… How'd you get turned? Like a bite or something?"

"Or something." Fallon's face contorted in pain.

"That bad, eh? Sorry." Just as she'd been feeling confident, Giselle had stuck her foot in her mouth. "I didn't mean to pry."

"You're fine." Fallon reassured her. "See the hair? That's no dye job. My best friend is a vampire. Her blood was the only reason I made it through the transition."

Giselle's jaw nearly dropped to the floor. "Wait… You've met a vampire?" She'd heard about them, but no one in her family admitted to knowing one. For all she' known, there were no vampires in Vegas.

"Oh, you poor sheltered little thing," Fallon laughed.

So much for her attempt at being cool. Her noob-ness flashed proudly like a neon sign above her head. "Yeah. Pretty much. But if it helps, I'm dating a witch." That had to count for something, right? "Dating out of your species. Against family rules? Cool points for you then." Fallon chuckled. "Yeah, my best friend is a vampire. But I knew her before she was turned. And then they – her vampy boyfriend and his group – tried to turn me."

"What?" This wolf was turning out to be the most interesting person Giselle had ever met. Who the hell tells off a group of vampires and then turns wolf? No denying the Alpha in that lady. That was for sure. Instant respect earned there. "How did you survive?"

"I put my foot down." Fallon stomped a foot for effect. "Told them I was under no circumstances going to let them turn me into a vampire. My best friend backed me up."

"Good best friend." Talking to Fallon had the disarming effect she needed going into this. With her, there had been no need to playact at all. Giselle hung on her every word. If all Alphas could be as cool as Fallon was, this evening would be totally easy.

"Oh, Alyssa's the best," Fallon continued, as they walked. "And she let me tag along until we met Brady and Aiden." Fallon pointed a finger to two large men across the room.

Giselle couldn't believe her eyes – they were both hot. And as a bonus, young-looking, too. She'd have placed them in their twenties, though true wolfy age was so damned hard to judge. But based on their looks and casual dress, she assumed they'd be just as easy to deal with as Fallon was. "Nice!"

"Yep. Fell hard for Aiden, and then had to decide between humanity or him." Fallon sighed. "I think I made the right choice."

"Your story is way better than mine," Giselle said.

"Oh, I don't know. Lost little werewolf rises to become the Alpha of the western territory? Sounds pretty epic from where I'm standing. Like an Oscar-worthy movie plot."

"Well, when you put it like that..." Giselle had gone into the room feeling like the lowest of the low, and it had been one of the big scary Alphas who'd given her the courage she felt now. Things were definitely looking up. She could do this. She would win the votes she needed to secure her place as Regional Alpha.

"See? Now hold your head up high. I got your back. Wow those Alphas. Show them why you were born to do this!" Fallon gave Giselle another friendly wink. "Let's start with my guys." She guided their steps toward Aiden and Brady.

I can totally do this!

13

"Announcing Mrs. Vivian Silverman and her eldest son, Aeson Silverman."

The butler's call drew all attention to the new arrival standing proudly at the doors.

I can't do this!

The moment Vivian locked eyes with her from across the room, Giselle knew she was done for. And worse, Ace was with her.

How? Why? This couldn't be happening. She'd literally been thrown to the wolves and told to survive without even the smallest bit of help. And there was queen bitch herself ready to pounce on her dying carcass in front of the whole assembly of Alphas. Ace's presence confirmed one thing: they were going to push hard for Giselle to be passed over as Alpha.

She'd been staring so hard she'd failed to notice the angry glare on Misha's face. Fifteen minutes of sucking up to a modern day clone of Jackie Kennedy, the great Alpha of the Midwest territories went down the drain in one moment of jealousy.

"If you're not too busy, Miss Silverman, we'll get down to business." The tone of Misha's voice sent a spear of dread straight into her chest.

Standing taller than Giselle, Misha had the presence of a woman who lived and breathed wolfy politics. She was the one wolf Giselle sensed she needed to impress above all others.

She'd failed at it miserably, and before she could utter an apology, the annoyed wolf walked away to find her mate, Brianna.

The other half of this Alpha duo from the Central territories, Brianna had gained an audience of her own, surrounded by the Lobos. She was a pretty wolf, not as intimidating in stature or dress as her mate, but she had the charisma to get the job done.

Richard's words came back to haunt her: either be the biggest and baddest, or have someone to be it for you. It appeared Misha and Brianna were a matched set that exemplified that very principle.

Other wolves hung on Brianna's every word until Misha walked up and silenced them all with a look.

Once Misha had her mate Brianna by her side, they walked up to the center table. Just as Richard had said, Misha acted as organizer and moderator, calling loudly to the room, "If you'd all take your seats, we can begin."

Giselle hoped she'd do better in the official meeting and began looking around for Richard and Martina, who should already have arrived. Neither had showed. She'd drown without a life preserver soon, and the hateful looks Vivian was shooting her from across the room were like a promise to be the first to hold her head under water.

Remembering she was supposed to be playing her part, not wallowing in the sea of nerves, Giselle lifted her head, set her jaw, and walked as proudly as she could toward the tables, hunting for the little name placard to tell her where to sit.

Tables had been strategically set in two rows with seats set only on one side, forcing each party to look at another across the gap. She spotted her table and the names that were assigned to it. Hers was there, and so was Vivian's; but oddly, Martina and Richard had been left off. Her heart sank with the realization that no help would come. Had they known this ahead of time? Had they lied to get her to attend with false hope of backup? Or had something more nefarious caused their absence? The moment of worry broke her mask of confidence. Anyone looking at that moment might have seen her true terror, and the game would have been all but lost. That thought alone had her gritting her teeth to keep her jaw from trembling. A growling breath rumbled up her chest to push away the stuttered breath of fear. Giselle called on all the strength her wolf had to rise and endure the rest of this meeting.

Across from her sat Fallon and her two escorts, Aiden and Brady. She felt more at ease knowing they were right in front of her. Talking to them had been refreshing. Unlike the others, these were younger Alphas, though no less powerful. They seemed, at least on the surface, open to Giselle's taking the title as long as she had a few years' tutelage under a regent.

Talking to the packs of the south had been less comforting. Thankfully, the Rufus Reds were seated out of her line of sight. They had showed particular curiosity in her upbringing, which Giselle took as a bad sign, refusing to talk about anything but life as a foster child.

The Lobos were to her left at the next table over. Unlike the Reds, they were happy to hear that leadership would be moved closer to them if she were to be allowed to take her place as Alpha of the Long Teeth, though she'd had her suspicions about their intentions when they began talking up their oldest son and marriage prospects.

The whole evening thus far had been beyond stressful, and the one light at the end of the tunnel, her adoptive mother's return, she knew would never come.

In her place, Vivian and Ace had been assigned to her table as representatives of the Pacific Coast packs.

Vivian strolled up confidently alongside Giselle and took her seat. "My dear niece, your nerves are showing." Her tone had all the concern of a schoolyard bully and the wicked smile to match.

Giselle couldn't roll her eyes any harder. She refused to rise to Vivian's taunting and remembered to keep her head high. Backup or no, she was going to give off as much pride as she could, especially with the queen bitch at her side.

Ace at least had the decency to look sorry for his role in all of it, though he did not speak to Giselle directly.

Servers began to walk the floor, delivering appetizers to the tables: small plates of meats on skewers. At least they got the food right. Giselle's stomach was nearly ready to eat itself with hunger.

Misha stood at her table and addressed the room. "You all understand why we are here?"

Between the sounds of hungry wolves eating, murmurs of *Alpha* and *Regency* answered Misha's question.

"Precisely," Misha responded. "We must determine the legitimacy of this wolf's claim." She pointed a finger directly at Giselle.

"You cannot seriously consider this child for the leadership role of our territories." Vivian was first to speak.

"Is she, in fact, Orion Silverman's child?" Brianna spoke up. It was the first time Giselle had heard her voice, and instantly it was clear why she held everyone's attention. Singsong in its melody, her tone was pleasing to the ears but did not betray intent. Whether Brianna was asking for confirmation or condemnation, her Giselle couldn't tell.

"Yes," Vivian answered with noticeable reluctance.

"Then by birthright, she is entitled," Brianna affirmed.

"But she spent her years in human care. She knows nothing of our way of life." Vivian's anger manifested in a loud slam of her hand down on the table.

Across the row, Charles from the Rufus Reds territory stood. "I too take issue with the child's lack of upbringing." Where Vivian had blunt anger, he responded with soothing concern. "How are we to know she'll uphold our laws and values? Could she mount a defense if her territory were encroached upon?"

"That is something the child can learn." Aiden responded directly to Charles, adding a nod towards Giselle. "Are you planning to encroach upon her territory?" he added casually, though his words were anything but.

"Charles is speaking hypothetically, I'm sure," Misha answered before he could. "But that brings up an excellent point. We should consider her ability to control her borders as well as her birthright."

"That has never been a consideration before in the succession of a child when the Alpha dies," Aiden put in, addressing Misha directly. "We honor the lineage."

Thank the gods she had at least one pack on her side. The Boston wolves had, without really knowing her, thrown in their support with nothing but a nod from Fallon as reason to do so.

"In a special case such as this, where the child has been brought up outside our laws and ways, we cannot ignore it. Weak leadership opens the territory to threats not only from within but outside as well. Traditionally an heir is groomed for the position as they grow within a pack." Her words sounded sweet, but they held a bitter edge. Giselle wondered if Misha would really hold such a grudge over their earlier interaction, or if this was just her businesslike tone. "I would hate to see Pacific territory slowly fall apart and be enveloped into the surrounding regions due do dissent and border disputes that couldn't be handled properly."

"She's a Silverman wolf. She comes from a strong and proud family line, one who's governed over the Pacific region for a very long time. I highly doubt she'd lose territory with the support of her family in the north and southern portions of her territory." Aiden answered back as if he were prepared for her argument. "And she'd have the benefit of a Regent until her twenty-first birthday. Plenty of time to be educated and guided as has been stipulated in our laws."

Misha nodded thoughtfully, as if weighing the information rather than actually agreeing, but that was enough for Giselle.

She let out a breath, feeling grateful that someone with the knowledge of pack law had taken up her cause, as she had no idea what she could have said in defense. At that point, she'd become a spectator in the game of succession. Had Richard been in attendance, she had no doubt he'd have been upset she'd not taken a more active role.

The moment of relief ended when Misha opened her mouth to rebut again. "The Silverman family is an old and very proud family. Of that I have no doubt. But will she be guided by a Silverman wolf during her those formative years?"

Vivian scoffed. "Her mentor and regent is a wolf who already lives on the fringes – some backwater leftover of a turf war that's been raging for a generation. Hardly the shining example of how proper packs operate."

Rage had Giselle's hand flying up ready to smack the bitch for speaking so badly about her adoptive mother, who'd been the first person to ever make her feel like she belonged, but she was able to pull it back before she landed a hit.

"You see? She can't even hold her own temper in a formal meeting. How will she handle warring packs or territory disputes if she can't handle what I have to say?" Vivian's words earned murmurs of acknowledgement from the other Alphas.

Fallon addressed the group. "You can't expect her to hold her temper when she's being verbally attacked by one of her own. None of you, not a single one, is standing up for this girl. You discredit her for how she grew up, but have you taken into account exactly what she's had to endure all these years? She's survived as a lone wolf in the human world. A child. No knowledge of what she was or how she came to be the way she was. And she managed to stay off the radar all this time. That's more than you give her credit for. You can't expect her to adapt to our ways overnight. Give her a chance. She's proven she can handle everything else that's been thrown at her."

Gratitude tempered Giselle's anger. That Fallon chick was pretty cool to stand up the way she did, after knowing her for only a few moments. But it seemed she was the only one to appreciate it.

Vivian swooped right in with an equal measure of anger. "Yes. Please, half-wolf, tell us all how we should allow more unfit wolves to be Alpha."

"You want to see how much of a wolf I am? Bring it." Fallon rose to the occasion, fearless, with her wolf peeking out from behind her eyes, frightening in its beauty. Giselle had no doubt the Alpha spirit resided within Fallon, half-wolf or not.

Vivian smiled evilly, as if she'd won without a single swipe of her claws. "See? This is why we have to be selective about whom we chose for leadership. Those who have not been bred for it simply can't handle the politics. My boy here is the first son of David Silverman – the last presiding Alpha of the Long Tooth territory."

Fallon speared Vivian with a fierce glare. "Orion Silverman still lives, does he not?"

Vivian slumped back down into her seat as if those words had landed a direct hit. "He is… not capable of leadership. In his current state, he's as good as dead."

"But not *actually* dead," Fallon reminded the group.

"No." Vivian gulped loud enough for Giselle to take note. "He lives."

"Then David Silverman, as second son, was acting as steward of the Alpha-ship to your territory. He had no claim to the actual title. Your son, therefore, has no direct claim either." Misha's words held a tone of finality that none of the other Alphas dared question.

However, after a moment of uneasy silence, Vivian spoke again. "And this girl does? Raised by humans, unaware of her birthright until a week ago?" Desperation colored Vivian's words. Her eyes again found a target with Fallon. "We would welcome the same problems as the Olde Town pack if we gave leadership to her."

Fallon's snarl could be heard throughout the room. And that seemed to rekindle Vivian's lust for power. She rose again and speared Fallon with a look of pure determination. "A cursory review of the Olde Town pack would reveal a staggering number of wolf deaths and attrition since the young Whelan and his half-wolf took over."

Across the row of tables, Giselle watched the twitches of muscle that preceded a shift. But before Fallon could bring her wolf forward, Aiden gripped her arm and pulled her back down to sit next to him. He stood and met Vivian's eyes with deadly intent. "When the Acta Sanctorum comes knocking at your door, we shall see how well your little pack fares."

"Excuses." Vivian scoffed and took her seat as well, having won for the moment.

"The Olde Town pack is the largest in the country and we've always been the caretakers of our domain. The Acta Sanctorum has plagued us for many years because of this. And yes, while our numbers have dwindled, we've worked hard to keep all supernatural activity off the radar. My leadership is not under question at this time, but if you'd like to make it an issue, I'll happily accept your challenge."

Giselle waited for someone to dare to speak up, and when no one did, Aiden sat slowly, confident in his win.

Vivian whispered under her breath, "I doubt the little werewolf here would be capable."

"This whole thing is kind of ridiculous," Giselle mumbled and dropped her gaze to her plate of food sitting uneaten despite her nagging hunger. The way things were going, she assumed she'd already lost.

"Would you defend your position, little wolf?" Misha asked, smiling almost deviously as she offered the floor to Giselle. "I'm sure we'd all be enlightened by your view of our Council and proceedings."

She instantly regretted her little grumble of dissent. Strike two with Misha. She counted on her fingers the wolves who were against her: Misha, Vivian, Charles. It was inevitable she would lose, but she'd been offered the floor to speak her piece.

Richard would want her to; Martina too. She looked around the room, meeting all the stony faces of the Alphas already in power. They were already taking more interest in their plates than what she was about to say, and she nearly let it go. But, Giselle had promised her family that she would do her best, no matter what.

With a deep breath, she stood, feeling that was what they would expect her to do. She attempted to meet each pair of eyes equally. The power they emanated had her wolf feeling uneasy. Everyone here was an Alpha of alphas, representatives of their territories and leaders who'd been in power for more years than she had been alive. In truth, she didn't belong. But when had she ever? And that gave her the voice she needed to speak.

"I'm not like you. You've all guessed as much. But I'm also not like others, either. I've spent the entire time I've known about my condition being my own wolf. It's taught me to rely on instinct, to trust only when someone has earned it, and how to read between the lines of bullshit when someone is trying to pretend they are something they're not. That's what years of being a lone wolf will do to you. So when I sit here and listen to Vivian call me and my new family names, or preach that I am not qualified to lead, I don't see a leader of wolves making a valid argument. What I see is a petty woman who wants the position for her son. Someone willing to tear down anyone and everyone if that's what it takes to get it." Giselle looked at Vivian and smirked. "You all want a leader you can feel confident in. That's cool. Can I guarantee you I'm that person? Nope. But I'm also not the person trying to attack a young girl's character without knowing her. I'm not the person trying to attack other Alphas on the Council to cause their leadership to be called into question. You have to do what you feel is best. All I can say is that if you want me to take the role, I'll do what I can. I won't make false promises."

The room had again fallen into an uneasy quiet. Perhaps her words had hit the mark and the Alphas were mulling them over. Or maybe she'd just made a complete fool of herself. Only time would tell, but as she stood there in the silence with all eyes on her, the overwhelming urge to sit and take sudden interest in her food took over. "Thanks for your time," she finished, and quickly took her seat.

"How dare you?" Vivian started to say before Misha slammed a fist on the table.

"We've heard enough from you Mrs. Silverman. Is there anyone else who will speak?"

The room erupted in murmurs and whispers of dissension, but no one stood to speak for or against Giselle. The noise went on for more than ten minutes, and no one had yet come to an agreement on what to do.

Misha sighed. "Since this Council cannot agree openly, it will be put to a silent vote. At the end of our feast, we will write our answer on a piece of paper, and I will tally the results."

It wasn't an outright no... at least, not yet. But Giselle understood that she had not won the support of the Council of Alphas. And based on the murderous glares coming from Vivian, she'd made a powerful enemy in the process. At least she knew she had one wolf on her side. Fallon gave her a wink from across the table. It would figure the one to support her would be the other outcast of the group. But hey, at least she was in good company.

14

Suffering through a dinner next to Vivian had been hard enough, but when the final verdict was handed down just after dessert, Giselle finally hit rock bottom. Mentally and physically spent from hours of play-acting strength and power had left her so emotionally drained she could barely muster a polite "May I be excused?" before bolting out of the room and running like a mad-woman through the halls.

In the short span of time between the reception hall and the elevator, tears erupted from the dam of her eyes and poured like rivers down her cheek. Layers of mas-cara and liner melted around her eyes. In the polished brass of the elevator doors she could see the mask forming, but rather than conceal her grief it made the whole of her suffering apparent to any who passed her along the way to her rooms.

Sobbing like a small child, searching for some shred of comfort, Giselle burst through the door of her hotel room.

"Where were you?" she cried out the moment she spotted Martina.

Long faces and apologies caught her before she crumpled to the ground, a complete emotional wreck. She hadn't wanted this job. She didn't need the job. All she'd wanted was to see her father and bring him home. The payment for it had been utter humiliation. Being brought up before a council of Alphas, sat there, all evening, to be judged and ridiculed simply for being born and left alone in the world. If not for Fallon's kindness, the entire night would have been horrid, but even that small ray of sunshine had not been enough to pierce the thunderous Vivian and her downpour of hatred.

Martina pulled her into a motherly hug. "I am so very sorry. More than I could possibly say. This was not how it was supposed to go. Please know this." She lovingly stroked her daughter's hair.

Despite her anger at being abandoned, Giselle couldn't pull away from the motherly embrace. Her emotional well had run dry, and she melted against her adoptive mother's body, borrowing from her strength to keep herself upright. Tears fell silently, but her sobs echoed in the room where she stood, with Richard waiting in the wings to come forward.

Martina might have signaled him to wait; Giselle couldn't see if they were having some silent communication. His presence she recognized, but the old wolf made no advance nor voiced an apology for his part in her abandonment.

Martina alone had the floor. She held tight to Giselle, allowing her to bury her wet face and cry for as long as she needed.

"We had planned to be there, Sweetheart." Martina's gently stroked Giselle's back. "But our places were taken by Vivian... and her son. We only found out about it at the door."

"You could have pushed your way in." Emotions got the better of her, and Giselle's anger soured her words.

Martina countered sweetly with compassion. "You know as well as I that it wouldn't have helped your cause if we barged in like savages."

"What does it matter? I lost anyway." Giselle pulled back, meeting her mother's eyes for the first time. She wanted to find a reason to rail on her. How could she have stood aside and let that woman come in and ruin everything? Martina should have been there to protect her daughter. But Giselle's anger faded when Martina's eyes dripped with sorrowful tears.

Martina had no words. She didn't need to. Her emotions spoke louder than her voice could have, leaving Giselle to accept what had happened.

She backed away from Martina to find a seat on the couch, her legs no longer wanting to hold her upright.

Richard took the silence as his cue to enter the conversation. He took a spot alongside Giselle and patted her on the shoulder. "Tell us what happened."

"I'm unfit" Giselle began, trying to hold her voice steady as her sobs turned to hiccups, "at this time. However, if I can find a champion to fight for me" – she took a breath to try and control the spasms in her chest – "they will allow my regency should that champion win."

On a loud sigh, Richard slumped in his seat and caught his head in his hands. "I was afraid it would come to this."

"It's all that stupid Vivian's fault," Giselle said, more loudly than she'd intended. "You should have heard her badmouthing me, you," – she pointed to Martina still standing in the center of the room – "even other Alphas."

"Why?" Martina pulled a chair over from the small dining table to sit in front of Giselle.

Richard answered before Giselle had the opportunity. "Her son."

"I should have guessed." Martina let out an exasperated sigh.

"He can have it. I don't care," Giselle said with a hiccupping sob

"It doesn't work like that," Richard said.

Wolf rules and laws were too damn tedious, and Giselle had had her fill of them. She didn't want to admit it, but a small part of her was happy now that she knew she would not be the Alpha. "Why not? He's been bred for it."

"That he has," Richard agreed. "However… I'm assuming they denied him on the grounds that Orion still technically lives."

"Yeah. Some second-son crap." Giselle rolled her eyes.

"Yes. Which is why I announced you as Alpha back in Vegas when David died." Richard stood and began to pace the room. "Tricky little loophole, really. Because the true Alpha lives, the second son is not actually Alpha, even though he served in place for seventeen years. Had Orion died, the outcome might have been different."

Panic stole Giselle's breath. Orion had been left in Vivian's care until they had planned to return home. "You don't think she would try to kill my father, do you?"

Richard stopped dead in his tracks. His eyes widened for a moment, and Giselle's heart skipped a beat. Before she could open her mouth and tell them to grab the car keys, he spoke. "I don't think so. The verdict has been delivered, so killing him would do nothing at this point. Nor would his sudden death. It would only bring unwanted attention to their family, and I'm guessing that's the last thing they want tonight."

"But to be safe, we should pick Orion up early, and care for him here until we leave," Martina added.

"Yes," Richard agreed. "Might as well bring him in now. Vivian will be in a foul mood for certain, especially if..." He paused, and his eyes shot to Giselle. "What was the verdict specifically for Ace's claim?"

"He can participate in the trial by combat if he wishes to stake a claim, since he's of age."

"Did the Council say anything else, honey?" Martina asked.

Giselle shook her head. It had all been a bit of a jumble once she'd learned they didn't want her for the position. She hadn't really paid much attention to anything else they said.

"When and where will the trials be?" Richard asked.

If she'd paid better attention, she might have known the answer. "Misha said something... I think they're going to set a date for the trials tomorrow. And I'll be expected to attend even if I'm not fighting."

"They'll hold combat so soon?" Richard's expression turned grim.

"No. Um..." *Had she said tomorrow, or just that they would set a date tomorrow?* Giselle wracked her brain to remember exactly what was said.

"I will fight for you." Richard took his seat again alongside Giselle and put his arm around her. "You've not lost this yet."

"Don't," Giselle demanded.

"But I must," Richard said. "I am your sworn enforcer, and will gladly lay down my life in your service."

"No. I'm done," Giselle pleaded, hoping he would understand. "They didn't want me. That's fine." She turned her desperate eyes on Martina. "Let's just go home with my dad and be happy."

"But there will still be a trial by combat," Richard said.

"And that was what you feared would happen if I lost. So we're already at the worst case scenario. Let it be."

Richard sucked in a breath. He looked about ready to give a speech, but Martina silenced him with a look.

"She needs time to cope with what she's be through tonight. We will have no more talk of this. And tomorrow, I will go and meet the Council, so you don't have to deal with them. I'll arrange what needs to be arranged and find out the details of this trial by combat. You" – she pulled Giselle into a momma bear hug – "just go back to being you for the time being. Okay?"

15

Emotional exhaustion did wonders for insomnia. Giselle hit the pillow hard, and when she awoke to blaring light streaming in through her hotel window, she was shocked to find the day had passed her by – the clock on the nightstand read 1PM.

Even in the middle of summer, without a plan for the day, she'd never been allowed to sleep that late. It was a true testament to Martina's sorrow for her abandonment. She sank her head back into the pillow and tried to let sleep take her a little longer, while she could still play on her mother's guilt.

But as always managed to happen once the seal had been broken on her sleepy eyes, the moment they glimpsed daylight, her mind started running, and sleep declined the invitation to return.

Refusing to acknowledge defeat, she shuffled around in bed and found the remote for the television. If she couldn't rest her body, she'd rest her thoughts with mind-numbing TV.

In the adjoining room, sounds of her family returning caught her attention, but she wasn't ready to deal with them just yet.

Taylor was there; she could tell by the tap-tap of her horribly uncomfortable but no doubt fashionable shoes. Then came a sound she did not immediately recognize–wheels rolling over soft carpet with a little hint of a squeak.

"Go and check on Giselle." Gavin's voice boomed with the order. "We'll be five minutes tops. I need to see to the nurse."

So much for peace and quiet now, Giselle sighed. But on a positive note, based on what she'd just heard, her father had arrived. That perked her up enough to rise and start hunting for clothes.

Her back was turned when the door to her room opened.

"You can't stay in here forever," Taylor said softly. "I heard what happened. It's not the end of the world."

"I know that. And I didn't even want the stupid role anyway." Giselle rifled through her luggage, not wanting to rehash her failure from the previous evening.

"You can't lie to me. I've known you too long."

When she looked up, Taylor was giving her the full *I don't think so* stare, complete with hands on her hips. Surprisingly for a teenager, she had the angry mother look down pat. Giselle feared for any future children her sister had. They'd never get away with shit.

The silence between them was like a challenge. Who would speak first? Giselle turned away, hoping that would be enough, but her sister pressed the matter. "Admit that you wanted it. Admit that you're bummed. It's okay to fail. Don't you dare bottle that up inside."

She was right. Damn it! "If it hadn't been for that Vivian lady, it would have all been cool."

Taylor's hands fell from her hips and she came in for a sisterly hug Giselle hadn't been expecting. "She's probably trying to get the role for herself."

Thank the gods for sisters. You could always count on them to go defense for you in any situation.

Giselle pushed away from her sister's bear-like grip. "She's not qualified though. Her son is, though… Ace."

A little glimmer of excitement flashed in Taylor's eyes, and despite all the negative emotions Giselle felt at that moment, the thought of her sister being happy smoothed things over. Both Taylor and Di had been flirty with the guys. If she couldn't be Alpha, maybe they had a shot. Assuming Ace fought well. The moment that sobering realization hit her, the hope was gone again. It would come down to brawn if the Alphas had their way.

Taylor busied herself in Giselle's luggage, picking out a new outfit for her instead of the one Giselle was holding. "As much as I want to hate her for it, moms will do anything they can to help their kids."

"I get that. And I'm cool with that. But does she have to be such a bitch about it?" Giselle scoffed, remembering how nasty Vivian had been, trying to discredit her at every turn as if she had a personal vendetta.

Di sauntered into the room with a bag smelling suspiciously of chocolate in her hand. "Who are we calling a bitch? Not me, I hope, because I brought medicine!"

Giselle laughed. "Not you… this time." She winked evilly at her sister.

Di set down the bag and pulled out a custard-filled chocolate iced donut. "It's good for what ails you," she announced, handing it to Giselle.

"And this is why I love you so much." Giselle snatched the donut and nearly inhaled the entire thing in one shot. "Any coffee?"

"Not this time." Di sat down on the bed with an over-filled crème delight. "Now, dish!"

"All right. Word is there will be a challenge for Alpha."

"Right. Martina told me they are having it back home in Vegas at the end of the month," Di said between bites of her donut.

"Wait… what?" Giselle stuttered. "You're asking me to dish when you clearly have all the juicy gossip."

"That's all I know." Di shrugged. "Mom's been pretty tight-lipped. But she was talking to Dad about it like she was really scared."

"Why would she be scared?" Giselle asked.

Taylor butted in. "Because it puts us all on display."

Giselle sighed, feeling like she'd be strung along on this Alpha bullshit forever. "So. I guess I'm not out of the woods yet. Apparently I'm allowed to choose a champion to fight for me. And they, if they win, will be my regent until I turn 21."

Di sucked in a deep breath. "Not the end of the world, I guess. You're still in the running."

"How can you say that?" Giselle shot back at her sister. "I'm not asking Martina or Gavin to fight for me. These battles are to the death."

"Oh. Right." Di's shoulders slumped. "So what are you going to do?"

Giselle flopped back onto the bed. "I dunno. Crying like a little baby seems like a fun option."

"Right. Because that's exactly what you'd do in this situation. Give up and lick your wounds. I know you way better than that. What's your plan?" Di waved another donut in front of Giselle's face.

"I got nothing. Seriously." If only they'd just let it go. All of them. She had been denied once, and as much of a kick to the nuts as that had been, dragging it out and making a spectacle of it was infinitely worse.

"Liar."

Giselle shot up from the bed, annoyed at the situation more than her sister's insistence, but her words came out angry all the same. "This is a world I know nothing about, and I'm not arrogant enough to say I could fight the big boys for the role. I've got nothing here."

"What about Richard?" Taylor's voice seemed almost a whisper against Giselle's outburst. "He seemed eager to help you."

"As a bodyguard, remember? He had no desire for the leadership role. And I can see why." Giselle exhaled loudly. "Bunch of assholes, if you ask me. All of them. Well, except the one chick."

Di's eyebrows shot up. She handed over another donut for Giselle and took a spot on the bed next to her. "You made a friend?"

She certainly had a good way of changing the subject. Who could resist chocolate and custard? No one, that's who. Laughter replaced Giselle's annoyance, and she took a bite before dishing on the new wolf she'd met. "Yeah, she's the mate to the Alpha of the Boston pack. Fallon. She was a human once."

"Oh, that's rare. Hardly anyone survives turning wolf." Di looked horrorstruck.

"She had a vampire help her or something," Giselle said casually.

"Damn!" Di shook her head in disbelief. "She must be connected. Friends with vamps, too."

"You think she'd be willing to stick up for you?" Taylor asked.

"I talked to her for like five seconds, you guys," Giselle snorted, nearly choking on her donut. "I doubt that's enough to inspire her to defend my right to rule…to the death."

"Couldn't hurt to talk to her before we go home." Di shrugged as if the question were as simple as that. "You have to do everything you can to keep your place as Alpha!"

"No." Giselle shook her head as she stuffed the last bit of donut in her mouth. "Not happening."

"This is so not like you!"

Di sounded disappointed. And for what reason? It wasn't like she was up for the title. She wasn't being paraded around in front of all the other Alphas. She wasn't being degraded and sniped at by Vivian. She knew better, but her mood got the best of her, and Giselle snapped. "And how would you know? You've known me all of what? A year! Don't proceed to tell me what is *like* me to do." Giselle stormed out of the room and into the empty living room of the suite.

At least, she'd thought it was empty.

16

She'd heard the wheelchair being brought in, but in her emotional outburst she'd managed to forget the whole reason she'd gotten out of bed in the first place. Her father.

Secured in his special chair, Orion sat silently. He'd been turned so he could see the scenery though the window outside of their suite's adjoining living room.

"Sorry. I didn't mean to interrupt you." Whether or not he could respond meant nothing; she spoke to him as if he were listening. It was the least she could do.

Giselle walked toward him, looking at him, emotions warring with each other inside of her: love, fear, sadness, desperation. Here sat a man who'd once ruled. Once loved. Once hoped for family.

And what had he gotten for all his aspirations?

Sentenced to a life of nothingness.

She walked around to face him, staring into his glossy eyes, hoping to find that spark of life within. "Is it worth it?" she whispered, as she knelt in front of her father. "You know I didn't want this. When I first learned that being a wolf was okay, I was fine with it. When

Martina accepted me into her pack, I was ecstatic. Then I learned that I had a mother... sort of... Cassandra."

As if the word had sparked something within Orion, his body twitched. She'd have thought it a trick of the light except for the sweat ring that had formed on the leather armrest of her father's seat. His finger had moved, leaving that telltale sign of what had once been there.

"Do you remember her?" Giselle asked. "Cassandra?" She hoped hearing the name again would cause the same reaction, but Orion remained motionless, still staring blankly out of the window.

Forgetting her own thoughts for a moment, she turned her mind to her father and his needs. He was in there. He had to be. And maybe instead of being so self-centered and worrying about petty fighting among wolves, she should leave her focus on him. That's what she'd always wanted: a family. Might not be perfect, but he was her flesh and blood. And he needed someone to treat him like something more than a statue in the room.

"Would you like me to tell you about her? I understand you two were in love once. You were willing to walk away from everything to be with her. A regular Romeo and Juliet." Giselle laughed at the thought of Cassandra standing out on the balcony, calling his name longingly.

Orion's body sat unnaturally still. His breathing so shallow he might as well have been stone, but Giselle refused to give into the ruse. She sat down cross-legged in front of his chair and looked up at him.

"She's alive and well. The witches back in Vegas have her on a tight leash for abusing magic, but she's happy to be part of a coven again. You'll get to meet her when we go back home."

Fate had been cruel to them both, stripping Cassandra of her magic and Orion of his sanity – all because they'd wanted to start a family.

"And of course, we'll have plenty of time to get to know each other better and make up for all those lost years. I'd thought I was unwanted and unloved; but as it turned out, I was more wanted and loved than most, I just got lost." She laughed nervously and then caught the twitch of his hand again.

"You can hear me, can't you?" She expected him to respond again, but it seemed every time she looked for it, it was gone, as if she and he were passing trains only destined to connect for a brief second and then rush away again.

"I don't blame you at all," Giselle continued. "I want you to know that. The situation got royally messed up. And I get that. Totally. So just remember that. I love you and know you loved me too. I don't want you blaming yourself or whatever. I grew up just fine. I mean, look at me." Giselle stood and spun for effect. "I'm happy and healthy."

Taylor came into the room unexpectedly and caught Giselle mid-spin. "What are you doing?" she asked cautiously.

Giselle's first instinct was to bow to embarrassment at having been caught play-acting for a silent audience, but instead she owned her silliness and gave another spin just for good measure. "Just telling Dad that despite what happened, I'm cool." Somehow being out here with her father, even in this state, was comforting and a welcome contrast to the tension and stress she'd been put through the previous few days.

Taylor laughed at her sister's antics. "You're more than that, Elle. Which is why you need to talk to someone about being your champion. You owe it to your future self, if nothing else."

"No. I've made up my mind. I'm going to let them fight amongst themselves. I've got my dad now." She placed a hand over his. "And that is all I need."

His hand twitched and shifted under hers, and when she looked down he was holding on to her.

"Oh, crap, Taylor!" Giselle yelled, and though she jerked back instinctively, she did not pull completely out of his grasp. "Look!"

Taylor strolled over cautiously and peeked at Giselle's hand. "How did you do that?" Her eyes lit with amazement.

"Do what? *He* did it." Giselle couldn't believe what she was seeing. The rest of him still sat in the same limp position on the chair, but his hand had strength, and he'd clearly moved with intent to hold on to her.

"We have to tell Martina and Gavin when they get back!" Taylor said.

Giselle bent and whispered in her father's ear, "Thank you for showing me you're still with us." This was far better than becoming an Alpha. The spark she'd felt was there, and that meant he was there, and if he was... she had to talk to the witches! "Where is Martina? Or Gavin, for that matter?"

"They had to go make arrangements for the nurse to come in and check on Orion a few times before we leave tomorrow. Vivian was not happy with us, but allowed us at least one more day's care. They're waiting to meet her in the lobby."

She'd all but forgotten about his special needs. And those would have to be taken care of when they settled into normal life back home. Her excitement dampened a little with the reality of his needs, but bolstered by her new mission to see if she could change his situation, she kept a smile on her face. "Okay, well, then as soon as they get back, I have to tell them. This is huge news."

17

In a few short hours, she'd be back to the dry dusty desert. That thought kept her eyes riveted to the window as the van cruised along the highway toward the airport. She'd be homesick for it, as she had been the first time she left, but that would be the only thing she'd miss. Giselle might have been born here, but it was not home – only a place filled with bad memories and nasty people. The one good thing about it was her father, and he was coming home to live with her forever. That was a much better prize than winning the title of Alpha, though she knew that battle was long from over.

Richard pulled the van into the parking lot, and the finality of their time in Washington became a reality.

Martina and Gavin pulled in next to them driving a specially equipped rental they'd had to pick up at the last minute to transport Orion. They busied themselves with unloading and inventorying their bags for the walk into the airport.

Giselle took one last look at the trees, burning the greenery into her memory, as that would be the last she'd see of such things for a while.

Di and Taylor didn't have the same reverence for all the natural beauty of the trees and grass surrounding them; too many years spent as desert rats. They struggled on the sidelines to balance the multiple suitcases they'd brought.

She could hear Gavin telling everyone he was going to get a cart, and she knew she'd have a few more minutes to enjoy the last glimpse of nature around her.

Richard came around the front of the van and stood next to Giselle as if waiting for her to finish her thoughts. The feeling of eyes at her back made her turn around quickly to face him.

"This is where I leave you for now," Richard said, placing a hand on Giselle's shoulder.

"Thanks for all the help. I'm guessing I won't see you again."

He scrutinized her face as if trying to look beyond the veil of her teenage indifference. "You'll see me sooner than you think, little wolf. I'll be attending the trials."

"I won't," Giselle said with finality. She'd set her mind the previous night. She'd attend if they forced her, but she would not fight.

"You have time to change that stubborn mind of yours," Richard replied. "And my offer still stands if you wish me to fight for you."

"Why?" Giselle asked.

Richard winced as if the sharpness of her words had cut him. He took a step back and turned his gaze to the field just beyond the parking lot. "I knew your father well. Served him until the day he chose to leave. And his brother after him. This is an honorable family, despite a few bad mistakes. I will continue to serve."

"Why not fight for Ace? You know he's planning to fight," Giselle said. If Richard was so dead set on fighting, it might as well be for someone already in power.

"Aeson is of age. He cannot have a stand in, though I would if I could," Richard said with a wink. "But you are first in line, by blood of the eldest son."

If Giselle had to hear that one more time, she would scream. Blood this and blood that. It was all anyone seemed concerned with. What about smarts? What about experience? She was no more guaranteed to be a good Alpha than Taylor would be. But because her father had been an Alpha years and years ago, she had claim to it by blood. And even then, her blood had accounted for nothing. The whole Alpha selection process was stupid – even more so now that it would be left up to the last wolf standing in a battle of strength. And they wondered why she didn't want the job? Who in their right mind would?

"I'll never be what they want me to be. And I don't want anyone to fight and die for me."

"You have the potential." Richard sighed deeply. "Sad the Council did not see it. You are so much more than the lone wolf they see you as. If only they'd taken into account what you have accomplished already in such a short time for your family."

"Any more talk like that, and I'll blush. You give me way too much credit."

"I only give it where it is due. Remember that."

Richard did have that going for him. Blunt honesty was exactly what she liked about him.

"Should you change your mind, all you need to do is call on me, and I will come to your aid." He held a hand to his chest.

"Thank you." Giselle felt proud, though she could not reason why. "I don't deserve it. But I do appreciate it."

"If you promise to think of the options made available to you – really think on them – then you do deserve the help I offer."

Giselle smirked. "You should be Alpha."

"I'll let you in on a little secret. I was offered the job many times." Richard smiled back.

"And you think me a fool to reject it?" Giselle asked.

"No." Richard's eyes narrowed. "You're a fool to not fully consider the options for your future."

"And you think I haven't?" Giselle asked.

"I know you haven't," Richard said with no hesitation. "And you'd be lying to me if you said you had."

"Curse you, Merlin." Giselle laughed.

"At least you're beginning to recognize my aged wisdom." Richard chuckled. "But sadly... no magic."

"I'm going to miss you." Giselle spoke truthfully. She might not have enjoyed the lectures, but he was real. Nothing held back. No ulterior motives.

"We'll see each other again before you know it," Richard replied. "Now go home and think. Promise."

"Yes. I promise." Giselle rolled her eyes and joined her family, offering to push Orion's wheelchair into the airport herself.

18

Giselle had left some of the pressure back in Washington, but knowing the trials were coming kept the shadow of anxiety close. As soon as she could break away from her family, she retreated to the one thing that helped to burn away the layers of pent up negativity, and headed over to her favorite running mate's house to drag him out with her, willing or not.

"So should I kneel, or would that be risking my Alpha's ire?" Asher joked as he greeted her at the door.

"Like you don't already know." If he'd expected a laugh out of her, he was in for a surprise. She'd hoped to get some peace from the whole damn situation, but it was the hottest gossip, and she was the cover story on the latest issue of *Wolf Weekly*, it seemed. "I was unacceptable to the Council due to my lack of experience as a wolf," said Giselle pointedly.

"But you were to have a Regent." Confusion added a tilt to the way Asher held his head. Like a cute little puppy who'd seen you throw the ball but never spotted where it landed, he looked to the horizon for answers. "They knew that, right?" When his eyes found her face again, disappointment had darkened them and added a wrinkle to his brow that aged his face.

He really hoped I would make it. Giselle had never seen Ash look so bothered. And it wasn't even something that he'd benefit from. She'd shrugged off his picking at her as playful teasing because he knew how much she didn't want the role. It hadn't occurred to her he might actually want her to be Alpha just to see her succeed on her own. And all this time, she had selfishly prayed for a way out. More anxiety settled on her, and she sighed as she began to rehash her failure again. "They felt that since I was raised human, I was not wolf enough for them."

"That's not what they said, was it?" Asher asked.

Giselle puffed out her chest and narrowed her eyes on Asher, giving her best impersonation of Misha. "'She bears a wild spirit cannot be tempered by the bonds of nobility and duty. Hers will be an exciting future, of that we have no doubt, and we look forward to the great deeds she will have in her time, but leadership must be finalized immediately and permanently.'" Giselle blew out a breath and sucked in a deeper one before continuing. "'Should she inspire loyalty enough for someone to step into the trials and fight in her stead, we will honor that wolf as Regent and assign Alpha-ship if they are victorious."

"Well, at least they tried to be nice about it." Ash cringed as if waiting for Giselle to strike him.

She'd considered it. Every time she came across someone who hadn't been at the meeting up north, she had to recount her failure. First with Christine then Jeffrey when they'd arrived. Next she'd spoken to Cassandra on the phone, hoping to tell her about Orion, and ended up spending more time with her sort-of mother's attempt at consolation for over an hour. If she'd had her way, Giselle would have retreated into Jeffrey's old caves in the mountain and hidden out until it all blew over, but no one would let that happen.

And worst of all, it wasn't a job she'd wanted, whether or not she was meant for it. *Blah, blah, blah and all that bullshit.* Having to relive the fact that she couldn't have it made it all that much worse.

"Well, for what it's worth, I thought you'd make a good Alpha." Asher at least was not making her go into too much detail. He leaned against the brick wall outside the door, not even attempting the courtesy pats or the sympathetic hug. Good for him. She'd probably have punched him if he did. What she needed was a run.

"It's cool." Giselle shrugged, hoping that would be the end of it, and turned, ready to take off and get a run in the desert.

"Father too," Asher said to her back.

"What?" She turned sharply.

"Father believed in you too. He thought you'd be great."

Not sure whether his words were meant to be inspiring of if he had some ulterior motive, Giselle walked up face to face with him. He was too tall; she craned her neck to meet his eyes. "Even better than you or your brothers, perhaps?"

If he had an ulterior motive, he wasn't showing his cards. "What?" Asher asked with that puppy dog tilt to his head again.

"I knew you were playing dumb about knowing what happened to me." She scrutinized his face and came up empty. "I doubt your father would have left out the last bit, though."

"What the hell are you talking about?" Asher snapped at her like she'd just accused him of conspiracy.

She took a step back. Maybe he had been left in the dark. That didn't seem possible. Knowing Nathaniel Thrace as the by-the-book Alpha, surely he would have told his son…."The position has been opened to all of age within our borders who wish to fight in combat to take the position."

"Shit, really?" Asher's jaw nearly hit the floor.

"Your dad didn't tell you?"

"No. He hasn't mentioned anything at all to me." He spoke truthfully; his body language screamed confusion. "Maybe he has an eye on one of my brothers vying for the role."

The door to Asher's home opened, and Mr. Thrace himself walked out. "Has it crossed your mind at all that I do not wish any of my sons to die in an Alpha war?" He spoke as if he were already part of the conversation.

"Mr. Thrace. I…" Caught off guard by his sudden appearance, she stuttered, trying to find the right words.

He sighed and placed a hand on her shoulder. "I meant what I said when I originally backed your claim. I feel you have some excellence inside of you… once some of your youth and defiant spirit are tempered by age and wisdom. Which will come through apprenticeship to a Regent." He could intimidate with a look, but his eyes merely confirmed the truth of his words when they met hers. "And by virtue of your birth, you should be first in line for that role."

For a man normally disapproving of everything she did – loudly and angrily most times – to hear him speak so highly of her now felt beyond awkward. Her fight-or-flight instinct had Giselle squirming from his grip. "But I've been deemed too wild." She chuckled nervously.

"That you are. But a wild spirit is not always a bad thing." Mr. Thrace smiled broadly, as if enjoying a private joke. "We need a little shaking up every now and again. You've shown me that my stubbornness and blind hatred were wrong. You stood up to me, and I cause lesser wolves to cower in fear."

"Well, now you're giving me too much credit." If he only knew how frightened of him she was most days. Stupidity more than bravery made her stand up to him that first time, even though the results had worked in her favor.

"I'm truly sorry it came to this," Mr. Thrace said, with a heavy sigh. The smile faded as quickly as it had flashed across his face and the stony look of resolution returned. Girls would call it *resting bitch face*, but it didn't seem right to use such words where Nathaniel Thrace was concerned. At least, not within earshot. "An Alpha battle is not for the weak…at all. More often than not, brawn wins where brains would do far better."

"See, I don't stand a chance," Giselle admitted.

"You would be murdered, little wolf." Mr. Thrace answered with no hesitation.

Asher nodded, but did not voice an opinion out loud.

"Because I'm a girl?" Giselle hadn't thought about the fact that girls and guys would be fighting in the same trials. She wondered how male-dominated the whole thing would be.

"No. Because you're not trained for combat." Mr. Thrace swatted her comment away like an annoying fly. "I've seen you fight. Remember?"

Giselle's face reddened, remembering old Jeffrey nearly ripping her to shreds. She'd had no chance against him. And he was old. She chuckled with nervous embarrassment. "Yeah."

Asher stood by, quiet as the grave. *Smart boy*. Best not to antagonize her now. She might not be able to fight a full-grown wolf, but she'd at least try to put Asher in his place, and his silence confirmed he knew it.

"The fight for Alpha is to the death," Mr. Thrace said solemnly. "Last wolf standing takes the prize. Purely archaic, if you ask me, but that is the way of our people. Bloodlines passing down their leadership helped avoid many a battle like this, but in your case... I truly am sorry."

Giselle shrugged, hoping to appear as if she couldn't care less, though deep down she was still disappointed. "It's fine."

Whether he believed her or not, Mr. Thrace spoke no more on the subject. After a moment, he cleared his throat. "I heard your father has come home with you. I would very much like to see him."

She couldn't tell by his tone if his interest were genuine or morbid. Seeing a great leader laid low could be of interest to another Alpha. Or perhaps he was just hoping to pay his respects. She hoped for the latter, and smiled at his request. "We're settling him in. He's in need of round the clock care, but as soon as we have him comfortable, I'm sure arrangements can be made."

"If Martina or Gavin needs any assistance, I'm quite happy to help." That she could tell was genuine. Since their truce, both the Hernandez and the Thrace packs had done well by assisting each other, almost as if they'd grown as close as family. Maybe one day they would join the packs as was originally intended; but for now, the truce was being upheld beautifully, and Mr. Thrace's continued support appreciated.

"I'm sure they would be grateful. I know I am." Giselle nodded.

"I'm a phone call away." Mr. Thrace gave a half smile and returned to the house.

"Well, that was awkward." Asher said, finally breaking his silence.

"Was he spying on us? Giselle asked.

"Yeah."

"Why?" Giselle asked suspiciously.

"He wants to know what goes on between us. We're apparently too friendly for things to be innocent."

"Fancy an alliance, does he?" Giselle punched Asher in the arm playfully.

"You've met him. What do you think?" Ash shrugged.

"Face it: you and I will always be under scrutiny. Taylor gave her permission, though, so at least my end is clear."

"Permission? Seriously?" Asher looked intrigued.

"Yeah, before we left. She said if I was going to be Alpha and all, I would have to have a wolfy boyfriend, and since she no longer wanted you…"

"Oh, well, if you like sloppy seconds," Asher laughed.

"Definitely got the sloppy part right." Giselle smirked.

Asher feigned insult with a huff, and playfully tucked in his shirt. "That better?"

"Idiot." Giselle laughed. But she had to admit, even if just in secret, that she was happy Asher was free and clear as far as her sister was concerned.

"So. All joking aside, how are you dealing? Losing the Alpha. Finding your Dad. Taking care of your Dad? Damn...you've got a lot on your plate these days."

"Honestly..." Giselle blew out a breath filled with pent up anxiety. "I'm a mess. And thanks for asking. Not about the Alpha bit. I don't care about it... really," she lied. "But Dad. I knew he'd be a vegetable. But I didn't know he'd be like this."

"Like what?"

She debated for a moment whether she should tell him. When she'd told Taylor, there had been apprehension. Even after witnessing her father holding onto her hand, Taylor still chalked it up to unconscious twitches. Martina and Gavin too. They reminded her that he did still shift at the full moon, and occasionally moaned or twitched. She wasn't supposed to put too much stock into it or get her hopes up. In truth, they didn't want her doing something stupid like going to the witches, which was in fact next on her to-do list. So as usual, she was alone in her speculation, and until she could prove anything, she felt the need to keep silent.

But Ash was different. Like Richard with his blunt honesty, Ash had always been one she could go to for the truth. And he was more likely to believe her crazy ideas.

That set her mind at ease. "He's a prisoner in his own body. I can feel it. When I touch him, he reacts. There's life behind his dull eyes. And I don't know what to do to help him."

Asher leaned against the stone wall of his house. "Have you talked to your boyfriend?"

"He knows what everyone does – that Orion's a vegetable. You have to see it to truly understand. He's coming over later, and I'll show him then."

"Oh so he gets to visit you, but we don't?" Asher said playfully hurt.

"Nope. You're sloppy seconds, remember."

Asher's eyes narrowed almost angrily at her.

Giselle let out a sigh. "You know how it is with the wolves. They hide the weak from each other. That whole alpha thing."

"Yeah, I get it. But you should allow us to pay a visit. You heard my father. He wants to see Orion."

"It will be up to Martina to sanction that."

"And what about me?" Asher asked. "Am I to be treated the same as he?"

"Let me clear it with Martina first. I'm sure she'll be cool with you, Ash. But I have to be respectful in her home."

"Your home too," Asher said.

"Yes, it is, but you know what I mean. I overstep on many occasions. Right now I want to make sure to keep on their good side."

"Because they're taking your father in?" Asher asked.

He knew her better than she thought. "Enough talk. I need to run. Are you coming?"

"I didn't mean to piss you off."

"I know. Everything is strange right now with my father, with the whole Alpha thing... I'm still sorting through my own feelings."

"It's cool. Just know I have your back. We're friends first... wolves second." Asher pulled out the keys to his truck. "Let's go find that dry creek bed."

"I'd like that," Giselle answered, already walking down the path to his truck.

19

Running had worked its magic on her, and after she'd gotten home and showered away the layers of desert from her body, she emerged feeling almost herself again.

Her sisters had taken the afternoon to enjoy their favorite pastime, shopping, and left her with the house almost all to herself, so she could have some alone time when Damien arrived.

She needed that. Most of her dates had been crashed by her sisters, and uncertain as their relationship was at the moment, due to wolf politics and the example of her own parents failure, they needed to have a little peace.

The doorbell rang just as she was pulling her hair into a ponytail. She rushed down to be first to answer it, and skipped outside to talk before inviting him in.

"Glad you're back." Damien greeted Giselle with an extended hug before she could even say hello. His hands sank from the small of her back down to her butt, finishing with a squeeze. "I missed you."

Giselle giggled to herself. He'd make a great wolf with the confidence he exuded. If only he was, life would be so much easier.

"Missed you too." She pulled away and met Damien's eyes with excitement. "And I have someone to show you."

"Is that why you met me out here instead of inviting me in?" Damien stole a quick peck of a kiss and took hold of her hand to walk alongside her as she led him further into the house. "Have a new man in your life and you want me to share?"

"If it were anyone but my father, I might say that was pretty kinky, but… uh… mind out of the gutter, okay?" she smirked at him.

"Okay, that was not one of my better jokes. Will you forgive me?" He batted his puppy-dog eyes at her, and she couldn't help but smile.

"Just this once." She rolled her eyes. "Okay. Here's the deal. You're going to be one of the first to meet Dad. And I need some of your witchy mojo."

"What now?" Damien's playful smile hardened.

"I'll explain. But… you have to keep an open mind." Giselle held the front door as if guarding it with her life. "Can you do that?"

"Do I have a choice?" Damien's tone darkened.

"No," she replied forcefully.

"Okay." He sighed.

"Don't be so… grumpy. This is a good thing." She opened the door and pulled Damien along to the couch. "Sit here. I'll be right back."

Damien looked as if he'd been trapped and might escape the moment she left his sight. She pushed him down and almost said *stay*, but stopped herself at the last moment.

"Before you see him, be warned. He's not... well... um... the magic took its toll on him. Just act normal, okay?"

You've got me all worried now," Damien said.

"Just be cool, okay?" Giselle ran to the guest room and pushed Orion's chair out into the living room.

Damien stood the moment Orion came into view.

"Meet my father, Orion Silverman," Giselle said proudly.

Not missing a beat, Damien waved his hand at the seated wolf and introduced himself. "Glad to meet you, sir."

Giselle pushed the chair up to the edge of the couch and took a seat nearby. She took hold of her father's hand, and as soon as their skin touched, she felt that spark of life. He twitched as if trying to grasp hold of her as well. More confirmation that her father was there, alive, and in need of help.

"So. You're probably wondering about him," she began to say.

"Cassandra told us what happened. Has she seen him yet?"

"No. But soon," Giselle answered.

"Can he... does he... I mean..."

Giselle's smile waned. "It's hard to see him like this. I know. But he's in there. I can't really say how I know, but I feel it. And I have to help him."

Damien's eyes widened suspiciously. "Giselle..."

"Don't you dare," she snapped at him. She'd heard enough from everyone else. She'd be damned if her own boyfriend would lecture her.

"I just want you to think."

"You think I don't?"

"You're impulsive," Damien said.

"And my instincts... have they been wrong so far?"

Damien sighed. "Not yet. But there's always a first time."

"Shut up and listen, will you?"

Damien held his hands up in surrender. "Fine. I'm listening."

"Don't listen. Feel." Giselle held her hand out to Damien.

He hesitated for a moment, but when a growl rumbled up Giselle's chest, Damien took hold of her hand as if afraid he'd have his head bitten off if he didn't.

"Okay. I want you to concentrate. Do you feel anything?" Giselle asked.

"Does nervous count?" Damien shot back with a laugh.

"Seriously?" Giselle *would* bite his head off if he didn't stop screwing around. "I mean it. Concentrate. Can you feel what I'm feeling?"

Damien shook his head. "I don't know what you want me to do. Honestly."

Giselle growled in frustration and dropped both Damien's hand and Orion's.

"Maybe if you tell me what I'm supposed to feel?" Damien said hesitantly.

"When I touch his hand, I can feel... something. There's a connection. I can't really explain it better. It's a feeling."

Damien stood. "Maybe if I held his hand." He reached out and gingerly laid his hand over the top of

Orion's. Closing his eyes he stood still, silently, and slowed his breathing.

Giselle watched with interest, hoping he'd get that same sensation she did. Maybe he, being a witch, could communicate or something. Make some kind of connection.

The moment passed, and Damien opened his eyes and retook his seat with a sigh. "Sorry. I just… Maybe I'm not the witch to do this."

Disappointment sank her hopes like a stone. Surely a witch could feel it if she could. Maybe he wasn't the one for the job. She could try Cassandra; but then, again she had no magic. The one bright spot she'd had, saving her father, seemed to dim before she had the chance to fully formulate a plan for him.

"Please don't be mad. I can try again." Damien's puppy-dog eyes were in full force now.

"I know he's in there." Giselle sighed. "Magic is the reason he's trapped like this. He's a prisoner in his own body. And if magic did this to him, then maybe there's some magic that can release him."

Sadness turned to stone in the blink of Damien's eyes. "I knew you were going to say that. Let me stop you right there. He's like that as a punishment." No pleading. No placating. Damien had always tried to help her, but this time, his words were delivered with a finality she wasn't used to hearing.

"It's still the result of magic," Giselle responded.

"There's a difference, though. When a witch casts magic, it can be undone by that witch. When the cosmos works to undo magic because a contract is broken, it's not something a witch can fix."

"So what you're saying is I need to offer something to the cosmos, then? How do I do that?" Giselle asked, hoping she'd understood what he'd implied.

Damien signed and smacked himself in the head. "No. You don't understand."

"Where do witches get their magic from, if not the cosmos? Are you not uniquely blessed to channel the magic?"

"Someone has been researching the web for info, haven't they?" Damien groaned.

"I wanted to be prepared for your argument," Giselle said.

"I see. Okay. Yes. We are blessed, as you say, with the ability to *channel* magic. We pay homage to the gods and make our offerings to please them in return for these gifts."

"So, then, if someone has pissed off the gods and got the magical whammy because of it, would it not stand to reason that offering up something in exchange might work to alter the magic done?" Giselle asked.

"There's a lot of *ifs* there in that sentence."

"*Ifs* are better than *nos*," Giselle said, and looked lovingly on her father. "I would do whatever I could to help free him from this prison. Cassandra got the magical whammy and she lost her ability to channel magic, but she still walks among the living. She can still have a life. What of my father? Look at him. This is more punishment than any deserves for what he did."

"He abused magic to create life," Damien said, with unusual coldness.

"When you put it that way, sure, it sounds bad, but remember Cassandra did the same. Why did she get off so lightly?"

"You speak as if she should have equal punishment," Damien said.

"No. I would never wish this on anyone. I'm using her as a point of comparison. Anything would have been better than this. Hell, they could have taken his wolf and left him human, and it would still have been a horrible punishment, but more fair than this."

"I get that. Really I do." Damien nodded. "But I don't make the rules. I'm not a god."

"But you commune with them," Giselle insisted.

Damien sighed, pinching the bridge of his nose. "It's often just a one-way conversation, and more chanting than shooting the shit."

Giselle snickered.

"Let's play devil's advocate here. If the gods were the bargaining type, what would you offer in return?" Damien asked.

Giselle shrugged. "I don't know. What would they accept?"

"Hard to say. But…" He gritted his teeth, "For arguments sake…you'd have to offer something good. And that's assuming they *would* take a trade."

"Could you look into it?" Giselle asked, batting her eyes, hoping that by putting the girlfriend card in play, she'd ensure his cooperation.

Damien sighed. His shoulders slumped. "You would ask this of me."

"I'll ask your mother if you'd rather I go that route." Giselle's temper flared, feeling she'd lost already.

"You'll still have to deal with her," Damien said. "What does Martina say? Or Gavin?"

"They don't know…yet."

"Of course they don't, Giselle. Why? The damn secrets. This is why you weren't named Alpha. You always operate on your own."

"That was a low blow," Giselle snarled.

"It's the truth, and I hope that, as your boyfriend, at least for the time being, you can appreciate my honesty."

"Are you going to help or not?" Giselle demanded the answer rather than let him steer the conversation away.

His jaw tightened as if wanting to argue, but after meeting the determination in her eyes, he let go of a breath and responded. "You clear it with your Alphas, and I'll talk with my mother."

"Fine."

"I mean it," Damien insisted. "No more lone wolf. You do this. You have the backing of your family."

Giselle looked at her father. Seeing him like this broke her heart. She would do anything for him. "You have my word," she lied, with a victorious smile.

Damien turned away. His body language screaming anger, but when he spoke his voice held only sadness. "I'm sorry if I ruined the mood. I just don't want to see you in any more trouble. I care."

"I get it. I do." She stopped her eyes from rolling before he saw them. If he had truly gotten it he'd have been first in line to help. But whatever, at least he had agreed.

"Our lives are complicated in so many ways. I just want to get past these rough parts with as little opposition as possible. If you have the support of Martina, I will help."

"I'll do my part as long as you are willing to do yours," Giselle agreed.

"Well, now you sound like a diplomat." Damien couldn't have been more dead on with his statement.

"Hardly. Just someone who hates jumping through hoops. I see; I do; I get it done."

The smile she so loved about him returned to Damien's face. "And that's what makes you awesome. But you have to make sure you don't mow others down in the process of your *getting things done*, lone wolf. Think of the others who might be affected by your plans."

"Now I get lectures from my boyfriend?" Giselle was done with the conversation, but he kept dragging it out.

"You want lectures, try living with my mother. Life as a witch is not all magical fun. With great magic comes great blah, blah, blah… Everything is a lecture. Respect. Family. Loyalty."

"Wolves are not much different," Giselle said.

"I get that. Okay, fine. I'll do my part as long as you do yours. No more talk on this subject tonight. Can we agree on that?"

"Please!"

"Still on for a movie, then?" Damien asked. "Or have I pissed you off too much?"

"Let me just take care of Father and let Martina know I'm leaving. Then we can go," Giselle said, feeling less and less like going out while her dad sat trapped in that stupid chair. With Damien's assistance or without, she would find a way to help him. He deserved so much better than that life.

20

The week away and her weekend at home with father had flashed forward, and before she realized it, Giselle found herself sitting in Mr. Harper's class, staring up at the fluorescent lights and wondering how she'd gotten there.

Like an echo at the end of a long tunnel, someone was angrily calling out, "Miss Richards," and it took her a moment to realize they were speaking to her. The northern packs would only refer to her by her father's last name, and she'd grown fond of the way it sounded. Giselle Silverman.

"Miss Richards, are you here with us this morning?" Mr. Harper's face came into view, snapping her back to reality.

"Sorry. What?" she asked, confused, as the bloom of embarrassment colored her cheeks.

The entire class stared at her, some laughing, some mumbling about her. Words like *crack head* and *stoner* were whispered, but still found their way to her ears as Mr. Harper ground his teeth above her.

"Reports were due this morning. Your absence last week did not change when your work was expected to be turned in."

No teacher had ever hated a student as much as he hated her. There was no reason to single her out for missing an assignment, and yet there he stood holding a hand out, publicly humiliating her for a minor infraction.

Worse, she had nothing to give him. With all the wolfy politics she'd been privy to in the last week, she had completely forgotten school and her report. Hadn't even started it. And she needed to pass this class.

Despite her desire to throw anger with the full force of her wolf behind her, Giselle dropped her head and took a breath. "I'm sorry. We had a family emergency, and I wasn't able to complete the report. Can I hand it in tomorrow morning?"

"Tomorrow it will be half credit."

She couldn't look up. If she met the hatred of his eyes, there would be no way to hold back. The venom of his words was nearly enough to send her over the edge. "You'll have it first thing."

Her heart pounded with anger, overpowering any remnants of the embarrassment she'd felt. The entire school could think whatever they wanted of her. She knew better. She dealt with so much more than their simple little lives demanded of them. But Mr. Harper... his effect on her life was much more pressing. A bad grade from him could derail her future. She hadn't even wanted to be in his class again this year, but her counselor had said she needed Chemistry 2 on her transcript. And of course, he was the only teacher.

Before becoming a pack wolf, she'd never had trouble in school. Keeping a family might have been problematic, but school had always been a constant. All this trouble over family and Alphas and Council meetings had stolen her attention away from the normal part of her existence. But she was not one to fail at anything, least of all this.

The squeak of a whiteboard marker told her Mr. Harper had turned his attention elsewhere, and she let out a breath before looking up to see what he'd written.

Guarana seed.

Asher nudged her shoulder but she didn't dare look in his direction nor speak. One more disruption and Mr. Harper would go off, and her wolf was already too near the surface.

"Continuing our exploration on stimulating substances, we'll look at South America." Mr. Harper continued to write on the board: *Yerba Mate, Suma, Coca…*

Asher nudged her again. Why he was trying to get her in trouble was beyond Giselle, but she would not give into the temptation.

In her notebook she wrote *Talk after class* and slid it to the side, hoping it would be enough to stop Asher from doing anything more to get her in trouble.

"The chemical compositions of these substances work to stimulate the nervous system…"

She tried to pay attention as Mr. Harper spoke, knowing at any moment she'd be called on for some further spotlight embarrassment, but as he droned on about stimulants, she felt an overwhelming desire to nod off. Di hadn't stopped for coffee this morning, and Giselle had stayed up way too late with her sisters talking about her date with Damien.

She'd crossed a line playing the girlfriend card to force him to work toward fixing her father, and that had overshadowed the entire evening. It brought up more concerns she'd been hoping to ignore about their relationship. Since learning about Cassandra and Orion, she'd felt more and more like being his girlfriend was stringing him along. Alpha or no, a relationship between a wolf and witch could go one of two ways, and her father was a shining example of the most likely result of continuing the relationship.

Despite her desire to do the right thing, she'd already abused their bond. How far would she go to get what she wanted from the witches? If she hadn't been his girlfriend, would Damien have given in to her demands? Probably not.

Those thoughts mixed with Taylor's and Di's agreement that no matter what, she'd eventually have to settle down with a wolf had kept her up to the wee hours of the morning.

"You will pick one substance from this list and describe its chemical makeup, effects on the body..." Mr. Harper continued to drone on in the background as her thoughts drifted in and out of reality.

Asher again nudged her and out of annoyance she finally turned to him, spearing him with a look of annoyance.

His eyes flitted down to the paper where she'd written word to him earlier. Just under her scribbles was a line written in his hand.

I have notes. Write your paper at lunch and turn it in before the day ends.

Her annoyance melted into gratitude. Asher might have saved her GPA if Harper would accept her paper turned in today. That meant skipping lunch and spending the entire period in the library, but she could pull it off with his help.

Her knight in furry armor. She snickered at the thought and straightened up the moment Mr. Harper's eyes zeroed in on her. Feigning a cough, she hoped she'd pulled off the ruse, but just to be sure, she raised her hand. "What's the due date for this next assignment?"

He didn't answer in words, but Mr. Harper's scowl and the quick glance back at the whiteboard where the information was written gave her all the information she needed.

"Thank you, sir. I don't want to miss a deadline again." It took all she had to keep her voice level and sound sincere. She'd jokingly said she'd rather deal with him than a room full of Alphas. Vivian and he were cut from the same cloth. And now she'd much rather be back in the presence of all those intimidating heads of territories. At least with them she was able to state her case.

All she could do here was keep her head down and pray she made it through the rest of the year in his class. At least Asher had her back. She'd thank him for it later.

21

With time against her, Giselle rushed to the library as soon as the bell rang for her lunch period. Her stomach ached from hunger. She'd hardly eaten before the school day had begun, and now more than three hours into the day, her wolf was scratching at the surface for any scrap of food. But knowing how prickly Mr. Harper was, she chose duty over sustenance. If she typed as fast as her fingers could, she just might get something decently resembling a report finished and on his desk before the next bell. Vending machine food would have to suffice – her reward if she completed her task.

She wasn't the only one with that idea, it seemed. As she entered through the double doors and passed the checkout desk, she spotted a packed row of computers.

Shit! She scrambled, rushing over, hoping to find one empty.

One by one, she walked slowly by, looking over the shoulders of each person sitting there. One researching parts of speech; another working on a complex spreadsheet.

And then she spotted the end of the row. A guy packing up his bookbag.

"Is that one free?" she asked, before she'd even reached his space.

"Give me a minute," the boy protested, and slowly folded his notebook.

Hunger and patience did not pair well, but she held her tongue rather than bite his head off and make him move.

She paced close while he took his time putting away his belongings as slowly as he possibly could. He smirked at her as if enjoying making her squirm, knowing his was the last open computer in the library.

Jerk.

She was just about ready to voice her annoyance when he shouldered his bag and walked away.

It was a testament to her newfound maturity as a potential Alpha that she hadn't made a scene. At last, that was what she told herself.

A quick glance at her phone told her she was running short on time. Giselle whipped out Asher's notes and sat down to the computer, opening up a blank document and started typing out her headings.

Not even five minutes had gone by when Giselle felt the weight of eyes against her back. She smelled wolf instantly but chose to ignore them, hoping her body language alone would scream *I'm busy*, but no one ever listened to that. Not even a wolf.

"Whatcha doing?" Di poked Giselle in the back.

Nose down, typing as fast as her fingers could fly over the keys, Giselle had no time for distractions. Lunch period only lasted forty minutes, and that left no time to edit her work. She grunted at her sister as she took her eyes of the screen for a moment to glance down at Asher's notes.

"You're missing lunch. You know that's a bad idea. You get cranky when you're hungry." Di pulled up a seat next to her.

"Don't care," Giselle mumbled, trying to concentrate.

"Damien was looking for you," Di taunted her.

Giselle let out a loud sigh. "Look. Harper is out to get me. I have…" She looked down at the time on the computer screen. "Shit! Twenty minutes to finish this report and turn it in before next class. I don't have time for this right now."

Di held her hands up in surrender. "Okay, lady. I was only trying to be helpful."

"No, you weren't. You were trying to be nosey." Giselle turned her attention back to the computer screen.

"If I was being nosey, I would have told you that *metabolize* is spelled with a z," Di said with as much snark as she could. "But by all means, shoo me away when I'm being sisterly."

Giselle growled in frustration and corrected the misspelling. "Fine. You have five minutes. What do you need from me?"

"Just to tell you that Martina has laid down the law. I got a text from her about an hour ago. Between Orion's care and the event we have to plan, we're all grounded for the next month. Or as she says… Our calendars are full. Don't plan anything."

"Overreacting much?" Giselle cracked a smile and finally looked at her sister.

"Just a little. I get it, though. We're in the spotlight. Hosting all those Alphas."

"Right, and I saw how stressed she was over the dinner with David not too long ago. I wonder how long before her head explodes," Giselle snickered.

"At least Christina is back and can help," Di said.

She couldn't argue there. Martina was a completely different person when her sister was around. Less stressed, for sure. Not even Gavin had that same soothing effect. "And she'll take the pressure off us. Let's face it, without her, we'd all be drafted into slavery."

"Oh… we still will. Part two of the text she sent said to prepare for assignments at dinner tonight." Di rolled her eyes.

"I'm already full up with assignments. Last week killed me. And…" Her eyes flitted over to the computer screen. "If I don't get this report done now, I'm screwed."

"Harper is a jerk." Di's words were true, but that brought no comfort to Giselle. She had to pass that class this year. Somehow her sister had managed to avoid his class entirely. Lucky.

"Thank you, Captain Obvious."

"Whatever. I'm on your side, remember?"

"Sorry. Just stressing."

"I get it. I'll take off. But before I do… Damien was looking for you."

"He'll have to wait. Busy."

"Moving further and further down the list of importance, is he?"

"Shut up." Giselle sighed.

"Just saying." Di turned to walk away, and despite her best efforts, Giselle lost her train of thought.

She let her head fall to the desk and banged it a few times. Life did not have to be this damn complicated.

With a groan of frustration, she picked up Asher's notes and tried to refocus. *All metabolic reactions can be broken down into two general categories: catabolic and anabolic.*

She reread the line five times before the words sank in, all the while wondering why Damien was looking for her and if he might have found an answer. No. He couldn't have found an answer that quickly. He probably just wanted to spend the lunch hour with her, like a regular boyfriend would.

But in the back of her mind the wonder was there, and Giselle desperately wanted to find out. As time ticked away, though, so did her chances for a passing grade, and she needed to finish this damn report.

Di's words mocked her. *Moving down the list of importance.* Where the hell was she on the list of important things? Somewhere below the last line, that was for certain.

No. She had to do this. School would have a lasting effect on her life. She needed to finish the report. She could always find Damien later.

22

The day escaped Giselle, a blur of words and papers, angry teachers, and missed connections with her boy-friend. Before she knew it, Giselle found herself washing up dishes in the kitchen while her mother called for a meeting in the dining room.

No rest for the wicked. Since returning home she'd hardly had a moment to sit and relax. Thanks to Di's warning, she already had an idea of what this meeting would be about: more Alpha bullshit.

If for nothing else, at that moment she wished she'd been awarded the title just so she'd have the power to tell people to leave her alone for a little while.

Homework from a week of missed school had piled up. She'd appeased her chemistry teacher for the moment but she still had literature, geometry, government, and Spanish to make up work in. All that on top of whatever Martina would want her to do, and research for her father. Just the thought of all she needed to take care of had her head spinning.

"Hurry up." Christina poked her head into the kitch-en.

Giselle was standing like a zombie at the sink, a dish in one hand and a scrubber in the other. "I'm coming."

"Martina's on the warpath. Don't make her wait. She'll have an aneurysm." Christina chuckled. Frozen in time as Martina's sister had been, Christina looked more like an older sister than her adoptive aunt. It was hard sometimes for Giselle to remember that in their little pack, Christina was an authority. Wolves, she'd recently learned, were hard to judge by age alone, often looking as old as they felt inside rather than displaying their physical age. It was if age was a sign of exhaustion; in flux rather than linear. Those who'd been through hard times appeared older. And in the truly old, times of little stress added vigor back to their features. Even old Jeffrey, Christina's mate, had lost some of the gray in his whiskers since their return from vacation.

Things to ponder at a different time. One look to Christina made her realize she'd lost herself in thought again, and Giselle set the dish down in the sink and headed out to the dining room.

"Assignments, ladies." Martina called the room to order. "We'll be under scrutiny for these trials, and I want to make sure we wow them. I mean it. Wow!"

Giselle groaned as she walked toward the dining room table, earning a disapproving glare from her sisters.

"Are we going with a theme?" Taylor asked, with a flash of excitement in her eyes. Party planning and décor was her calling in life. Captain of the cheer squad, Student Council, and head events coordinator in high school had given her quite the resume for setting events up. Personal stylist and shopper for Giselle was the way she practiced and honed her skills on a daily basis. Pen at the ready and a notebook in front of her, Taylor practically vibrated in her seat with energy.

Di, whose talents lay in the finishing touches like makeup and accessories, looked equally excited and eager to get started. "Oooh, yes. I'm thinking something rough and rugged, given the setting."

"Right. We're going to be in the desert, so maybe we play that up." Taylor squealed with delight.

Martina cleared her throat. "I appreciate your enthusiasm, ladies, but let's do remember that we are hosting heads of all the powerful Alpha families in North America, not the glee club at school."

Martina's words hit Taylor with the intensity of a smack across the face. Her jaw dropped slack as her eyes widened, glistening with tears. "But…"

Di placed a consoling hand on Taylor's back. "Of course we'll keep it classy." Her tone betrayed her wounded feelings, though Di's face remained a mask of calm.

For all a wolf's touted abilities to read between the lines with body language, Martina didn't seem to see how her sharp tone and quick dismissal of Di and Taylor's idea had hurt them. To Giselle it was plain as day, but she didn't dare speak up for either side, though she thought Martina's quickness to put down her sisters' idea a little rude. If nothing else, those girls were good at making anything or anyone look their best.

Christina set down a few spiral notebooks on the table and shoved one in Giselle's direction. "Maybe we could all sit and brainstorm for a little bit before we jump into what ideas are good or bad."

Thankfully someone was playing peacekeeper. It wasn't like Martina to be so judgy, but then again, it wasn't every day that they were under such scrutiny. Part of the reason, Giselle felt, that she had been rejected as Alpha was that her family was so unknown. This was a good way for them to show just how capable the Hernandez pack was at diplomacy and spectacle.

"I'm fine with whatever the group decides. Really. Just tell me what and when. I'm easy like that," Giselle said, to maintain neutrality.

Taylor snorted. "You? Easy?"

"I can be. If given the right circumstances." Giselle bit her lip to avoid smiling.

"Ladies. Focus!" Martina sat heavily in her seat. "We have a short while until this city fills up with wolves. We must look and act our best during the time they're here."

"Are they staying with us?" Giselle asked.

All eyes around the room settled on her. She hadn't thought it was a bad question, but the minute the words left her lips, she realized how silly it was of her to ask. It was hard enough getting the Hernandez pack and the Thrace pack to get along. Why ever would she expect foreign wolves, Alphas in their own right, to be any easier to deal with?

"Sorry," Giselle said sheepishly. "What I meant was, are they staying close, and will we be responsible for their entertainment the entire time they're here in this city?"

Lines in Martina's face softened. She nodded to herself and consulted the paper in her hand before answering. "We've booked the hotel at Bonnie Springs for guests since we'll be handling the event in the desert. The place will be ours for the week. Our responsibility, though, is to the event, not to the attending Alphas and contenders for the role. What they do in Vegas is up to them, so long as they keep to the golden rule and stay secret."

Giselle snorted. "Like anyone would break that rule. Especially if they were trying to be the next Alpha."

"You'd be surprised," Martina said sternly. "But I expect no less than perfect behavior from you all."

Giselle, Taylor, and Di exchanged looks that promised innocence, though below the surface a little mischief simmered. Beyond the stress of foreign visitors, there was that edge of anticipation. What did wolves get up to when they got together for a party? Because, after all, when the dust settled and an Alpha was chosen, there would be a party.

"I mean it. One toe out of line…" Martina channeled her full power as pack Alpha with that command.

"Scout's honor." Giselle hoped a joke might lighten the overpowering tone of seriousness in the room.

"Already on the wrong foot, young lady. Might I remind you that your past and proclivity for trouble is part of the reason your claim was rejected?"

Not even a week ago, Martina had consoled her and told her to return to the wolf she had always been; and now she was throwing her failure back in her face? "Why am I being attacked here?" Giselle's stress level jumped to eleven, and she was on her feet. "What have I done to deserve such treatment? I made a joke. That's it."

"No one is attacking you, but if that's how you feel, maybe you should examine why it is we have such ammunition to lob your way." Martina's voice carried a growl at the edge Giselle was not accustomed to hearing. "You don't take anything seriously. This is nothing but a joke for you. A job you didn't want. And one you'll never have. That's your choice. This event puts our pack in the spotlight. We will work as a pack. We will all take our jobs seriously. I have no time for joking. And you will not bring any embarrassment on this pack."

Part of her, the teenager who'd rather not be bothered by any of this shit and felt life had dealt her enough crap, wanted to retort in kind. But another part of her felt Martina's stress. The pressure to perform. Feeling the weight of all eyes, unwanted, on her. This she knew intimately. Though she was loathe to admit it, Martina's hurtful words came from a place of truth, and though the fault should not rest on either of their shoulders, Giselle understood its effect. She allowed the calmer part of her to take control, and chose the path of peace rather than retaliation.

After tense moments of silence passed, Giselle retook her seat.

"As I said. Best behavior! All of you." Martina sighed and continued. "The hotel will handle sleeping arrangements. Our job will be to locate and set up a suitable place for the reception, trials, and end of ceremony."

Christina spoke up. "I've already put in an order for some special gates and barriers to be created to make an arena. The Thrace boys will be setting that up as soon as we've scouted the best place to locate it."

Martina checked something off on her sheet of paper. "Good. They'll need to come up with some kind of seating space as well. Do we have a head count yet?"

"No, but let's say an even hundred to be safe," Christina replied.

That would be more wolves than Giselle had ever met in her entire life. "Do we have the witches casting protection spells on the area to keep it secret?" she asked, suddenly realizing just how big an event this would be.

"Of course, dear." Martina's tone had lightened, thankfully.

"I'm guessing we can't just hire a human catering company to run the event?" Giselle asked, wondering how all those wolves were going to be fed.

"We do have a trusted company who will run the event, and their secrecy comes at a high price," Martina said.

Giselle thought about asking who'd be paying for all of this, but money was not her responsibility, so she kept her mouth shut. The less she spoke at this point the better, she figured. Martina was on a hair trigger as it was.

"So what exactly do you need us to do?" Di asked timidly, though her eyes begged for something important to be handed down to her. "Sounds like you have everything taken care of."

"Ideas. Themes. And once we've settled, I'll send you all out to gather supplies," Martina said.

"I'm thinking white tents. With a little bit of UV lighting, they'll glow like the moon," Taylor said, waving a hand in the air as she envisioned it. "Everything linen should be crisp and white. Accented with silver to really pick up that glow. And maybe pewter-colored plates to provide that lovely roundness and remind everyone of the moon."

Martina smiled. "That sounds lovely dear."

"And very classy," Christina approved.

Di nudged Taylor and winked.

"Okay, girls." Martina pointed a pen at Di. "You will manage the table décor. Let's say ten tables seating ten a piece. Napkins, plates, silverware, centerpieces."

Taylor quickly scrawled down the list as Martina called out the items.

"The catering company will provide the table and cloth as well as seats. Christina, can you coordinate with them on the details? Tents, accents, and what lights did you say?"

Taylor responded. "Like a backlight. If we set the lights to shine on the tent walls, they'll have a glow to them. But we will need regular lights for the rest of the space, so people can see."

"And candles," Di chimed in. "Lots of lovely candles on the tables."

Giselle shook her head. "Fake candles. Lots of rowdy wolves… and linen. No fire."

Martina nodded. "Good point. Get the flameless flickering ones."

Di sighed. "They'll have to be pillars to put off enough light. Tea lights will be too small."

Taylor continued to write things in her notebook. Giselle looked over her shoulder. She wasn't just writing, she was sketching out what she thought the setting should look like.

Martina's initial apprehension that they would not impress the wolves was well off the mark. By the looks of Taylor's drawing, they would have a space to rival any celebrity wedding.

"Sounds like we're well on our way here. The initial reception will be for all attending to meet and greet." Martina read from her notebook. "No battles will be held that day. It will be a full moon, so we'll have quite a few in the partying mood. Dress code will be high class."

Di nudged Taylor, and both girls exchanged excited glances. This was like crack to them.

Giselle smiled and nodded, knowing she'd be outfitted by the best, with no need to even consider what she'd wear.

Martina continued. "Night two will be the start of the trials. They'll last until there are no wolves left to challenge. Ideally only one night, but this can spill over to a second night if the battles take too long. Sundown to sunup. We'll be providing refreshments only for this event. A small tent with open bar, and finger foods. Nothing fancy."

Christina held up a hand. "Are we going to set up any first aid station, and have we arranged for the bodies?"

"Thrace is handling that," Martina said, quickly moving on to the next topic. "And once the trials are over, we'll have a final night to crown the victorious and celebrate."

"Same style party as the initial reception?" Taylor asked, flipping to the next page in her notebook."

"I'd say so. Dinner, dancing, and the ceremony to crown the victors. Yes." Martina nodded. "If we can, re-use anything from before."

Taylor set her notebook down. "We'll find what we can to reuse."

Martina looked at Giselle. "You are still a contender for this event, so your presence is mandatory for the receptions; however, if you don't wish to be part of the trials, you may stay home. In fact, all of you girls may stay home for that."

"What if we want to go?" Taylor asked.

"This will not be a place to ogle boys. Alpha battles are to the death. Only one person leaves the ring alive,"

Martina said. "But I will not stop you from going. You're wolves. This is part of who you are."

Giselle sighed. "I have no desire to go."

Martina said, "I respect that choice. I, however, must go."

"I don't want anyone fighting for me," Giselle said, as if she needed to remind everyone of her choice. "So I'll stay home with father while the others do battle."

"Your choice has been made. And it will be honored," Martina said.

"Thank you," Giselle said. "I'll do whatever else is needed of me, but I'd like to have as little involvement as possible beyond duty. I hope that's acceptable."

"Quite." Martina nodded. "Then let's get your duty out of the way, so you can leave the unpleasantness behind."

23

Lunch was the only time Giselle had free now that Martina had set them on their tasks. She'd tried to meet with Damien before school that morning, but the girls had barely pulled into the parking lot by the time the first bell had run. That left her scrambling for her worst class of the day, and between classes was a four-minute dash that left her little time to pee, let alone hunt down her absentee boyfriend.

Between bites of the sawdust-flavored burger she'd waited more than ten minutes to get in the lunch line, Giselle searched the cafeteria for Damien.

For a boy who'd been looking for her, according to Di, he'd been surprisingly absent in the usual places, and equally unresponsive via text message as well.

The cafeteria had proven a dead end. Giselle tried the library and even took a walk around the parking lot before heading back inside to find him at his locker.

"Long time no see," she teased with a smile.

He returned the greeting, but his eyes lacked their usual glint of joy at seeing her.

Bad news. She knew it before even bringing up the subject of her father. It had been the last thing they discussed, the topic Giselle had been too eager to push. Magic had caused his condition, and magic had to be the key to correcting it. And in that line of thinking, Giselle had beat herself up for the last day and a half over how pushy she'd been with Damien over it.

"Been busy?" Damien asked, though his focus was on the locker and the books he rifled through inside.

"If you only knew." Giselle laughed nervously, hoping that a change of subject might alter the current awkwardness between them. "I'm not even part of this whole Alpha event, but I've been drafted into slavery to make sure it goes off without a hitch."

"Slavery? I seriously doubt it's like that." Damien's tone hinted at boredom, or perhaps exhaustion. She couldn't really tell. His whole vibe was weary, as if he'd pulled an all-nighter and seriously needed caffeine.

Giselle kept her tone light and friendly. "Well, if you asked Di or Taylor, they'd say they were in heaven. Party planning is their crack."

Damien closed his locker and shouldered his backpack. "Sure. I can see that."

"Colors and lights and fashion… blah, blah, blah." Giselle waved a hand flippantly. "They're all my family is talking about."

"Really? The wolves care for all that?" Damien asked with genuine curiosity. He nodded his head toward the end of the hall and started walking.

Giselle walked with him, matching his pace. "The spectacle, sure. Mostly they'll be there for the battles, but between those are the parties."

Damien nodded. "Parties are the fun part. Are you going to enjoy any of it?"

"I may." Giselle shrugged. "The pressure is off of me as an Alpha, so I'll get to go as a guest."

"That's the spirit, I think," Damien said.

"Hard to really get into the spirit when you're watching people fight to the death."

"You wolves..." Damien grimaced.

Giselle sighed. "Yeah."

"Well. Besides the killing, what else does Martina have you planning? Wait... that didn't come out right." He cracked a smile, and she could see some of his personality shining through the fog of exhaustion.

"I'll just check killing off my list." Giselle snorted. "Next."

"You know what I meant," he chuckled.

"Yeah. There's a big... moonlight revelry, I think that's what it's called it. As part of the closing ceremonies. I'm supposed to be gathering materials for that. Service for one hundred or something. Gavin is scouting locations out near Bonnie Springs. They have a hotel, and it's close enough to the mountains for our kind to get lost in for the real event."

"Too bad you couldn't just book a hotel on the Strip."

"Oh, yeah, and charge for tickets like a prize fight," Giselle said.

"Wouldn't be the worst show on the Strip."

"Too true." Giselle sighed. "But it would break the golden rule of secrecy."

"Rules be damned." Damien stopped walking and pulled Giselle close. He planted a kiss on her before she could push him away.

Happy for the little distraction, she welcomed the kiss. Enjoyed it, even, lingering a little closer in the hopes their lips might touch again; and when they did, she finished with a little nip.

"Sorry," he sighed. "I had to get one last kiss in while I could." The weariness returned to Damien's eyes as they separated.

"What do you mean?" The moment broken, she was slammed back into reality and her heart nearly stopped in anticipation of what his next words would be.

"Since…well… Cassandra showed up, you've been more than distant." Damien's eyes dropped to the ground. "Like we've moved into the friend zone, but you hadn't said as much in words."

He was right. She'd been holding him at arm's length for the last few weeks. Duty as a wolf demanded it. The truth of what their future would be had played out in her father's condition. They were doomed as a couple, though she did feel strongly for him.

Love? She couldn't quite call it that… yet. They were still so young, and that was a concept she had yet to understand. She knew she would never be the same if he were removed from her life, but as a friend, she'd still have him there. She had no answers to say out loud. But in her heart, she knew she wasn't ready to let go of him. And that had played a huge part in why she'd been so odd about their relationship. Giselle opened her mouth to put a voice to those thoughts. She wanted to let him know that she had no desire to break things off right now, but Damien cut her off.

"And…you were right to do so. Your return from Washington only added more clarification to our positions as witch and wolf."

"I've said something wrong, haven't I? When I asked you to help me with father? I abused my privilege as your girlfriend, didn't I?" She'd struggled with her feelings for him for so long. The thought of ending things broke her heart as much as the thought of them turning out like Cassandra and Orion. Now he'd turned the tables on her. She knew the blame resided solely with her. She'd abused the relationship. She'd held him at bay and then teased him with it when she needed him.

"No one is at fault here." Damien spoke as if he were reading her mind. "We're both just kids. Our relationship is new. And fun. And believe me when I tell you that you mean the world to me."

"But?"

"The truth is we're better off as friends." Damien finished the sentence for her. "Your family has already put pressure on you. And mine are doing the same. Cassandra as well. The reality is there, in both our faces. It's time we admit it."

How many times had she had this conversation with herself? Practiced saying the same thing to Damien. Every time she looked at her father, a voice in the back of her mind whispered it. But even with the reality staring her in the face, she hadn't given in.

Damien had. And as she stared into his eyes, her heart broke, seeing the steely resolve there. She'd triggered this. He wouldn't admit it, but she overstepped. She had pushed him over the edge and caused this.

Tears threatened to fill her eyes, but she held them back. She'd save them for later and allow them to flow in private. Giselle gulped down the ache in her throat and answered back, "Maybe you're right." Her shoulders slumped. "But I'd liked to remain friends, if that's still something we can be."

Damien looked as if he wanted to lash out. Strange wrinkles formed across his brow. He set his jaw, clenching his teeth tight. "Of course." He turned away. "But I need to take some time."

His body language gave away what he was fighting to hide. This was hard on him too. A small consolation. If that could be considered consoling at all.

The worst thing, though, was her guilt. She'd wanted this on some level. And maybe that was what had caused her to act so flippantly with her relationship. Despite what he'd said about family putting pressure on him, she knew she was the source of it.

Giselle hoped, as she watched Damien walk away, that after a little time, they could be friends. She still needed him. For more than just magic. He was a part of her life.

24

Soldiering through the remainder of the day without shedding a tear ranked up there with one of the hardest things Giselle had ever done. And when the bell rang at the end of her final class, Giselle opted to walk home rather than deal with her sisters nosing into her business. News traveled faster than the speed of light in high school. Without a doubt they'd already heard, and she'd have to face that conversation soon enough. It would be on her terms, though, when she was ready to deal with the scrutiny and the platitudes about it being better to end it now than later.

Giselle held it together all through the long walk home and even as she entered through the front door of her house. Passing by the happy couple Jeffrey and Christina lounging on the couch nearly sent her into a fit of waterworks, though, and it was all she could do to make it to the room where her father was staying before she completely lost it all.

He was her rock, silent and steadfast, a pillar of strength despite the fact he was little more than a vegetable.

Orion's room was large, a second master in Martina's two-story home, complete with a set of French doors looking out onto the patio. His seat had been turned to face the back yard so that he might enjoy the view; if in fact he was able to see. Giselle hoped deep down that he could, and it was easier for her to think of him doing so. He looked so much at peace; whereas her emotions were at war on a scarred battlefield with no hope of survivors.

"He dumped me!" She melted into a sobbing pile of emotions in front of her father. "Is it always going to be like this?"

If ever there was a time she needed an answer, it was then. A comforting pat on the back, or some kind words of encouragement. She'd get none of that from her family. None of them had ever dated out of their species. Even if they had, it wouldn't matter. Martina had the entire family in a frenzy of planning so that they might appear perfect for the Alphas' arrival.

A dirty little thought snuck into her mind at that moment. What if she hadn't pressed her luck at all with Damien? He hadn't seemed all that mad the last time she'd been with him. Annoyed, maybe, but not mad enough to break things off. How much of this decision to break up had been pressure from both families for the sake of appearing perfect for the Alphas?

"I wish I could talk to you, Father." Giselle squeezed her eyes shut in the hopes of stemming the flow of tears. "I wish I knew what you'd faced. How to deal with all of this."

He'd been guilty of loving a witch. The family had made no secret that it was the reason he'd had to abdicate this title. But there had to be more to the story. All she had was blank spaces with no answers. Love didn't bloom overnight; relationships took time.

Even with Damien, she wasn't ready to call what they had between them *love*, but it had certainly developed into more than just a friendship, and they'd taken a year to get to that point.

And both families had been neutral about them all this time.

Well. Neutral enough.

"Please just wake up. Talk to me. Tell me how do deal with this," she pleaded, hoping the universe might see fit to grant her just a few minutes of fatherly advice. Something. Anything.

But for all her sobbing and begging for an answer, all she received was silence.

Giselle, as always, was the lone wolf having to figure the world out by herself. She ran the last month through her mind searching for clues. There had been many times when she'd been nudged in the direction of breaking things off with Damien. Especially right before she'd left for Washington.

Damien had never said anything, but it would stand to reason that he'd been nudged in a similar fashion. But by whom? Anyone in her family could be counted guilty. And for that matter, his family too. Perhaps they had colluded to make this happen.

She couldn't tell what hurt worse: being dumped, or the fact her family might have conspired to rip her heart out behind her back.

She laid her head on her father's lap, still trying to rein in her tears. Anger began to take the place where sadness had resided, but she had no target for her newfound fury. "Please give me strength." Giselle breathed the words, trying her best to maintain control.

Orion didn't move an inch. No twitch of muscle. No spark this time where there had been all the others. Just the slow and steady rise and fall of his chest, the only sign to confirm life still remained within him. As if he were trying to stay out of it even in his vegetative state.

25

If she had any hope of ferreting out answers to what had happened between her and Damien, she'd have to try the only other person who'd been in the same predicament.

Cassandra.

The rumor mill had already churned out the reason behind Giselle's sullen mood, and Martina mercifully gave her leave for the night to shirk her wolfy duties. That alone bred suspicion, but Giselle accepted the evening reprieve and the quiet in the house as the others left to tour the site where the trials would be held.

However, rather than sulk, she called over her other mother, offering time for the two of them to see each other as bait.

Cassandra wasted no time, arriving minutes after receiving the invitation.

Her wounds still fresh from Damien's dismissal, Giselle opened the front door tentatively, putting on a brave face in case Cassandra had not yet heard what had happened.

The moment their eyes met, Cassandra knew. "Sweetheart. Come here and let me hug you!" Motherly instinct or perhaps the lingering part of the wolf residing in her gave her that innate ability to delve deep into the window of the soul and read her pain.

Cassandra wrapped Giselle up in exactly the hug she needed. Warmth and love radiated from her in a way that Giselle could not only feel but draw strength from. She'd been so close to crying before, but now with this bolster of support, she pulled back from the pain and took a cleansing breath of calm.

"Thank you," Giselle said, as she let her arms fall to her side.

Cassandra gave one more squeeze before letting go. "The pain is real. But I won't make you dwell on it."

"It just happened so quickly," she said.

"You know that's not true. It's been in the works ever since you learned about me. Admit that at least." All mothers must be blessed with that *tell the truth* glare. Cassandra might not have had much practice, but the look she gave Giselle made her want to admit she'd eaten all the cookies – even though there weren't any.

"Not from him, though. I might have thought about it once or twice, but he's been Team Giselle. All the way."

"Until the reality of it smacked him in the face. When he came home after seeing Orion, there was a noticeable change in him. That's all I'll say." Cassandra held her hands up.

There had been a change, all right. But it wasn't just from seeing Orion. A wolf could smell a lie, and Cassandra gave out all the right signals. She wasn't wolf enough to hear the uptick in a heartbeat the way Giselle could, but she had to know that her sudden drumroll sounded like an alarm to wolf ears.

That saddened Giselle. She'd hoped her *other* mother would be more open and honest. But whatever the reason, she'd confirmed that Damien had been influenced toward his decision.

With a defeated sigh, she changed the subject. "Before we go in there, how long has it been since you've seen him?"

"Since the day I left," Cassandra said solemnly.

"It might be hard for you to see him initially, because he looks so fragile. But I know his spirit is still strong within him. I can feel that," Giselle said.

"What do you mean?" Confusion stole the sadness from Cassandra's tone.

Giselle struggled with the words at first, trying find the right way to explain his situation. "Like he's there, looking out of his eyes like a window. His body is broken, but his mind is still there."

Cassandra covered her mouth with her hand. "Oh, dear gods. That's a fate worse than death for him."

At least she had the appropriate reaction. Everyone else she'd told had acted as if she were crazy to imply such an existence. He was a vegetable to them, incapable of thought or feeling, simply existing in a void until his life expired – which to Giselle sounded infinitely worse.

No. He was alive. She knew that much. And he was conscious on some level, as terrible as that was to think of.

"Right. I could imagine it's hell," Giselle said.

"Given the years a wolf can live…" Cassandra paused, as if unable to find the right words. "He could be like this for an eternity."

The gods truly were cruel if they could do that to someone. Eternity in a prison of your own mind – no crime was worth that kind of punishment. And at the very least, it seemed that Cassandra understood that as well.

"Is there any way to fix him? Like, true love's kiss or something?" Cheesy yes, and a completely childish question; but Giselle had no other way to broach the subject tactfully. And if nothing else, she'd earned an amused chuckle with her inquiry.

"You are way too old to believe in fairy tales. All magic has its price, and we all paid that price for you."

Amusement lasted all of two seconds before nose-diving right back into harsh reality for Giselle. "Way to make me feel crappy."

"I don't mean it like that," Cassandra said. "But magic has no emotions. It is what it is, and demands a price be paid. That's the bottom line."

"There has to be some kind of a magical currency system or something. Pay a price for something else?"

Cassandra had the look of someone really trying to avoid saying *no* and failing miserably. "Even if that were a possibility, what would you pay? And for that matter, how?"

Giselle shrugged, not having an answer herself. She'd hoped to glean more information, and just like with Damien before, she'd come up short. Everything got lobbed back at her like an endless tennis match. If only she could find her ace. What could she offer in payment? What did she have that was worth the life of her father? There had to be something. She just couldn't allow his condition to continue. He deserved so much better than this life.

Cassandra squeezed Giselle's shoulder. "I know you want your father. And if there were a way, I would tell you."

"Stop reading my mind."

"Not hard to do. It's written all over your face. And though you might not believe it, I feel exactly the same. I would give anything to have my husband back."

"What would you do if you did?"

"Live happily ever after," Cassandra said, with a chuckle.

"Me too," Giselle agreed. "Alpha or no, I don't care."

"I'll be happy just to see him again," Cassandra said, eyeballing the space behind Giselle as if she were blocking him from view.

"Right. I'll take you in there." Giselle led the way to Orion's room.

"And please know I will do whatever I can to take care of him." Cassandra followed close behind Giselle.

"We'll take care of him," Giselle said, almost defensively, although after she spoke, she wasn't sure why. Still prickly over why Damien had decided to leave her had everyone looking suspect. She didn't want to trust another man she cared for to anyone else. But Cassandra was not just anyone else; she was his wife.

"Yes. *We* will." Cassandra stopped Giselle, making a show of pointing to herself and Giselle in turn. "My vow was *in sickness and in health*. The only reason I left was to stay alive long enough to track you down. Now that we're all together again, I will uphold my end of the bargain. I will be by his side, ensuring his health and care right along with you."

Giselle smiled. "I can't tell you how happy it makes me to hear you say that." If Cassandra truly meant it, she

might be willing to help Giselle with her magical research. But she'd broach that topic again after her *other*
mother had had the chance to really soak in Orion's
condition.

"Here he is." She opened the door and allowed Cassandra to enter the room ahead of her.

26

A week of awkwardness had gone by at school. Giselle kept tight-lipped about her situation with Damien, though she was certain everyone already knew. The initial pain of being dumped had faded with the overwhelming duties she had to perform for the upcoming trials. And when time permitted, she threw herself into research on magic. A busy mind had little time to dwell in the doldrums, and hers was running a marathon at top speed from morning until night.

Without a guide, however, on what was real and what was purely fiction, Giselle came up short on answers.

When her father had been an abstract concept – a strange, faceless man she'd never met – and she had been told of his condition, she'd felt sorry for him. But now, day after day, seeing him the way he was, helping to make sure he took his fluids, watching hired nurses showing the family how to change him and perform the tasks required to maintain him, the sense of urgency to fix his condition took over all other thoughts.

She didn't want to approach him so soon, but she knew she had to do it. Damien was her best link to finding answers, or at least sorting out the truth from the magical mumbojumbo she read online.

"Hey." She tried to sound casual as she ambushed him outside of his classroom. "Want to grab lunch... talk?"

"Depends on what we're going to talk about." Damien sighed with the weariness of someone who knew they were trapped.

"Not about us. You've made your position clear on that." Her heart ached, remembering him walking away, but she held her head high.

At least he looked as If he were hurting too. Boys loved to hide their feelings, but his puppy-dog eyes betrayed him. "I meant it. I want us to be friends. I just need time."

Giselle harnessed her heartache to put desperation into her words. "We will be friends, in time. Right now I need an ally."

"For what?" Damien asked, and nodded his head toward the lunchroom.

Thankful he had not turned her away at the door, she followed his lead, taking a moment to think of a tactful way to approach the conversation.

"I cannot stand by every day and see the shell of a man my father has become."

"We've already—" Damien started to say, but she cut him off.

"No. You don't understand. I feel this in my bones. I have to do something. I've—"

"Gods, you're so stubborn. Please don't ask this of me." Damien's fist came up, rearing back as if he were ready to punch the nearest locker, but he stopped himself and took a breath.

"So, have you found out something?" Giselle asked, ignoring tact now that curiosity piqued her interest. Only something truly bad could have elicited that kind of response. What did it mean, though?

"I really don't want to say," Damien said. "You and I are in a weird place. But no matter what happens between us, I care."

"Which is why you must tell me. Because you know when I set my mind to something, I have to do it."

"Why do you have to be like this?" Damien didn't hold back this time, slamming his fist into the locker. "I'm trying to protect you. I thought if we… but no. Of course you can't be swayed. You're so god-damned…" He finished with a growl.

"It's in my nature." Giselle shrugged, hoping to give off an air of indifference, though she hated having to put Damien in this position. He cared; that was more than apparent in his outburst. And so did she. But there was truth to her words. When she set her mind to a task, there was no stopping her. All the way to possible ruin, her drive to see things to their end was rooted in the very fabric of her being. Reflex more than action. She had no control to stop herself.

"If I said there was nothing you could do, would you believe me?" Damien asked. The coldness in his tone betrayed him. Lying to a wolf was near impossible. Scent cues and body language always gave away the truth.

"Of course not. Why insult me by trying to imply it?"

"Because I had to try." Damien started to walk away.

Giselle wouldn't let him off that easily. She caught up and matched his pace. "Fair enough. And I appreciate your care for my wellbeing. Really, I do. But family needs me. My father needs me."

"How can you know this?? He's been a vegetable for your entire life." His words were like a slap in the face.

In truth, she'd only known him for a short while, but the hidden tail of seventeen years of childhood longing for a family – real family – drove her to accept nothing short of success. "So I should leave him this way?" Giselle snapped at him.

"No." Damien stopped short and turned on her with fear rather than anger in his eyes. "That came out wrong. I believe in saving those who can be saved, but you cannot know for sure that he can."

"Damien, I feel it. I sense him in there. He responds to touch. To *my* touch. He's a prisoner trapped in his own body. I know it deep within my bones, and I have to do anything I can to reverse what's been done to him."

Damien sighed. "I don't want to lose you."

"You've already given me up. Remember?" She hadn't meant to throw the words at him with such spite, but heartache, coupled with his lack of empathy for her father only deepened the wound.

"I might have lost us, but I haven't lost you. Yet."

"So I have to sacrifice myself?" Giselle's heart sank. Somewhere deep down she knew it would be a one or the other thing. His life for hers and vice versa.

Her resolve weakened as self-preservation reared its head. She could give up nearly everything to save her father, but could she give her own life? And after all her grandstanding, would she be seen as a fraud for backing out, if that were the case?

So many questions plagued her mind, and in her silence she could see Damien watching her. He'd yet to answer for sure. And there was something in his hesitation that pulled her from the downward spiral she'd begun.

"Details," she said with a sigh. "I need to know everything."

Damien closed his eyes and took a breath. "To help your father you would need to offer up something in exchange."

"You've said that before. But what, exactly?" Why could he not just give her an answer? The unknown frustrated her more than his lack of specificity because her mind instantly went to a worst-case scenario: her life. But until such words were uttered, she wouldn't accept them.

"That's the tricky part." He turned away, as if not wanting to meet her eyes when he delivered the bad news, but she pulled him back with a hand on his shoulder.

"Just tell me."

"This isn't like paying a debtor a specific amount owed. You have to look within and make your offer. If it's accepted, then my family can act as the broker for the exchange."

"So I have to come up with something...?" Giselle asked cautiously. Maybe he was overplaying the doom and gloom angle. She didn't have to offer her life, then. Maybe something smaller. Her eyes trailed down to her hand. Could she offer a part of her? A pinky finger, perhaps? She could live life without a finger. It was useless anyway. Though that of course negated the idea of it being valuable. When she didn't hear an answer, she turned her gaze back to Damien. "Something of value to me?"

"Yes. And only you can offer it. I cannot even tell you what might be acceptable. It has to come from within."

"What if my offer is not acceptable?" Giselle asked.

"That I can't say. Magic isn't a black and white thing. Your offer could be taken and nothing given in return. Your offer could be rejected. It's up to the cosmos." Damien waved a hand to the sky. "The universe holds the great power. We, the witches, are merely conduits of that power. We might look as if we control, it but we simply ask for things to be done." Damien's shoulders slumped.

"You're still holding something back. I can see it. You know the sacrifice would have to be something big… like my wolf or my life to make this work. Don't you?"

Damien shook his head. "I wish I could say. I only know that your father is in deep. Cassandra too. She'll never recover the magic. The path to the cosmos is closed to her forever. And so it is supposed to be for Orion."

"Have you told Cassandra?"

"Of course I did." Damien rolled his eyes. "She lives with us. She heard me poking around."

"Fair enough. I should have expected as much, though she never mentioned it to me."

Damien shrugged and turned away, looking at the people walking past them in the busy halls rather than directly into Giselle's eyes. "Why would she?"

His overt avoidance of meeting her gaze sent red flags up, warning her that despite his attempt to feed her information, there was still quite a bit more he was keeping below the surface.

"Because she promised to do all she could to help Orion. She comes to visit nearly every day."

"She may not have known you long, but she's already got your number. I think she figured if she lay low, you might not do something rash."

"Really?" Giselle all but rolled her own eyes at Damien scrambling to give her a believable story. More deception. More half-truths.

"Okay. No."

"So what does Cassandra say to you about all this?"

"What do you think?" Damien sighed.

"Stay out of it?"

"Yes." Damien finally looked her in the eyes and she saw what he was hiding. Fear. Desperation. Beyond just being worried, there was true terror there. As if he knew her life lay on the line, and he could do nothing to prevent her demise.

What she saw within the depths of his sweet puppy-dog eyes scared her too.

"Stay as far away from magic as you can," Damien pleaded. "Learn from history. Magic can backfire terribly. The gods can be cruel."

Her resolved waivered, hearing what he said, but she couldn't ignore the nagging thought of her poor father trapped for eternity, or however long wolves lived. No. As scared as she was, doing this was the right thing.

"Thank you," Giselle said.

"Please... don't." Damien held his hands up.

"What I do is my duty to family. That I think you can understand. So as far as your assistance there goes, I do thank you. And for myself... I thank you for caring enough to be worried for me." Giselle said.

"We might be done, you and I, as a couple, but I will always care for you." Damien looked as if he wanted to pull her into his arms and keep her safe, but he made no motion forward.

"The feeling is mutual." Giselle offered a half-smile.

"If you choose to go through with this, call on us at the night of the full moon. You and your father."

That was barely a week away. She'd have to decide what to do soon. Another abstract concept turn reality before she was ready to accept it. Could she find something of value before then? Terror of a different kind wrapped tendrils of doubt around her mind. "That's the night of the trials," Giselle said, realizing too what else would be going on at precisely that same time.

"Are you going?" Damien asked curiously.

"No." Giselle shook her head. "I had hoped to stay home and avoid the trials. Spend more time with Father while the rest of the wolves killed each other for his title."

"Don't decide now. Take your time. Maybe even wait a month. There's a full moon every month, you know. You have time."

That gave her some peace – knowing that she could delay a little if she needed, even though that meant more time that her father had to be trapped. "I'll think on it and let you know the day before."

"I need to go now."

Giselle could see his desperate need to escape, and although she'd asked for him to share lunch with her, prolonging their time together would only make things worse. "Of course. We'll talk soon."

He turned away from her without so much as a hug or a word of good-bye. Watching as he walked away again felt just as raw and painful as the last time he'd done it. But at least she knew he cared.

27

I'm not worthless, so what is it that I can bring to the table? Giselle sat staring blankly at the computer screen. *What would the universe take in trade?* She'd run though all the web searches she could on offerings to the gods and magical pacts and still came up empty. *Blood sacrifice. A life for a life. First-born child.* Most of them sounded like the stuff of fairy tales. Knowing the great majority of what she read was bullshit didn't help either. In the past, she might have texted Damien to ask him or maybe stopped by his house to chat. But their breakup had ruined that, and pressing the issue with him would only push him further away.

She couldn't ask her family; wolves knew next to nothing of magic.

Giselle really needed the advice of a witch – one that wouldn't advise against what she planned to do out of motherly love, so Cassandra was out too.

Still her fingers hovered over the keys as her mind drew a blank of what else she could ask the vastness of the web. She'd been holed up in her room for the better part of an hour before the door opened behind her.

Giselle ignored her sister's approach. Didn't matter which one it was, she was busy. They could go about their business and leave her in peace. She was supposed to be studying and catching up on missed work still; at least, that was the cover she'd used to get Martina to give her alone time.

Nothing could stop her prying sisters, though.

"I'm not going to bring it up, because I know it's a worthless cause, but you have to snap out of the funk soon," Taylor said to Giselle's back.

Damn! Just go away. Giselle wanted to scream the words. She'd rather face the Spanish Inquisition than invite her sister to open her chest and rip her heart out again talking about stupid boys.

"Okay," she sighed at her sister's awkward attempt at pretending she didn't want details. It ate her up inside, and Giselle knew it. Her and Damien's breakup had been the quietest one in school history, with neither talking about it to anyone in the families. In public they acted as if all was business as usual, except that it wasn't. Seeing him ripped the band-aid off her bleeding heart. Each time she was reminded that she was not allowed happiness in anything.

Behind her, she heard the soft squish of the mattress. If Taylor was getting comfy, this conversation was happening whether Giselle wanted it or not..

"Ash was looking for you at school today," Taylor teased, as if hearing his name might spark something in Giselle.

Not the boy she's expected her sister to bring up; but she didn't feel like talking about him either. "Ash knows where to find me," Giselle sighed. She started typing the words *magical sacrifice* into the search bar then deleted them just as quickly, knowing she was being watched.

"Maybe he wants to go run? I could cover for you with Martina." Taylor sounded genuine, but hints of unease were laced within her words.

"Yeah. Sure. Running is good," Giselle said absently, trying to locate her train of thought. "Not now, though. Busy."

Taylor groaned behind her. "If I were Di, I'd just demand you turn around and tell me what the hell is going on in your head."

Giselle squeezed her eyes shut, holding back the angry reply she wanted to give. Taylor was right about one thing: Di would try to steamroll her, but that wouldn't necessarily change the results. She took a breath and decided to fight fire with fire. Taylor wanted info, and so did she. "Am I worthless?" Giselle turned to face her sister.

"I didn't mean…" Caught off guard by her reply, Taylor choked on her words. "That's not… No… Look. I'm sorry." She stood as if she were planning to walk out of the room, but Giselle beat her to the door.

"What makes me valuable? What is so damn important about me?" Giselle asked. "If I'm so damn important, as everyone has tried to tell me, why has the universe chosen to shit on me?"

Fear replaced shock in Taylor's eyes. "What? Why are you asking that? Are you okay?"

She'd taken the bait. Giselle smiled inwardly as she kept the hurt in her voice. "Everyone tells me I'm so special, but recent events have proven otherwise, right? I mean the Alphas… Damien…"

Always the sympathetic one, Taylor's bleeding heart gushed, hearing Giselle downplay her self worth. Tears glistened in her eyes as Giselle finished speaking.

"It's been a crappy month, Elle, but that doesn't mean you're worthless."

"Sure seems like it." Giselle added a little extra sulk into her voice.

"You're awesome. I mean it. Forget the whole Alpha blood debacle. Forget Damien and his stupid family for breaking you two up."

"So they did break us up?" Giselle cut Taylor off before she could realize what she'd revealed.

"Uh…" Taylor's shoulders slumped with guilt. "Yeah. He was asking too many questions about Orion and Cassandra, and his mom finally said it was time things ended."

"I figured as much." She'd long since accepted that truth, but it still pained her to hear it.

"He really cares about you. So don't think it had anything to do with your worth." Taylor reached out, but Giselle pulled away before she could make contact. Annoyance flashed across Taylor's soft face, and she let the smack of her falling hand hitting her thigh echo in the room before speaking. "No one wanted you and him to end up like your father and Cassandra."

Giselle let the words sink in. Everyone always worked with her best interest at heart, but good intentions weren't always the right path. Damien's questions were no doubt the ones she'd had him ask, and the truth that was being so closely guarded had ended their relationship – a truth she had still yet to discover. Something of value to her. She had to offer something. But what in her was worth anything? Her blood? Her spirit, maybe? She could only offer herself. And maybe that was it – part of her soul or something, scary as that was.

Taylor's annoyance faded in the silence of the room as the two girls stared blankly at each other. "I know life is throwing crap your way, but you have to try and shake it off. In less than a week—"

"I'm sorry I'm being a bitch." Giselle cut her off. "I'm just wallowing. Feeling worthless. I mean, I was all but guaranteed to be royalty and then dumped like hot garbage… why?"

"That Vivian lady." Taylor flipped a switch and went back on the defensive for her sister. "She's poison. You should have been Alpha. You have the blood of Orion Silverman in your veins. You were born of freaking magic and all. You're like Super Wolf."

Giselle snorted at her sister's gushing. "Super Wolf? Really?" Her words hit closer to home than Taylor had probably intended. She was a special kind of oddity in the wolf world. Magic had been her catalyst, and though her mother had lost it, Giselle had not had life stolen from her. So perhaps some spark of it resided within her.

"I could totally whip you up a fabulous cape if you wanted." Taylor's smile returned.

"Do it. Seriously. Hot pink." Giselle threw words out to keep Taylor speaking, while her mind worked out what Damien had said about being able to channel magic as a witch. She might not be one, but if that quality resided in her blood, it might be part of the equation.

"Ewww. No!" Taylor cringed, and then took her place back on the bed. "If anything, you need a cool blue."

"Either way, I'm Super Wolf, right?" Her sister had unwittingly given Giselle the answer she had been looking for. But damn. She had no way to confirm her suspicion.

"Yeah, I'll say. Super Annoying Wolf." Taylor laughed. "You're awesome when you're happy; but damn, girl, you can mope with the best of them."

"Well, I did lose Alpha and my boyfriend in like the same week. Am I not allowed to have feelings?"

"Nope." Taylor chucked a pillow at Giselle. "You suck it up like a big girl."

Giselle lobbed the pillow back at her. "Right – you're one to talk."

"That's a low blow." Taylor scrunched up her face, but there was no real anger to be seen.

"It is, isn't it?" Giselle mocked her. "All is fair in love and war."

"Speaking of love…" Taylor asked. "Ash?"

"Really? You'd ask me that now?" She knew she shouldn't have brought it up. Taylor might have said she was okay with anything that might happen between Giselle and Asher, but the truth was, she'd be hurt.

"He was asking for you."

"Because we both love to run when we're stressed."

"And he likes you," Taylor said with a tinge of jealousy.

"I just lost my boyfriend. I'm not ready for a rebound. Especially not with Asher Thrace."

Her stern rebuttal had a calming effect on Taylor, as if her sister needed to hear the truth to temper her own fears. "Okay. Just trying to get your mind off of Damien. You know… sister solidarity."

Giselle's mind had lingered on Damien for too long because he was directly tied to all the failing aspects of her life. She needed him to help find information. She missed having him around. And she knew that beyond his family's support of their breakup, hers was secretly cheering it on as well. One less embarrassment when the Alphas came.

It hurt. All of it. Like a dagger to the heart, over and over. And there was nothing to be done about it because they were all right. She couldn't be with Damien in the future anyway, Alpha or not. It just wouldn't work. That much was certain. Saving her father would only further drive the wedge between them, as she now had an idea of what she'd have to ask Damien and his family to do for her. She only hoped by the end of things that friendship would still be possible... if she were capable of it herself when the dust settled. A small part of her wondered if she'd end up trading places with her father when all was said and done.

"I swear I will get Di in here with more chocolate if you don't stop moping." Taylor's annoyed voice rang sharply in Giselle's ear.

"I'm not. I just lost my train of thought."

"Could have fooled me."

"Sorry. I do need to run. Burn off some steam. That will get my head right again." Giselle tried to smile, but she saw the light fade from Taylor's face. It didn't take a genius to know why, either. "And I hope you and Di will run with me. Sister solidarity." She winked.

"You don't want to go with Ash?" Taylor's voice betrayed her true feelings.

Giselle prayed her sister would get over Ash. She hadn't even dated him that long, but her pain lingered despite her many attempts to refute it. "Why would I want to be around a boy right now? They're dumb, remember?"

Taylor had come in to perk her up, and Giselle had ended up being the one to make her sister smile by the end. She laughed about it as she grabbed her sister by the hand and hauled her up from the bed. "Let's take the night off and go find the dried-up stream."

28

Time betrayed Giselle. With her mind set on what she would do and the uncertainty of the results, time hurtled her at breakneck speed toward the full moon, when she'd be forced to go through with the sacrifice she'd have to make.

A thousand and one scenarios played out in her mind, pushing away the sadness of the loss of Damien and the stress of the upcoming trials. But what it replaced them with was the stuff of nightmares. The very real possibility of her losing herself to save her father kept her awake at night and made the day's tasks all that much harder to accomplish.

Out in the middle of the desert, where they would be shielded by mountains and miles away from an access road, Giselle had been tasked with helping to set up the reception tents for the party.

"I heard what happened with Damien," Asher said, as they worked to set the tables up under the large white tents.

As a punishment for all her sulking, or some secret plot by Martina to help her get over Damien, she'd been partnered with Ash, while the others found better work to occupy their time.

"I don't want to talk about it." Giselle set a stack of chairs against the side wall of the tent.

Asher hoisted up a table as if it weighed nothing and set it right on its newly attached legs. "For what it's worth, I'm sorry. Being a wolf sucks sometimes."

"I said I don't want to talk about it," Giselle snapped at him.

Asher held up his hands. "My bad. Just trying to be friendly. We are friends. I might think you're pretty hot, but I do care about your feelings too."

"It's just weird talking to you about boy things. Ya know." Giselle tried to lighten her tone. Her negativity had more to do with lack of sleep than his good-natured flirting.

"Right. Bad topic. Let's pick something more wolfy, then, because if I have to spent the day setting places and arranging a dance floor in silence, I will die."

"How did you get stuck on table duty? Piss off daddy?" Giselle snorted.

"I asked, actually. I wanted to hang with you," Asher responded.

"Why? What did I do?" Giselle said. "Or is this a rebound thing?"

"Wow. I'm hurt." Asher thumped his chest as if he'd be shot and feigned pain.

"I doubt anything could hurt you. Not with that massive ego for a shield." Giselle laughed.

"Okay, maybe I wanted to see how you were doing with your newly single status, but I'm not trying to be sloppy seconds. Just wanted to be there for you."

"Right. Points for being the knight in shining armor for when I have recovered from heartache?" Giselle said.

"Right." Asher caught himself. "I mean, no. Sort of. Is it working?"

Giselle laughed hard. "If anyone can make it out of the friend zone, I'd put money on you. But not today."

"Either way, I get to hang out with you rather than set up the pit." Asher's eyes flitted over to the opening of the tent. Outside, manly grunts to the tune of Nathaniel Thrace's shouting orders made table duty sound so much more appealing. At least inside the tent, they had shade and a cooler filled with water.

"The pit?" Giselle asked, heading straight for the cooler to grab a bottle for herself.

"Arena. Pit. Cage of death. Call it what you want." Asher shrugged.

Barbaric. How could anyone think this was the right way to choose a new leader? Beat each other bloody until only one was left standing? Stupid!

"Are they really going to fight to the death?" Giselle asked. She understood the rule, yet she couldn't quite imagine anyone going through with it. Not in this day and age, at least; maybe back in medieval times.

"Death or submission. But most wolves would rather die than be seen as weak. So…" Asher let the words hang in the air.

"That's terrible." Giselle grabbed a bottle of water for Ash and tossed it over to him before opening her own.

"Yeah. But for good reason. It does keep the applicant list small." Asher slugged down the entire bottle in one go.

"I guess." She hoped she wouldn't see anyone she knew in the arena. And then her mind brought Ace's face front and center. Her cousin. He was a good guy. His mother might be rotten, but he was a decent guy and probably better suited for the role. The idea of him having to step into the arena and kill or be killed scared her. She'd never seen him fight.

Asher had continued speaking, even though she'd nearly lost the thread of conversation when her thoughts unraveled. "You don't want just anyone reaching for the title."

"True, I guess." Giselle scrambled to bring her mind back on point. "But if only the strongest muscle-bound wolf goes after the title, how does that bode well for leadership in general?"

"To be in the running, you have to be more than just a fighter. Only those with the potential to be an Alpha can try. To be an Alpha, you must have it within you to lead. All the applicants will come from good families with breeding and education. I guarantee you they will not be meatheads," Asher assured her.

"I still have my doubts. Ace and Jay will be in the running. What did you say about them?" Giselle reminded.

Asher grimaced. "They are of the right birth and good family. I'm sure they're smart, too."

"You say whatever it is you need to say to convince yourself. I think this whole ordeal is insane." Giselle rolled her eyes.

"And that's why…"

"If you say I didn't get the job, I will smack the fur right off your face, Asher Thrace."

"Yes, ma'am," Asher said mockingly, cowering in fear while chuckling.

She thought of hitting him, just to smack that grin off his face, but she knew better. His act of cowering was just that, an act – he could overpower her in a second if he wanted to. That boy was built hard and strong. "I know I'm not right for the job, despite everyone except the Council saying I am."

"You have potential. And breeding. You just have to let go of the…"

"What? Say it. I have to let go of the need to ask questions and reason everything instead of blindly following tradition?"

Asher shrugged and crushed the water bottle in his hands. "Basically."

"Jerk." Giselle punched him in the arm.

"I've been called worse." He winked at her.

"Well, I'm not going to watch the bloodshed," Giselle said. "I plan to kick back and hang at home with dear old Dad."

"Lucky. Dad demands we all witness."

"Must be a boy thing. Martina gave us all a pass if we wanted it."

"But you're still going to the reception, right?" Asher asked with more interest than he'd shown in the rest of the event.

Giselle grumbled. She'd hoped to get out of every part of it, but Alpha or no, she had to make an appearance and wish the combatants and the eventual winner good will. "Of course. I have to be at that one."

Excitement flashed in Asher's eyes. "Then be my date."

Giselle narrowed hers. *Sneaky little wolf!* Trying to turn this into a formal thing. *No!* Even if she wanted to. *Hell, no!* She was in no position at the moment for that kind of thing. And he was a jerk for even trying to play that game now.

"Not a *date* date." Asher stumbled over his words. "I just wanted you to... ah... help introduce me. You're much prettier than Dad, so it will make me look better."

It was hard not to laugh at him totally trying to pull his foot out of his mouth, and she snorted. "Keep going. This is epic backpedaling."

"Shut up. Yes, I want us to go together; and yes, I am trying to get on your good side. You happy?"

"Yep. Totally. But I have to arrive with my sisters. So I'll meet you there, and we can just hang out together. The four of us." She emphasized that last part to make sure he understood how *not a date* this would be. Even if she wanted to entertain the idea of Asher, she couldn't. There were other far more important things she needed to do, and in a few short nights, she'd find out exactly what the repercussions of her sacrifice would be.

"Works for me." Asher forced a smile and turned his attention back to the tables that still needed to be built.

His ego might be bruised, but he'd recover. Giselle's thoughts turned back to the task at hand, counting down the hours until *go* time. She'd have to make an appearance at the reception, but the night of the full moon would be the start of the trials. With the family all watching, it would be the right time to execute her plan and bring over the witches to wake her father up.

29

The light of the moon called to her. Simple, pure, and true. Giselle couldn't explain the connection between the moon and the strength of the wolf within her, but as each cycle came and went, it was unavoidable.

Nearly full as it was, the urge to shift and bask in that silvery light took hold, and she was powerless against its pull. No one in her family could, in fact, especially under the amount of stress as they all were.

Martina called the family together and even invited Nathaniel Thrace and his pack to join their run – the first joint pack run Giselle had ever been a part of. Which by itself was an oddity. Their packs had become friendly, but they'd never run together in the time she'd been there.

"How long are we going to wait?" Giselle asked impatiently, wanting to shift and take off the moment she stepped outside.

Strategically placed as it was, the last home in a development on the edge of open desert, the Hernandez pack house was the perfect place to meet. Straight out the back gate, a service alleyway led right to the empty land that had somehow managed to remain undeveloped. For miles it went on and on until it met with the base of the Sheep Mountain range. Other developments were nearby, but there was plenty of space for her pack to roam and avoid being seen.

"Mr. Thrace runs on his own time, apparently," Martina responded, just as impatiently.

Giselle, her sisters, Martina, and Gavin were all waiting out in the back yard for the Thrace boys to show. Christina and Jeffrey had opted to stay behind with Orion.

They all could do with a little stress relief, and nothing worked better than fresh air and a good hard run in the desert. Martina, though, looked ready to snap.

Di pulled Giselle close and whispered in her ear, "Something's up."

"I know," Giselle said. "I can feel it."

"Word is the city is overrun with wolves for tomorrow's reception," Di put in.

"I know. It's all Martina's been talking about since we left today."

"It's worse than that," Di whispered. "But no one is saying why."

Giselle shrugged. "Just nerves. So many people here for a fight. That's all. And honestly, I couldn't care less. I want to be as far away from the fighting as possible."

Di's eyes grew wide as saucers. "Please tell me you're not causing trouble for the Alphas."

"Nope. Scout's honor." Giselle held up her hand in salute, hoping to appear as genuinely innocent as she could. "I'm staying home with Dad." She chose her words carefully, knowing how easy a wolf could smell a lie.

"Why don't I believe you?" Di asked.

"Because you never do." Giselle giggled. A half-truth was not technically a lie.

"But you would tell me if you were planning something stupid. Right?" Di asked.

"Of course." Giselle smiled innocently.

"So?" Di asked.

"I'm going to invite Cassandra over too," Giselle said. "She is Orion's wife, you know."

Di narrowed her eyes suspiciously.

"I don't feel like dealing with the wolf politics. So I'll babysit Dad while you all go be wolfy," Giselle said.

Her sister continued to look suspicious but did not pry further, a fact Giselle was quite happy about. She hated keeping her sisters in the dark, but she knew what would happen if she told Taylor or Di what she was up to.

Besides, there was no point in her being part of the Alpha tournament now that she'd been disqualified.

Di was right about one thing: something was up, at least with her adoptive parents. The whole time they'd been waiting outside, Gavin paced the yard like a caged animal.

"They'll be here soon, I'm sure." Gavin sounded as if he were trying to convince himself as well as calm Martina's nerves. "This was a last-minute request, after all, and we did put in a full day of work on the site."

"Not enough, clearly, for the Alphas who expected to be chauffeured around today," Martina resentfully. "Forget all the hard work we've done to coordinate this whole affair."

"My love, let it go. You've worked very hard. We all have," Gavin said from the sidelines of the back yard. "They'll be impressed when they see the results."

"Will they?" Martina threw her words back at him.

"Yes." Gavin's tone sharpened with a finality that almost dared Martina to continue her spiral into self-loathing.

Naturally it was the Hernandez pack's fault that the arriving Alphas had to fend for themselves for transportation. Giselle had listened to Martina and Gavin arguing over it all afternoon. That had set the tone for the whole rest of the day, and no one escaped Martina's anger.

"We run as a pack tonight," Martina said, her gaze landing squarely on Giselle as a target for her negativity. "I don't need anyone stepping a paw out of line. Do you understand?"

Having taken more than her fair share of solo jaunts, Giselle wasn't surprised that her adoptive mother would single her out, and as the warmth of embarrassment rose to her cheeks, she turned her gaze away. Better not to say anything and further anger her mother.

Footsteps approaching in the alley had Giselle breathing a sigh of relief. Reinforcements. And not a moment too soon.

"Excuse our tardiness." Nathaniel Thrace opened the gate and allowed his boys to walk in past him.

He was always so rigidly proper that Giselle wondered if he ever let loose and relaxed. From the look of his family, the answer was a clear *no*. They filed in like perfect little soldiers, coming to an almost military parade rest, awaiting their father's order.

"If we're all ready…?" Martina replied, rather than greeting her guests. She, more than anyone else, needed this run. "Let's go, now."

Giselle couldn't even muster up teenage attitude to throw back at her mother. Stress had been the name of the game these last few days, and as head of the family, Martina had taken more than the lion's share. And Giselle had been in her own world, thinking of her father rather than helping to hold up her end of the bargain. She was, after all, the reason all this had come to pass. That more than anything else made Giselle hold her tongue in the face of Martina's temper.

"We'll follow your lead." Nathaniel Thrace's head dipped slowly once, as if bowing to her wishes, but not enough to drop his eyes in submission.

"I'd like us to stay closer to home this time," Martina said. "With so many others in town, I'd rather avoid any potential confrontations."

"Are we expecting problems?" Giselle asked with genuine curiosity.

"I don't anticipate any," Martina started to say, but Mr. Thrace cut her off.

"Where our kind are concerned, it's better to be safe; especially when the reason for the influx of wolves is a tournament to establish new leadership."

Martina nodded. "In old days, it would have been a worry. We're much more civilized now, but I won't risk anything with you pups."

Giselle couldn't remember the last time Martina had called her a pup. It was a word Jeffrey was fond of, and even Mr. Thrace when making a point to age and seniority, but Martina had rarely used such a belittling word. She cast a suspicious eye toward the Thrace group.

Asher stood with his brothers like soldiers at attention waiting for their general's order. Life in his house had to be unbearably strict. Martina might be on the warpath at the moment, but even at her worst she was hardly a drill sergeant.

"We'll all run a tight group." Mr. Thrace looked at Martina as he spoke, but Giselle saw the nod of agreement from his boys.

A sigh of relief escaped Martina's lips, and Giselle began to wonder exactly how worried her Alpha was. This should have been a simple run; sure, they had the addition of the Thrace pack with them, but that meant little more than a few extra people in the group. With the signs Martina was giving, she seemed ready for a fight, even though she'd just spoken to the contrary. Were the Alphas really that mad at her for not being there to greet them? That seemed such a tiny infraction to get their fur all mussed up over. Maybe Di had been right, and something else was up.

"Do you want me to stay behind with you during the trials?" Di whispered again in Giselle's ear, as they waited for instruction to shift and run.

"Nah. Go enjoy the spectacle," Giselle said, hoping her sister would drop the topic.

"Okay." Di shrugged. "I tried."

"Points for that." Giselle winked. "Now let's go run." Giselle quickly disrobed and shifted to join the rest of the pack, who were already starting to head through the back gate.

She shook off the slight chill that tingled as her body took full wolf form, and stretched her legs to prepare for a sprint to catch them.

Ahead, Martina led the pack into a light jog. Even in her wolf form, Giselle saw the differences in her Alpha's approach to this run.

As a pack, they often allowed each wolf to venture out of sight, but still within howl range. Martina was already rounding on the pack as if herding everyone into a tight group.

Totally not conspicuous. Anyone who happened to see them would notice the weird movements of this pack. Thank goodness they were deep into the desert already.

She enjoyed the breeze through her fur. The air had a slight chill to it; fall was beginning to overturn the oven-like heat that even after sundown clung to the barren desert ground. In a month's time, the weather would be perfect, and summer would be all but a bad memory, with its hundred-and-twenty-degree temperatures.

They ran tightly, nearly tripping over one another's paws; far from the free-spirited jaunt her wolf needed. That was the point of a moonlight run – to allow the beast its time. This was hardly even a tease.

A jackrabbit caught her attention, and it took all she had in her to not chase after it, knowing Martina's retribution would be swift. She'd risk nothing that might ruin her plans for the following day. Best behavior no matter how badly she wanted to enjoy freedom – that was her mantra while she ran with the pack.

After ten minutes of slow jogging, however, Giselle was ready to shift back and go home.

Most. Boring. Run. Ever.

And then a scent caught her nose, and she nearly forgot her oath to Martina to stay with the pack. Deep and cloying, like the earth after a good rain, natural and musky. More wolves.

She whimpered and jutted her nose in the direction of the new smell, hoping to catch a glimpse of another pack or the Alphas who'd come to visit. Anything was preferable to running in a straight line while her pack Alpha nipped at the heels of anyone daring to step out of formation.

Martina looked back at her and growled. The message was clear: *No!*

Their run went on for a few more minutes as they rounded back through the boulders and past the dry creek, heading for their neighborhood.

The smell followed too.

Whoever it was, they were going to meet very soon.

Excitement more than nerves had Giselle's head on a swivel, desperately trying to catch the slightest peek of the unknown wolf or wolves nearby.

Even with the flatness of the desert landscape, she found it hard to make out any shapes or dust trails kicked up by paws. Whoever was following them, they were not revealing themselves just yet.

Martina shifted as soon as she reached the edge of the alleyway and immediately held out her hand to the rest of the pack. "Stay in form," she commanded.

Mr. Thrace was the only other one to shift. Gavin stayed as a wolf, taking a position in front of the girls.

The other scent grew stronger until Giselle could finally make out three wolves heading their way.

Her kind were larger than the average wolf, with thicker coats. But other than those features, they carried the same coloration as the wolves of their territory. Two of the approaching wolves followed this pattern, but one stuck out – brilliant red with black tipped ears and socks, like a fox rather than a wolf. She'd never seen such coloration before and stood in awe, watching eagerly as the visitors approached.

The red wolf shifted, and Giselle instantly recognized her.

Against Martina's order, Giselle shifted too. "Fallon! Good to see you again," she said, excited to see the one wolf who had stuck up for her in the Council back in Washington.

Martina, however, looked murderous, with all her anger directed at Giselle's disobedience.

30

"Stand down, Giselle," Nathaniel ordered, placing himself between her path and Fallon. Giselle halted her steps, but continued to address Fallon. "What are you doing here?"

Nathaniel Thrace had an imposing build and the commanding presence of an Alpha, but that didn't faze Fallon in the slightest. She looked past the angry wolf, meeting Giselle's eyes instead. "Told you I was a Vegas girl. Couldn't resist the chance to visit," Fallon responded with a wink and then turned to Nathaniel. Her demeanor altered the moment her eyes met his. He might have been an Alpha of this local pack, but she was a mate to the Regional Alpha of the Olde Town and radiated that power as she spoke to him. "We didn't mean to startle you. We should have announced ourselves before showing up in your territory. However, it would do you and your pack more credit to be courteous to guests when they do arrive."

Mr. Thrace's teeth ground together loudly. Giselle doubted any woman had ever put him in his place before, and if Fallon hadn't been mate to the Regional

Alpha, he might not have held his temper. "Of course. How rude of me."

"Please don't let our desire to protect the pups reflect badly on our pack, Mrs. Whelan." Recognition of the red wolf had Martina's eyes nearly bulging from her sockets. Martina lifted a hand behind her back. A small movement, but enough to put Gavin at ease. He remained standing guard for the girls, but his posture relaxed and his tail lifted. "You're most welcome to join us back at our home." Martina continued, "I don't wish to remain in the open during this uncertain time, though. I'm sure you will understand."

Fallon's gaze jumped from Mr. Thrace to Martina and finally settled back on Giselle.

She nodded eagerly for Fallon to join them, excited for the prospect of introducing the infamous wolf to her sisters. Giselle had told them so much; now they could see for themselves how cool she was in person.

Fallon gave Giselle a wink and cast a glance back at the two wolves accompanying her. "Of course. We will follow."

Martina blew out a relieved breath. She looked as if she might faint. Her adoptive mother had always been so strong, but lately it was as if she were cracking under all the pressure.

Maybe Giselle should have listened. Shifting without being instructed to do so had probably made her mother look like a weak Alpha. There were so many nuances to being a good wolf that she had yet to master, and only after she screwed up and saw the results did she understand why. Fallon might not care. But she couldn't gauge the other two wolves standing by her. One thing was certain: she'd embarrassed her mother and needed to play nice before Martina had a heart attack over all this stress.

Giselle whispered, "I'm sorry" as she shifted back to her wolf.

The pack began to run again, making quick work of heading down the alley behind Martina, toward the house. They quickly re-dressed, and Martina found suitable clothing for their guests.

Inside the Hernandez pack home, Martina led the trio to the most comfortable spots on the couch, falling instantly into the role of hostess as if it were her calling.

Giselle recognized the two men who had accompanied Fallon, but in an effort to be respectful, she waited to speak until Martina had addressed them and Fallon had made her introductions.

All smiles and just as friendly as she'd been back in Washington, Fallon seemed eager to hang out with Giselle's pack. "Let me introduce the Whelan brothers: my mate and Alpha of the Olde Town pack, Aiden, and his brother, Brady."

Aiden, was the older and darker-haired brother with almost midnight black eyes. Giselle had already had the pleasure of chatting with him and knew him as the sort of wolf who gave off an air of curiosity. Silent unless he had command of the room, his eyes were always moving, scanning his surroundings, absorbing everything he saw. But when attention settled on him, the studious gaze melted away, and the Alpha was present.

Aiden nodded as Fallon made introductions, but he didn't make any individual greetings. Giselle couldn't read his intentions, but sensed he was not a happy as Fallon to be here.

Brady, on the other hand, the second son with dirty blond hair and chocolate brown eyes, looked as carefree as any wolf could. He smiled and shook hands with Christina and Martina, and then pulled Taylor and Di into a bear hug. He finished with a hand out to Giselle before addressing the men. "Nice to see you again, little wolf. Still causing trouble, I see."

"Unintentional." Giselle shrugged, hoping to end the conversation there.

Aiden might have been the calculating one, scrutinizing everything around him, but Brady's gregarious nature made everyone let their guard down; though for Giselle, it set off an alarm bell in her mind.

Jay's words had haunted her from the moment he'd spoken them. She needed to watch her back where the Alphas were concerned. And she had to be careful about any wolves she met, even if she was out of the running for Alpha. It was easy to learn what made a person tick when you were their buddy. And Brady was almost too friendly, at least for someone she'd only met once before, acting as if he'd known her forever and way over the top with her sisters.

If you asked Di or Taylor, of course, they'd probably have taken another one of those manly hugs. Jaws on the floor, they were practically drooling over the big blond wolf.

She let the curiosity about him go as Martina pushed her way to the center of the living room after packing everyone into the space.

"You've caught two packs tonight." Her voice warbled ever so slightly with tension, but Martina was still the Alpha in this house and doing her best to show it. "The Hernandez and the Thrace packs share the Las

Vegas territory these days. I'm Martina Hernandez, and this is my mate and co-Alpha Gavin. We share these three girls and my sister Christina and her mate, Jeffrey. He belongs to my pack." She cleared her throat and held a hand out. "Nathaniel here is Alpha of the Thrace pack."

Nathaniel stepped forward, radiating all the Alpha he held within him. No stress, not even a bead of sweat marked his brow. He met Aiden's eye as he spoke. "I bring my boys: Asher, the youngest; the twins, Devlin and Hamish; and my oldest, Jason."

The boys nodded with a military uniformity that reminded Giselle exactly how strict Mr. Thrace was at home.

"We appreciate the generosity of your shared leadership to host this event. It must be a huge undertaking," Aiden said, addressing Martina directly.

That sign of respect was not lost on Martina. Her whole body seemed to relax at that moment, and the strain in her face faded into a warm smile. "It has been a challenge," Martina said, holding her head high. "But we never fail to rise to a challenge." her hand flitted behind her back, and Christina caught the sign, immediately backing out of the crowd heading for the kitchen.

Aiden had taken his seat in the center of their main couch, commanding the room with his presence, and whether by instinct or just to get a better room, everyone shifted around him to be in view.

"How is it that you two are separate packs, yet both claim equal lordship in this territory?" Aiden asked.

"Both our packs have been in this area for a long time. Neither of us desire to leave nor will either submit to the other," Nathaniel began to say.

"We learn sharing in kindergarten," Giselle whispered jokingly to Taylor, who was standing next to her.

Taylor either didn't get the joke or was too scared to laugh. She stood still, eyes forward respectfully toward Aiden and the others.

Wolfy hearing ensured that everyone in the room might have heard what she'd said, and it was Fallon who responded with a snort. Her gaze landed on Giselle's face with a wink.

At least someone got the joke.

"We're at peace," Martina said confidently. "Neither of our packs desires rule over the other. We act as council to one another."

"It's not unheard of," Aiden said, "Admirable, for sure, but oftentimes short-lived."

"One day at a time, then," Giselle whispered again, as if the idea of peace was something of a 12-step program for wolves.

"You," Aiden addressed Giselle directly. "Ideals are for the young. And they are a good thing, but time often snuffs out that spark, and reality makes cynics of us all."

Giselle's smile faded. He wasn't calling her an idiot outright, but the sentiment was there.

Christina returned with a tray of beers and a bowl of nuts, saving Giselle the embarrassment of being singled out by a Grand High Poobah of the Alpha world.

"Why don't you all relax? Take a seat," Christina said.

While the group all attempted to squeeze their butts into the remaining couch and love seat space or grab a scrap of carpet, Giselle slowly backed away until she could make an escape. She wanted nothing to do with this pack-style meeting, especially after she'd stuck her foot in her mouth not once but twice. Martina would pay her back for that later, once she finished fawning all over their royal visitors. But while she and the others were busy, Giselle could solace in the glow of the refrigerator light and the last bottle of caramel iced coffee within.

"Thought you could get away easy, eh?" Fallon caught her off-guard, and Giselle nearly dropped the small glass bottle.

"Not really my place in there, is it?" Giselle shrugged.

Fallon leaned against the arched frame leading into the kitchen and crossed her arms as she watched Giselle drink.

Not knowing what to say, Giselle hoped the distraction of sweetness would give her time to think of a more clever reply, so she prolonged out each gulp as she emptied the bottle. Fallon might be cool and all, but she was an Alpha, and a big deal at that. "If you haven't guessed by now, I'm the troublemaker in this family."

That earned a laugh from Fallon. "Some of the best people are. I told you about my friend Alyssa, right?"

"The vampire? Yeah!" She'd never forget that. The moment vampires had been confirmed as a real thing, Giselle had had set her mind on meeting one.

"She's a world-class troublemaker, not unlike yourself." Fallon pointed a finger straight at Giselle. "And becoming a vampire did not change that."

"And I'm sure her people loved her for it, right?" Giselle scoffed. No one liked the troublemaker.

"Oh, yeah," Fallon laughed. "She pissed off the entire Peregrinus clan on a daily basis. Especially Nicholas. It was like her calling in life to make that guy mad. Mine too, once I got to know him. He's just too easy a target not to poke. But I'm getting ahead of myself. Alyssa got herself and everyone else into trouble more than she should have, but she also pulled us out of a lot of jams, too, because she threw caution to the wind and was willing to do what others wouldn't."

Alyssa sounded just as cool as Fallon. No wonder they had been best buddies when they were human. Just the thought of that sent her mind spiraling. Human transformations to supernatural creatures was something no one really talked about. She hadn't even known it was a thing herself until Fallon had confirmed it. When she'd spoken to her sisters, they acted more shocked that it worked than surprised it was a thing.

That reminded her of just how much a noob she was. There was so much to this world Giselle still had to learn. Her thoughts took her down a path she'd not intended, but by the time she realized that Fallon was still talking, she'd recovered enough to catch her before she'd finished her speech.

"So don't discredit yourself by saying you're just a troublemaker. It's not always a bad thing, Giselle."

"I'll wear it like a badge of pride, then," Giselle joked, hoping Fallon had not caught her glazed-over expression while her mind had wandered.

If Fallon had, she didn't let on, but she didn't laugh at Giselle's bad joke either. "And don't let Aiden get to you. He's not a bad guy. To be honest, we wanted to see you take leadership. Youth has its advantages."

"But didn't he just say—"

"That you're young and naïve?" Fallon cut her off. "Sure. But no one said that was a bad thing. You just assumed it was."

"Now you're talking like one of the old ones out there."

"Who are you calling old?" Fallon asked.

"Not you, obviously." Giselle giggled "I'm not pissing off another Alpha tonight."

"How many do you piss off on a regular basis?"

"Everyone I meet, it seems." Giselle said. "It's kind of my job."

"I believe it. You are so much like my friend Alyssa." Fallon said wistfully. "I'll have to let you meet her someday."

That perked Giselle right up. She'd drop everything to go meet a real live vampire. Were they live? Guess she'd find out. "Really?"

"Someday. Yes," Fallon agreed. "I haven't seen her in a long time."

"But if she's your friend, why haven't you hung out?"

"She and her group are in Europe. Taking care of vampire business." Worry crossed Fallon's face, darkening her features for a moment, before she snapped out of it and gave Giselle a mischievous wink. "If you can, try to avoid pissing off too many more people in the near future, at least while the Regional Alphas are around and presiding over the trials. I think your rashness and temper were facts that counted against you in the vote."

Giselle sighed. "Probably. And Vivian for sure."

"Nah. She was gunning for you. It was clear to us, but Misha had to accept some of her points."

Running the memory of that night through her head again, raw anger swelled up within her. Vivian had been out to destroy her reputation. The claws were out for sure. "She wasn't even supposed to be there. Martina was."

"I heard. But the second son has option to challenge, too. So she was allowed Martina's place at the table."

"It's like they make up the rules as they go. How is anyone supposed to get anything done?" Giselle said in frustration.

"Wolf politics are tough to navigate. I had to make my sacrifices as well to be where I am." Fallon's hand moved, as if by instinct, to run through her red tipped hair. "I won't lie to you. Me and the boys showing up here tonight was no coincidence. I'd heard you backed out of the trials. I hoped those rumors were untrue."

"I've been deemed unfit by the Council."

"By *some* members of the Council, yes." Fallon stressed that point.

"Well, those members have spoken, and I am unfit. I can't defend my right by fighting, and I don't want to have someone lay down their life for me just to make a few old wolves happy." How could Giselle ask anyone to step into an arena and make the ultimate sacrifice for her?

Fallon's smile hardened into the mask of authority she wore in public. "That's part of being an Alpha. It's not all ordering people around; sometimes it means going into battle and inspiring others to take up your cause."

She might have been human once, and she was certainly the coolest wolf Giselle had ever met, but at that moment, Fallon was an Alpha through and through. Absolutely inspiring. If a human could make that transition, then the possibilities were there. Still, though, she'd have to ask someone to be willing to die for her. She knew Richard would; he'd already offered. But even with his support, the idea of him or anyone dying for her just didn't sit well in her mind.

"If you ask me, Giselle, you have a natural nobility within you. You're honorable in your intentions and reasons. I think you'd do very well in the role if given the chance."

Such high praise almost made her want to call up a champion. She appreciated the vote of confidence, but she'd already set her mind to other tasks. Just past the archway that Fallon had been leaning against was the door to her father's bedroom. That was where honor and duty were calling her, though she wished she could have both. "Thank you, Fallon. Your words mean the world to me."

"They're true words. I like you. And you remind me a lot of Alyssa. So how could I not want to pull for you?"

Giselle nearly blushed with all the praise she was receiving, but it would not sway her decision. "If circumstances were different, or maybe if I were older, I'd consider it, but I've been called to a different task now."

"Oh?" Fallon's face contorted in confusion.

"My father needs me." Giselle walked past Fallon and opened the door. Inside, Orion Silverman lay still as death in the bed against the far wall.

Fallon nodded solemnly. "You have more honor within you than you take credit for. I know you've set your mind against it, but the tournament will last three days. You have until the end to call forth a champion." She put a hand on Giselle's shoulder and squeezed. "I have to get back before I'm missed. Go be with your father. And please think about what I've said."

Giselle turned her eyes toward her father. If given the choice, she'd have both – but the prospect of healing her father meant more to her than a title. Even if Alphas like Fallon felt she was right for the role.

31

Giselle blinked, and somehow it was time to get ready for the grand reception before the trials – a night she had dreaded as it meant more pretending and playacting to wolves who had already dismissed her as unfit, as well as meeting with wolves who would soon fight and die in combat over a title.

However, as she was Orion Silverman's daughter, she had to go to at least this and the crowning banquet at the end of the trials.

Di and Taylor were over the moon, spending the entire day on spa treatments to make themselves radiate even more beauty than they already possessed. When it came time to get dressed, it might as well have been Christmas with all the squealing and oohing and ahhing they were doing.

"How are you not more excited for this?" Taylor asked, as she put the finishing touches on Giselle's outfit.

The girls had chosen to work with the cream and pewter tones of the party décor and work them into each of their outfits.

As always, Taylor and Di created magic with their designs.

Taylor wore a slender mermaid style crème dress with a light dusting of sparkles, topped with a faux-fur white shrug.

Di sported an off-the-shoulder, floor-length satin crème brûlée-colored sheathe circled by a shimmering silver belt.

And for Giselle, they'd chosen something a little more risqué: skin-tight and knee-length pewter with peek-a-boo lace at the shoulders, stomach, and around the hem. Paired with glittering heels, even she felt she looked fierce.

Di had set her hair in a simple yet elegantly tied side ponytail with a glittering clip to hold the loose knot in place.

If her mood hadn't been soured by the reason for the event, she'd have gladly strutted down the red carpet. It was hard to not feel confident and Alpha-like when you knew you looked *that* good.

"I'm excited. Sort of. I just want to enjoy the fun parts and forget the rest," Giselle said.

"Are you sure you're doing okay? I know you and Damien just…" Taylor said.

"We're fine," Giselle answered. "And he's not going to be here tonight, so that makes it all that much better." She breathed a sigh of relief.

"I know you're fine," Taylor said, with a consoling pat on the back. "And so is he."

Just thinking about him made her heart ache. Giselle had come to terms with the fact that their break up was inevitable, but she'd hoped she could have enjoyed what they had a little longer. It had been nice being so close to him. Magic or no, Damien was a good guy. And when the dust settled, she hoped they'd find that closeness again.

But that would take a while longer to happen, a fact that made her stomach churn with guilt and anxiety. She still had her plans in place. And that meant stirring up a whole shitstorm of dust that could take years to settle. Damien might have said he'd help, but she saw how much it pained him to do her bidding. He knew the sacrifice she'd have to make. And he alone knew what might happen. She still had no idea.

Her mind had played out so many worst-case scenarios: death; trading places with Orion; losing her wolf.

The list went on, each one terrible and frightening. She nearly lost her nerve thinking about it. But then, all it would take was one look at her father, seeing how sad he looked, a shell of a man, cursed because he'd wanted to start a family.

That fortified her resolve and pushed her to do what she could to appease the cosmos and wake her father.

Neither Di nor Taylor knew what was in store. They'd be off enjoying the trials. When next she saw Damien, she'd make her sacrifice, and pray to the gods they accepted it.

"Hello, Giselle." Di snapped a finger in front of her face. "We lost her. Damn it, girly, wake up."

"Sorry. Lost in thought." Giselle stood and walked to the mirror to inspect her sister's handiwork.

"Don't think about him. Tonight's about meeting new people," Taylor said. "So let's not dwell on those we already know."

"You're right, of course," Giselle agreed absently, as she admired the way the dress clung to her hips. She really did look fierce. She was supposed to make an appearance, and in this outfit, that's exactly what she'd be doing. "I'm interested in seeing a few familiar faces, though," Giselle said, her thoughts turning to the Alphas who'd attend, and Fallon, her new favorite. She could easily pass time chatting about vampires and her friend Alyssa.

"You think Ace and Jay will be there?" Taylor asked, knocking Giselle out of the way so she could continue preening in the mirror.

Hearing her cousins' names snapped her back to reality. "I hope not," Giselle said defensively. She'd hate to see one of her own taken down in the arena. She might not have known them long, but Ace was family.

Taylor hissed and turned on Giselle as if she'd insulted her. "What? Why not?"

Distracted by boys and the chance for some eye candy, her sisters seemed to have missed the plot. Giselle glared straight at Taylor, saying, "Those who come here are planning to fight to the death. I don't want to see either of my cousins fighting and dying for a title."

Reality struck hard, and Taylor hung her head shamefully after Giselle had finished. "Sorry. I forgot."

"But if Vivian has any say, Ace *will* be there," Giselle added, remembering her aunt's desire to see the title pass to her eldest son.

"There's a wolf I'd be happy to fight," Di said, clenching her fists.

"You? Fight Momma Bitch?" Giselle asked.

"Hell, yeah," Di said confidently. "She'd put her boys on the chopping block. She's their mother. How could she do that?"

Giselle felt the same way, but understood that a mother would do anything for the advancement of her children. "When you see her, you be sure to tell her that."

Di looked as if Giselle were calling her a liar. "I will. And you'll be there to watch."

"Will I now?" Giselle laughed. "You going to pull her into the arena yourself?"

"Don't tempt me," Di said angrily, closing her tube of lipstick.

"Seriously, though. We're supposed to be on our best behavior. No picking fights," Giselle said.

"Which is why we're your dates." Taylor laughed. "We're supposed to keep you in line."

"Good luck with that. I plan on causing all kinds of scenes," Giselle joked, but her sisters didn't seem to understand the punch line. Rather than laugh, they looked horrorstruck, as if she would really do something that stupid.

"Scout's honor," Giselle said with as serious a look as she could muster. "I'm not going to do anything tonight. Best behavior and all that. I promise."

Still they looked as if she were about to unleash hell. It was only Martina knocking at the door that pulled their attention away.

"Ready, girls? Let's get this night started."

Giselle heaved a big breath and reminded herself to be calm and play nice. Just as she'd promised.

32

"Breathe," Giselle reminded herself as she walked through the tents into the transformed ballroom.

Light music played from speakers set all around the room, loud enough to break any silence but soft enough not to disturb conversation.

Arm in arm with her sisters, borrowing their strength, Giselle strolled in as confidently as she could. It helped knowing she and her sisters were dressed to impress, a fact that spread like wildfire through the entire tent.

She'd not been announced as she entered, yet all eyes seemed drawn to her the moment she crossed the threshold into the room. A collective breath hushed, and Giselle again reminded herself to lift her head and walk proudly.

"Damn," Di exclaimed, taking the words straight out of Giselle's mouth.

Apart from the tension she felt having everyone staring at her, the splendor of what they'd created was breathtaking. Everything looked gorgeous, even better than it had when they'd been setting places and arranging the table décor.

Twinkling lights and the added ethereal glow from the special lamps lit the walls of the tent up like the night sky and set the tone for the following night's truly full moon.

Giselle scanned the faces of those closest to her, hoping to spot someone familiar and friendly so she could ease into this event. Her sisters had missed the tension of the Council dinner where they'd passed judgment on her. They had no idea who was here and who they should be respectful to.

So many faces. So many wolves. None of them recognizable, at least from where she stood, and that amped her tension up to eleven.

She needed Richard or Fallon to show themselves; at least then she'd know she had allies around.

"Are we going to stand here and wait for people to come to us? Or are we going to mingle?" Di asked, but her eyes were trained on a handsome dark wolf with piercing blue eyes across to her right.

Not wanting to be the bearer of bad news again, Giselle held her tongue rather than remind her sister that half the people here tonight would not be around come the end of the trials. It almost wasn't worth making new friends just yet.

Even if she did speak up, by the looks of Di's glazed over expression, it wouldn't have mattered. She let go of her sister's arm and was just about to push her in her new crush's direction when a familiar but unfriendly voice called out to her.

"I half expected you to hide in your den, little wolf," Vivian cackled.

Giselle gritted her teeth, reminding herself of her promise not to make a scene, and slowly turned to face her aunt. "I have no reason to hide."

"Of course you don't. Being rejected by your people is not shameful in any way at all." Vivian's voice was sickeningly sweet despite the poison she spewed.

"Usurping your husband's position and putting your children on the chopping block isn't either. But then, I knew you'd be first in line. Glad you could make it." Giselle responded in kind, matching Vivian's tone.

Behind her, Giselle heard the half snickers escape her sisters' mouths.

Lips parting to reveal her perfectly white teeth, Vivian's face contorted with a wicked smile. Frightening in the way she looked both pleased and murderous, Vivian's tone betrayed neither. "Fearless little werewolf. Pity you're unable to show your mettle in the arena."

Speechless for the moment, Giselle struggled for the right retort and came up empty, settling for, "Rain check?" and a smile.

"I look forward to it." Vivian snapped her jaw. "When you've finally cut your teeth, little werewolf, come and see me. I'll teach you the meaning of fearless."

Vivian sauntered away without a second look back.

Giselle's heart was pounding. She would love nothing more than to allow her wolf the chance to come forth and shut that woman up, but the truth was, she was outmatched. Vivian was untouchable. And the bitch knew it.

"You okay, Elle?" Taylor whispered in her ear. "You're shaking."

Giselle blew out a breath. "Yeah. I'm fine."

"Then let's go be fine somewhere else. People are starting to stare." Taylor tugged at Giselle's arm, but she didn't budge. "Let's walk."

That woman had burrowed deep under her skin with hardly more than a few nasty words. And all Giselle could do was lob a few empty threats her way. Humiliated and disgraced in the first five minutes she'd been there. To say the night had gotten off on the wrong foot would be an understatement.

"You want me to put that bitch in her place?" Di said with a smirk. "I promised I would… didn't I?"

If anyone was going to do it, it would be Giselle, but the irony was not lost on her that it was she who now would play voice of reason to her sister. Vivian might be a force to be reckoned with, but Martina's rage would be ten times worse if they caused a scene. "We promised we'd be good."

"Just saying. *You* can't rough her up. You're already on Martina's shit list, but I've got brownie points stored up for just such an occasion." Di winked at Giselle, and it was exactly the thing she needed to relax. Her sister would never do something that out of line. She might play tough, but she was a rule follower. The offer, however, was enough to soothe the trembling rage that had Giselle nearly vibrating where she stood.

"Let's grab something to drink." Di took hold of Giselle's arm and led her toward the bar they'd set up on the far end of the ballroom.

"Wait. There's Ash." Taylor stopped the girls in their tracks and waited as Asher and his brothers entered the tent.

Giselle might have been nervous coming into a room filled with the toughest of the tough wolves and Grand High Poobahs, but not Asher.

He strolled in as calm as if he were walking into Mr. Harper's class. How was he not sweating bullets?

His brothers too – they all walked in as if they owned the place, heads held high and dressed to the nines.

Asher spotted them and came straight over. "I thought we'd meet outside first?" He might not have looked flustered, but Giselle caught the little note of it in his voice.

Thank the gods. For a minute there she'd thought he might be a robot. Anyone with any sense should have been nervous walking into a den packed this full of deadly creatures.

"We had to make an entrance," Di said proudly.

Smiling slyly as his eyes made their way down Giselle's body, Asher looked more wolf than man, with his prey in sight. "Yeah. I'll bet you did."

Forgetting where she was and who might be watching, Giselle slugged Asher in the arm. "Don't be such a pig."

Di snorted and quickly covered her face to mask the sound. "Might want to take a step back before she murders you."

"Was it something I said?" Confusion played across Asher's features, making him look like a scared pup who'd been swatted with a newspaper for piddling on the rug.

"You're being a guy," Giselle threw at him, and then realized her own nerves and anger might have made her a little too touchy. "You're supposed to be a gentleman tonight. So maybe try less undressing us with your eyes and more escorting us to the bar. I need some water."

Asher and Taylor exchanged looks that ended with a shrug from her sister. He then tried his silent question with Di. She wasn't playing his game, though. "You heard the lady. Escort away."

Still looking utterly confused, Asher did as instructed and offered an arm to whichever girl took hold first.

Giselle was just about to hook her arm through his when she felt a tap on the shoulder.

"You guys go ahead. I'll be right there," she said, and turned around before they answered her. Jay stood smiling behind her. His mood had improved greatly since the last time they'd seen each other. A drink in hand, already halfway gone, he looked as if he was enjoying his evening.

"No hard feelings, little wolf," Jay said, as he slugged down a gulp of his drink.

"Of course not," Giselle lied. Her run in with his mother had soured her mood towards his family.

Jay leaned in and whispered in her ear, "It was best you backed down."

"For who?" Giselle asked suspiciously.

"You," Jay responded, wobbling slightly where he stood. "There are some on the Council who did not want you in power. And I believe they would have found a way to kill any champion you brought forward."

"How do you know this?" Giselle asked, wondering why he was so forthcoming now when previously he'd been so cryptic with his warnings.

"It's easy to hear things when you're presumed to be an idiot." Jay slugged back the rest of his drink, and it was then that Giselle realized he was drinking water.

It made sense now. Jay was the second son. He had no claim to anything, and that allowed him to be privy to other people's schemes.

She looked up and winked. "Thanks for having my back. But why, if I'm your brother's competition?"

"We're family," he said, leaning in close. "And some people in power would do anything to get their way. Even killing innocent little wolves."

"Who are you calling innocent?" Giselle feigned insult.

"Don't play the game. You will lose." His words had all the ominousness of a threat, but he wasn't making one. She was certain of it. Still, the effect was practically the same, and her wolf wanted nothing more than to rise to the challenge.

"What about your mother?" Giselle asked spitefully.

"She's playing the game quite well. For both sides. Ace will be stepping into the arena for our family." Again his words sounded off. There were strange inflections on certain words, as if he were speaking in a code she should understand but couldn't.

"Why make him?" Giselle asked. "Ace doesn't need to be subjected to this."

"He offered. It's his right to do if our family wishes to hold their seat on the Council."

"And what is the Council's view on his claim?" Giselle asked. She looked around but could not locate her other cousin in the crowd.

"They know our family. We've been in power for a while," he said, with a quick glance over his shoulder. "But there are others who've recently gained favor with other regions. Be wary of the Rufus Reds."

Giselle rolled her eyes, almost glad to be avoiding more of the wolfy political process. "I'm keeping out of it all."

"Good." Jay smiled and winked. "I must be off. If I hear anything, I'll let you know. Just be sure you are nowhere near here during the trials."

"I don't plan on it."

"Good girl." Jay swatted Giselle on the butt and whooped loudly. "I've always wanted to do that."

Giselle growled in response. Her instinct was to smack him, but she realized all too quickly he was still playacting. She could do it too. And with a loud huff, she turned and walked away.

"What was that all about?" Asher looked ready for a fight. He propped himself on his elbows against the bar, and his narrow eyes looked straight past Giselle, finding their target on the back of Jay's head.

"Nothing," Giselle grumbled, still pretending to be angry.

"I told you those guys were asses. Bet that Ace or whatever his name is ends up taking the leadership. It's all rigged anyway."

Giselle wondered if she should tell him the truth. She knew Asher was trustworthy, but in a room filled with wolves, all with extra sensitive hearing, she decided otherwise. He could learn the truth later. For now the charade needed to look real.

"Let it go. He's drunk," Giselle said. "And bragging. That's just what guys do."

"That's no excuse. He's an Alpha's son. He should know better." Asher's voice was loud enough for the room to hear.

"And one who will never be an Alpha. So let it go." Giselle pulled at Asher's arm, forcing him to turn away from Jay and the potential fight he was starting.

"What's got you all riled up?" Di asked, sipping her drink while scanning the room.

"Boys being boys," Giselle said. "You see anything interesting?"

Di giggled, her face turning a few shades darker with embarrassment. "Am I that obvious?"

"Only slightly. Might want to wipe your chin. You're drooling a little," Giselle smirked.

"Whatever. Some of the contenders look like meatheads, but I think I might have to pay closer attention tomorrow, there are a few pieces of eye candy out there."

Asher raised an eyebrow. "And you got mad at me for being a dude?"

"We girls are allowed to look too," Di snapped at him. "And I freely admit I will be looking, tonight and tomorrow."

Giselle laughed at her sister's blatant ogling. "Good for you. I'm staying home."

Taylor scooted closer to Giselle and passed her a soda. "You sure we can't convince you?"

Asher looked hopeful, but didn't say a word.

"Nope. I don't want to be anywhere near here. I was deemed unworthy. I don't need to have those that are worthy shoved in my faces." Giselle made sure to speak as loudly as was conversationally appropriate and still allow her voice to carry.

Across the room she spotted Fallon. Finally another friendly face in the den of soon to be killers. She wanted to get up from her seat and go talk to her new friend, but

Fallon looked disappointed. She'd fought the good fight, but Giselle had made up her mind. She would not make a challenge.

Their eyes connected for a brief moment, and though she looked sad, Fallon raised a glass in acknowledgement.

Giselle needed to make sure all in attendance would not miss her or question her reasons for not being there, because when tomorrow arrived, there could be no interruptions in her plan. Tomorrow night was for her father. That above all had her focus, though she did hope for Ace to take his place as Alpha. He'd do a good job, and he was the clear favorite for the Silverman family.

"Whatever. You're just as good as any of them," Di said.

"And the fact you guys think so is affirmation enough. But I'm still a kid, and I'd like to enjoy that for as long as I can." Giselle laughed boisterously, making sure others could overhear her conversation. "You know – make mistakes. Have fun. Do stupid things and get away with it."

Di laughed. "You're good at it, that's for sure."

"See? I figure I could make a career of being a stupid kid." Giselle winked.

"Already formulating your next idiotic scheme? Di asked.

Giselle shrugged. "Wouldn't you like to know?"

"No, I wouldn't, because if you are…" Di suddenly looked flustered. "You're bound to get us all in deep shit. Nope. I'd rather be in the dark and continue to enjoy my eye candy."

"As you wish." Giselle bowed.

A look of pure terror crossed Di's face. "You *do* have something up your sleeve?"

"No. But it's fun to see you get scared." Giselle giggled.

"You better not."

"Scout's honor." Giselle saluted.

"Why do I not believe you?" Di said.

"Because you know her too well," Asher finally chimed in.

"I swear. I have nothing planned to disrupt this trial. I couldn't care less who wins tomorrow or the next day." Giselle turned to walk away, but Asher caught her by the arm.

"Promise?" The look on his face made her wonder if he knew something. If he had talked to Damien. If somehow her secret had gotten out.

"What did I just say?" Giselle pulled away from Asher's grip and weaved her way into the crowd.

Not two steps in, she found Richard.

He stood talking with a drink in his hand. Three wolves she'd never met before surrounded her former mentor, hanging on his words as if he were a prophet. Young wolves by the look of them. Maybe only a few years older than she, but that was enough to give them the right to fight for their chance at the title. And maybe that was what Richard was talking with them about. She didn't want to stick around to find out.

Their eyes met, and without a word between them, Giselle made clear her answer was still *no*.

Everyone needed to know and understand that. She was here because she had to be here, but she would not fight or call anyone else in to fight her battles.

There was no point in dragging out the conversation nor interrupting his, so just as quickly as she spotted him, Giselle altered her course and veered deeper into the crowd of wolves. The goal of this evening was to be seen, and she would ensure she was.

33

"You all did so well last night," Martina praised her family, as they finished packing first aid kits and bandages in the living room. Twilight had come, and the trials would start shortly after. "Tonight I expect no less. You may not be part of these trials, but you are there to bear witness to them." She flitted around the room like a hummingbird on speed, packing her purse and checking on each of the kits to make sure there were enough bandages and ointments. "Splints. We'll need splints." She disappeared into the kitchen and came back with another box with padded wooden board splints sticking out.

Taylor jumped up from where she was sitting. "I'll carry those for you."

"Have fun with that." Giselle rolled her eyes thinking of the real injuries. They were going to need body bags, not bandages.

"Are you certain you want to stay behind? We can bring Orion with us if we all want to go." Martina sounded as if she really wanted Giselle to go, while trying her best not to force the issue.

Under normal circumstances, she'd have gone. Even knowing she'd be seeing unnecessary bloodshed, she'd have done it to show solidarity to her family. But not tonight. "I want nothing to do with this," Giselle said with finality. "I played my part, and now I'm done. I hope you understand."

Martina gritted her teeth and nodded in acceptance. She set the overfilled box on the couch and went to work trying to stuff in all the loose pieces.

Taylor snatched up a tape gun and hovered over Martina, waiting for her chance to use it.

Giselle walked over to the side table and retrieved Martina's purse while the others weren't paying attention to her. Her mother had been under so much stress with the whole Alpha situation. Her trials had been ongoing since they left Washington, and Giselle had been no help. She had so much to apologize for. She'd been a horrible daughter. And tonight would be no different. Giselle slipped a hand into Martina's purse and pulled her phone out as she walked the bag to her mother. "Don't forget this." She handed the bag over and gave Martina a one-handed hug while pocketing the phone. She'd make this up to her mother soon. She'd make up everything soon.

When her father awoke and was able to be a functioning member of the pack, they'd both make up for all the problems Giselle had caused.

But tonight, she still had one more thing to do. And she needed her family gone for it.

"Thanks, honey. Are you sure you'll be okay?" Martina asked.

Her adoptive mother's concern made what she planned to do all that much worse. Betrayal, disobedience, and carelessness were not her way, though she operated as if they were. Knowing that her mother cared went hand in hand with the understanding that that care would prevent her from doing anything deemed stupid. Which basically made up the majority of things Giselle did. Reckless, maybe, but certainly not stupid. Either way, if Martina knew what she planned, the answer would be *no*.

This was the only way.

She gave her mother one more big squeeze with both hands before letting go. "Of course. How much trouble can I get into at home?" Giselle joked.

Di stood ready to get going. She alone seemed to have missed the negative side of this event. Dressed to impress rather than to watch blood splatter, her sister looked as if she were hunting for an Alpha to make her mate. Giselle wondered how Di would feel after seeing a guy she'd been drooling over lying dead and bloody on the dry desert ground. Not that curiosity would tempt her to go see Di's reaction; Giselle would learn that quickly enough when they returned.

"Please. Just go and say good luck to Ace for me. I'll be fine," Giselle said, hoping to push them out of the door faster. All she needed was Martina's phone to go off in her pocket or some other form of Murphy's Law to strike, and her evening would be ruined.

Taylor settled down on the couch. "I might just stay too. I'd hate to see you all alone here."

Giselle's heart skipped a beat. Everything she had planned hinged on the fact that she would be alone in the house with Orion. No one but she and Damien knew what was going to happen, and even he hadn't been told the entire truth.

"You're so thoughtful," Giselle said giving a hug to Taylor. "I'm not going to be alone, remember? This is Dad and me time."

Martina's jaw tightened at the mention of her spending time with Orion. "Sweetheart, I'm glad you want to be closer to your father, but I feel like you've developed a somewhat... unnatural obsession with him lately."

Anxiety turned the volume of Giselle's voice up to eleven as she barked at her adoptive mother. "I spent seventeen years not knowing I had a father. Excuse me for acting like I care when I do find him. So what if he's not all there? He's my dad. Let me have this, okay?"

Martina held her hands up. "I didn't mean it like that—"

"How did you mean it, then?" Between the stress of what she was about to do and the fact her family was stalling to leave, Giselle was on the verge of a teenage emotional breakdown.

Martina too looked one moment from snapping, and the tension in her voice confirmed it. "We are happy to care for him. But that is all we can do. I feel like you want him to wake up and start talking back to you, and maybe the full extent of his condition hasn't quite settled in yet."

"No. It hasn't. Happy?" Giselle threw the words at her. "But is it so bad that I want to take time and warm up to the idea that this may be all I get out of him?"

Martina looked as if she'd been slapped in the face. "We need to go." She stood and headed for the door.

Taylor looked back. "I'll stay if you want."

"No. You guys go. I need alone time anyway." Giselle groaned and crossed her arms, making a show of turning away from the door.

"Call if you need anything," Martina said.

"I will." Giselle nearly rolled her eyes but caught herself before her mother could.

Starting a fight with her family had not been part of her plan. Martina was hurt and stressed out, and didn't deserve how Giselle was acting toward her. Nor did she deserve having her phone stolen. Giselle would have so much to atone for when this was done. A small voice in the back of her mind begged her to let it go and end all the secrecy, to call Martina back before it was too late and just attend the trials like the rest of the family.

But another part of her had been waiting for this opportunity and knew it might not come again. She had to act now.

Giselle waited for the door to close, listened as the car started, and then backed out of the driveway before digging Martina's cellphone out of her back pocket.

Her mother wouldn't miss it with all the craziness going on at the trials. She set it on the coffee table and pulled her own phone out and sent a text to Damien.

Giselle: It's time. We're ready for you and your mother to come.

Agonizing minutes went by while she waited for a reply. Damien had said they had to work under the light of a full moon. She'd told him it would probably be tonight. Why wasn't he answering?

Finally, right before she sent another message, Damien replied.

Damien: And Martina knows and is cool with it?
Giselle: Yeah of course
Damien: And there is no way to talk you out of this?

Giselle: Nope. We're doing this. Tonight. With the other wolves busy at the trials we will have no interruptions.

Damien: I will tell mother

Giselle sat and waited in silence, staring down at Martina's phone on the table in front of her. Damien had stipulated that their help would only come with the approval of her pack. The trials had provided such a distraction that she doubted Damien's mother Jasmine had any time to sit down and chat with her adoptive mother. She banked on it as she watched like a hawk, waiting to see a message flash across Martina's phone.

Damien might have taken her at her word, but Jasmine wouldn't be that easy to fool. Though she did hope this ruse would be enough.

As she predicted, a few minutes passed and Martina's phone rang. Giselle let it go to voice mail and waited another minute more before sending a text back through her mother's phone.

Martina: I'm sorry. Can't talk at the moment. We are beginning the trials.

Jasmine: Giselle is at home alone then?

She'd never pretended to be Martina before and thought before sending back replies. *How would Martina word this?*

Martina: She is not attending. You will have privacy at my house.

Jasmine: You know what she means to do then?

Pretending to be Martina was harder than she thought. Was she sounding too formal? What would her mother say in response?

Martina: My hands are tied. She's too stubborn for her own good.
Jasmine: We witches will not be held accountable
Martina: Understood

Giselle prayed she'd played a convincing role, even if only by text message. After a few more minutes of silence, her own phone buzzed again.

Damien: We will be there shortly.
Giselle: Thanks!

She blew out a breath of relief. At least for the moment, things were working in her favor. She'd pay later for stealing Martina's phone. And she'd definitely pay for lying to Jasmine. But if her father came alive, it would so be worth it.

34

Watching the clock like a hawk had no effect on time. It moved slowly, tick by tick, as Giselle waited for the witches to arrive.

Track lines from her pacing revealed the path she'd walked numerous times around the living room as she tried to do something to ease her mind.

Finally, she heard a car pulling up the driveway. She beat them to the door, pulling it open before they could hit the bell.

Jasmine stood in all her witchy finery, looking as if she'd stepped out of a Renaissance festival. Patchouli oil and citronella burned Giselle's nostrils; her least favorite of all the scent combinations, though it didn't seem to bother the others. Behind Jasmine were Damien, looking as if she'd killed his puppy, and Cassandra. She'd expected Cassandra to come along, though for what reason she didn't know, as Cassandra had no magic.

"Are you truly sure you wish to do this?" Jasmine asked, before stepping inside the house. The look she gave Giselle had all the hallmarks of a judge casting down his verdict of *guilty*. Giselle wondered if Jasmine knew of her deception.

All the lies. All the trickery. What if she'd given herself bad karma by setting things up this way, and it made the spell fail? *Oh, Crap!* Giselle nearly broke out in a cold sweat there. She gulped back as much nervous energy from her voice as she could, and answered back.

"It's because of me that he is in this state."

Jasmine had never been the kindest of mothers she'd met. Her demeanor ranked right up there with Nathaniel Thrace, only in a dress and wearing way too much perfume. But hearing Giselle's words and the undertone of worry that accompanied them had an effect. "Sweet child, you cannot blame yourself for the actions of others." She pulled Giselle into a hug that had more warmth in it than she'd ever thought possible from the tough witch.

When Jasmine pulled away and met Giselle's eyes, though, her all-business tone came straight back as if it had never gone. "Cassandra and Orion entered into a magical contract binding themselves."

"But for their trouble, what did they receive?" Giselle asked.

Jasmine looked back at Cassandra, standing like an obedient puppy behind her. "They received the greatest gift of all, a healthy child."

Cassandra's eyes lowered shamefully, but she nodded in agreement all the same.

"One they could never enjoy" Giselle shot back angrily, seeing her other mother in such a sad state.

"That was not their bargain with the cosmos." Jasmine turned her attention back on Giselle. "They abused magic to gain a child. Magic is something to be respected.

Great things can come of it, but there is a price to be paid."

"You think I have no respect for magic? But I do. It's why I'm asking for your help," Giselle pleaded, as she ushered them inside and shut the door.

Jasmine stopped in the middle of the living room. The witch clearly had the power in this situation, and she knew it. "You ask me to take away the enchantments that addled your father's mind. But what are you prepared to offer the powers that be for this magic?"

"What would the cosmos accept?" Giselle asked, already prepared for the answer to be her soul. She'd been born of magic; it resided in her blood. She'd offer that up and allow the gods or the cosmos whatever they wanted to be called to take what they needed to restore at least consciousness back into her father.

Jasmine wasn't budging from her spot. "That is not for me to say. You wish me to act as a channel for this magic, and I will go as far as that. You must be the one to make the offer and hope that it is enough for the gods to accept."

"I have very little in this world, but I would offer whatever I can to save my father." Giselle began to walk away and hoped that Jasmine and the other two would follow in her wake. She opened the door to Orion's room and walked inside. "I owe him that."

He was sitting still as ever in his chair, strapped down so he would not slump, nearly lifeless except for the gentle rise and fall of his chest. At that moment Orion's eyes had completely glazed over, appearing as if he were not there inside his shell of a body.

But Giselle she knew he was there; and that this life was no life to live. His debt was well beyond paid.

"Your love for family is endearing." Jasmine stood in the doorway, looking past Giselle at the weak figure of Orion. "Especially for one who never knew of his existence until now."

"It's because of the life I've led that I hold fiercely to this newfound family." Giselle placed a hand on Orion's shoulder, hoping to feel that same spark of energy she'd felt in the past. It was there – faint, but there all the same. And that was all she needed to bolster her resolve. "Growing up never to be loved because you were different will make you fiercely loyal to those who embrace and accept you," she said defiantly.

"Love is not always enough. Remember that, child, and do not hold to the hope that your love would be enough to pay the debt," Jasmine said.

"But my life would be, wouldn't it?" Giselle asked, cringing as she awaited the answer.

Part of her expected to see an emotional response register on the witch's face, but Jasmine looked as if she were bored by the revelation that Giselle would give her own life if need be. "No, child. You cannot trade your life for his; magic gave you life."

She let out a breath of relief. She hadn't wanted to make that ultimate sacrifice, and hearing she was absolved of that lessened her tension. But only by a little. She might not lose her life, but there were other things she could be cut off from. "I am willing to offer of myself whatever the cosmos needs to pay the debt. Take from my longevity, my immortality, whatever power resides in my blood."

Damien whimpered, as if he wanted to speak but had been ordered against it. Behind Jasmine, Giselle could see the pain in his eyes. They were all but screaming for her to take it back; to not go through with this.

Jasmine heaved a deep sigh and waved her son forward. "We may be able to bind some of your life force to an item as a sacrifice to the cosmos. If accepted, though, you'd be gambling your future on this spell working."

Damien carried a backpack of supplies. He came closer and set the bag on the bed, avoiding eye contact with Giselle. His body language said enough. He disapproved. He wished he had not been dragged into this. And she wondered if, after this was done, he'd ever speak to her again. She certainly hoped so.

"How will this work?" Giselle asked Jasmine.

"To bind your life to an object would be to create an item that could, in the most simplest of terms, hold part of your soul within it," Jasmine said.

"Will it hurt?" The question seemed insignificant the moment it left her lips, but Giselle's mind had shut down as she got closer to actually going through with the sacrifice. Fear nearly caused her to back out. It was one thing to say she was willing to sacrifice herself, but to actually go through with it was like standing on the edge of a bungee platform, waiting to be told to jump. Her heart beat erratically, and her eyes darted between Jasmine's stony expressions to the empty eye of her father.

"The effects are unknown. But if it works, you'd be giving part of yourself away. You'll be incomplete." Jasmine began to unpack the bag that Damien had brought in with him.

"But will it work?" Giselle asked, not bothering to hide the nerves causing her voice to crack.

"This I cannot promise. I can only try. The gods must accept your offering."

Giselle closed her eyes, took a deep breath, and said, "Do it, then."

"As you wish it." Jasmine held a hand out pointing towards the French doors leading out from Orion's room to the patio. "Open those, please."

Damien stood next to his mother, taking items she handed to him. He did not speak, but the way his shoulders slumped and the clear aversion of his eyes as Giselle passed by him were signal enough that he was not happy.

Giselle did as instructed and opened the back patio doors.

Jasmine turned her attention to Cassandra. "Find us a chair and bind Giselle to it."

Cassandra nodded and cast a weary glance at Orion and then to Giselle. "You don't have to do this."

Giselle looked at Cassandra. "I have to try."

"We've paid for our wrongdoing," Cassandra said.

"This is not payment. This is torture," Giselle said, casting her eyes to Orion. "He's locked in a prison of his own body. This is no life. This is the worst kind of hell."

Cassandra pursed her lips tightly, but behind her expression there was thankfulness in her eyes. She disappeared without another word.

Jasmine began pouring mixtures into bottles and assembling daggers and bowls around her makeshift altar.

"I may not agree with you, but I appreciate your efforts to try," Jasmine said.

Cassandra appeared in the doorway. "Will this chair be sufficient?" she asked, carrying a dining room chair past them and placing it out on the back patio.

Jasmine pulled out a hank of corded rope from her bag and tossed it on the bed. "Fine. Tie her hands and legs firmly."

"You're not going to try to stop me?" Giselle asked, as she willingly sat in the chair Cassandra provided and placed her hands on the arms, awaiting her binding.

"I've learned not to argue with you," Cassandra said solemnly. "And I have no right, as I have not been there to be a mother to you."

"I'll not be swayed. I've made up my mind. And besides, it's not like I'm going to be Alpha anymore, so I might as well enjoy my family. Now that I have them."

Jasmine looked at her altar and back to her son. "I'll need a quartz pillar. A small one to bind her essence."

Damien sucked in a breath and his eyes grew wide, but he did not say a word as he retrieved what his mother had asked for.

"Hold her arm," Jasmine commanded, and Cassandra finished her knot and took hold of Giselle's free arm. Jasmine held a large black dagger in one hand and a shallow bowl in the other.

Giselle knew without being told what was to happen. She held her arm still and allowed Jasmine to slice across her wrist. She held the bowl below Giselle's arm to collect the blood.

Giselle breathed deeply through the pain and watched every drop as her blood collected.

Jasmine set the knife into the bowl, not wasting a single drop, and tossed a roll of bandages to Cassandra to wrap her wound.

Damien pulled out a clear crystal not bigger than her pinky finger. The stone was pure and clear, nearly transparent except for a few blemishes. He handed the stone to Jasmine, and she placed it in the center of the bowl.

"Last chance to back out of this," Jasmine said, already turning away as if she knew the answer before Giselle said as much.

Cassandra finished wrapping Giselle's wound and then tied that hand down to the chair as she'd done with the other.

Jasmine whispered a prayer over the crystal, and while she worked, Damien and Cassandra lent their voices, repeating the prayer that Jasmine had started as a chant.

Jasmine finished her prayer and took her makeshift alter out to the patio, setting everything down on the concrete before setting herself down under the moonlight.

Damien and Cassandra worked in unison pulling out candles and setting them in sequence all around Jasmine. They lit them one by one, still chanting their prayer, while Jasmine held her hands over the bowl and gazed up at the bright moon overhead.

Giselle watched with rapt attention, half wondering if she should be feeling something and scared of what she would feel if she did.

Jasmine held up the bowl with the blood and the crystal and joined the chant of Damien and Cassandra.

Cassandra finished lighting her half of the candles and took a position behind Orion. She pushed his chair up towards the altar with Jasmine and unbuckled the straps holding him safely in his seat. Orion began to slide down, but she caught him before he could move too far.

Even from behind, Giselle could see the love Cassandra had for him. She didn't just hold him in place; her body wrapped around him. An embrace. Her strength was in her love for him and that helped her to keep him upright.

Giselle's stomach knotted. Her resolve was unshakeable, but in the back of her mind she feared her sacrifice would not be enough.

"Do you offer up the essence of your being to be collected and preserved within this crystal?" Jasmine asked Giselle, her voice turning deep and tinged with an otherworldly echo.

"Yes," Giselle responded weakly.

Jasmine placed the bowl filled with her blood and the crystal on Giselle's lap. "Look at the celestial commander of your race. Behold the goddess and make your intention known," Jasmine said, and her eyes flitted up to the moon.

Giselle gazed upwards. The moon had grown large and brilliant in its fullness. "I offer whatever is needed to save my father. Take from me what you will."

A surge like an electric shock flashed through her body. Her limbs attempted to flail out beyond her control, and if not for the ropes holding her in place she might have hit Jasmine. In that moment her body was not hers at all. She felt herself ripping in two, as if the gods were flaying her alive, slowly, with an invisible knife. The sound of screaming pierced her ears and, overwhelmed by sensation, she hadn't realized it was her own voice. Pain the likes of which she'd never felt before set every single nerve on fire. The human half of Giselle cried out, calling for death to end this, unable to withstand the torture ripping her apart.

Her wolf rose to the surface, the true strength in her soul, forcing a transformation that for the first time in her life felt excruciating. Bones cracked. Fur ripped through her skin as her coat came to the surface. She felt every excruciating second of it until her mind blanked of thoughts and concerns, turning feral and hungry. Using anger to fight the pain, she was able to withstand it a little longer, but the spell continued, and she could feel pieces of her being cut away and disappearing into the abyss.

Her wolf diminished and retreated with the pain, burrowing safely inside where even the gods dare not touch it. Her body shifted backwards, leaving her a crumpled pile of torn clothes and broken ropes in the chair.

Her first thought was to make sure her wolf had not left her completely. Weakened and licking its wounds, she still felt the other half of her still residing where it was supposed to be. But there was a hole there too. Not large – if one could even measure the size of their soul – but she felt it like a nuisance; a scab that begged to be picked at. Something was not right. But nothing could be done about it, even if she had the energy to do anything at that moment.

Utterly exhausted by the effects of Jasmine's spell, Giselle could hardly move a muscle. Bathed in sweat and her clothes shredded from a botched transformation, she was afraid if she did move she'd fall into a naked puddle on the ground.

No one came to her aid. No one asked if she was okay. Damien and Cassandra's chanting continued, rising to a deafening crescendo as the light of the moon seemed to focus on Jasmine and the bowl she held aloft.

"It is done." Jasmine silenced the chanting with her words and brought the bowl down eye level with Giselle.

What once had been a pure and clear stone had gone blood red and murky. All the blood that had pooled into the bowl was gone as well, without so much as a smudge on the inside of the bowl.

Her mind blown by what had just happened, Giselle tried to speak, but when she opened her mouth, words did not want to come out.

"You are bound to this object for your time on this earth. What is your wish?" Jasmine asked.

"Help my father," Giselle said weakly. Her body still on fire, it was all she could do not to cry out for mercy. She hoped the worst had been done.

"As you request," Jasmine said. She took the stone and brought it to a small cauldron and began adding ingredients and whispering more prayers.

The other two again began chanting, but these words were different; still unknown to Giselle, but musical in their cadence.

Cringing inside, waiting for round two of the torture chamber, Giselle watched with wide eyes as Jasmine brewed a drink of some kind using her new bound stone as the final ingredient. When she had finished, she siphoned out some and offered it to Orion with a medicine dropper.

One dropper at a time, she slowly fed the entire contents of the small cauldron to Orion. Then as Giselle watched and waited, Jasmine removed the stone. It had turned white again, as if it had never been blemished by her blood.

Jasmine placed the stone in a soft pouch with a long cord. "Whether or not the spell worked will be up to the will of the gods. But this you must keep safe. You are bound to it and it to you. What has been done here cannot be undone. You have sealed your fate with it."

Her words scared Giselle, but she would not let on how truly frightened she was. "Thank you." She wore the small pouch like a necklace tying the cord around her neck and set her sight on Orion. How long would she have to wait?

35

"Father?" Giselle asked, cautiously watching muscles twitching in his formerly lifeless limbs.

He moaned and jerked as if he were having a fit, and it was all Giselle could do to not rush to his aid, but Damien came up behind and held her at bay, whispering in her ear, "He'll be okay. Just give him a minute."

Moans turned into slurred speech – still unintelligible, but it was clear he was returning to the land of the living.

Cassandra stood by hopefully as well but dared not to move closer as Orion struggled to regain control of himself.

His twitching limbs sprouted fur, and his body twisted and contorted down into a shady brown wolf, his coat in varying shades from russet to sand and eyes of the deepest green that stared directly into Giselle's.

"Father. Orion? I don't really know what to call you right now." Giselle bent down to her knees and reached a hand out to the growling wolf. "I'm your daughter."

The wolf took a few wobbly steps toward Giselle and sniffed at her outstretched hand.

She remained as still as she could while Orion inspected her as only a wolf would. He circled her slowly twice before coming to a stop, sitting in front of his child.

Cassandra fell to her knees next to Giselle and mimicked her introduction, reaching out a hand and holding still for Orion to smell.

"What do we do now?" Giselle whispered.

"He needs time," Jasmine spoke soothingly. "Your sacrifice has awoken him, but only he knows how much he's endured for the last years."

Giselle turned back to her father, who was still sitting like a guard dog watching them. "I can't pretend to know what you've gone through. And I'm sorry."

That triggered something. The wolf began to shift again, fur fading, arms and hands replacing paws. "Do not be sorry." He choked the words out as he collapsed on the ground at her feet.

Giselle and Cassandra both reached out to him, but it was Cassandra who pulled the fallen man into her arms and gently stroked his hair.

He breathed weakly, as if any movement of his body was a struggle.

"I'm not sorry that you brought me into the world. I'm sorry for the twist of fate that punished your love," Giselle said.

"I... would endure..." Orion took a labored breath. "Hell. Anything... for my family."

"You have that now, love." Cassandra continued to stroke his hair.

"We're here," Giselle said, elated to see him coming back from the void. He remained weak and limp in Cassandra's arms, but life slowly returned to him.

Tears of joy streamed down Giselle's face. All her wishes had come true: her father and her other mother. Both alive. Together. The small void in her soul was there too, present in her mind, but it was so worth it to have her family back. She sniffled and wiped away a tear as she looked at Jasmine. "Thank you. Thank you so much. I can't say it enough. You've given me my family again."

Where Giselle and even Cassandra were elated, Jasmine's face held all the joy of a funeral. "I wouldn't be so quick to thank me. You've offered up a cosmic debt to the universe. Gambled your own soul for the life of your father. One day that debt will have to be repaid. All magic comes at a price."

Giselle sucked in a sobering breath. The hole was there. She felt it. Like a missing limb; only the part of her soul that had been taken was not visible. In her fervor she had not thought of any consequences beyond that evening. Her hand instinctively reached up for the pouch around her neck. Inside the stone she'd bound herself to rested like any other mundane object. She'd have to make sure to protect it with her life, as it could very well be her life she guarded. "I'll keep the stone safe. I promise. And am I too to be held to silence for this magical contract, as they were in the past?"

"The magic that enabled this transaction resides around your neck, dear girl. Telling someone would be revealing your own weakness to them; and in your society, weakness is always exploited. Keep that in mind."

"Understood," Giselle said cautiously. Protecting an object for the rest of her life might be hard, but in the grand scheme of things, it was worth it to have her family back. "Well, for your part in enacting the magic, I say thank you."

Jasmine nodded and cast her eyes to Damien. "We must leave now. Say your goodbyes and let the wolves have their peace."

Damien pulled Giselle into a surprisingly tight hug. She missed the closeness with him and allowed herself to melt against his body, hearing the steady rhythm of his heart. Since their breakup, she'd hardly seen him. Her only real connection to him had been her phone and the businesslike text messages they'd sent each other. She held on to him tighter, afraid of the truth that it was just goodbye all over again.

When he pulled back, tears stained his cheeks, but deep within his eyes she found a cold wall blocking true emotional depth. "I hope you know what you got yourself into."

"Do I ever?" Giselle joked, hoping to get him to crack that wall with a smile.

"I often wonder." Damien sighed as he turned and followed his mother.

"Are we okay?" Giselle asked, speaking to Damien's back.

He didn't answer; just kept walking until he was through the door, ripping her heart in two all over again.

Another price to have paid. Damien had warned her not to do this. She did it anyway, of course, as she always did despite the detriment to this or any of her personal relationships. Perhaps that was her curse. The lone wolf wasn't lonely out of desire, but because that was the only way they could be.

With that painful realization, she glanced over to Cassandra, who was still holding tightly to her father, bent over his prone form nuzzling his nose, while whispering apologies and confirmation of love.

Their love was pure; their emotions were written in bold across their features. Every touch, each connection of skin confirmed it. Orion, as weak as he looked at that moment, reached his shaking hands up to hold the tearstained cheek of his wife as he whispered, "I love you."

In that moment, though their daughter sat only a few feet away, Cassandra and Orion were the only two people in the universe.

Theirs was the kind of love that transcended all. To call them soulmates seemed a feeble understatement. Theirs was a love that had all the tragedy of star-crossed lovers, only death had not been the release to allow them to meet in the afterlife. Through the years they had endured their separation, their penance for daring to defy the universe with their union. Love was supposed to conquer all, but it had nearly destroyed them.

Yet that same destructive force had produced the one person able to bring them back together.

Things had come full circle now, and Giselle would sit and watch their love story unfold forever if not for the jarring command of Jasmine.

"Come, Cassandra." the witch said, from behind her back.

Cassandra looked up, hurt. "Must I?"

"The wolves need their time." Jasmine's voice held no emotion. "Giselle sacrificed her soul to see her father, not to watch you two make love under the moonlight." She continued to walk away, as if knowing Cassandra would follow as instructed.

A slap in the face might have been kinder. Cassandra looked as if she'd been hit hard by Jasmine's bluntness. She glanced from Giselle to Orion and back as if hoping one or both of them might tell her to stay. "I—"

"You can take your time—" Giselle started to say, but Jasmine cut her off.

"You'll have plenty of time later. I need you to help me pack the car now."

"But. I only just found him," Cassandra whimpered.

"Cassandra? You're bound to me as punishment for your own wrongdoing. You will do as you are ordered." Jasmine's voice turned dark.

"Maybe a few minutes would be good." Giselle tried not to sound too excited about it. She needed some time to soak in the fact she had a father. A real, live, and awake father. And one on one was best. "I'll make sure he's okay, and we'll get you two back together as soon as possible."

Cassandra looked as if she would not let her prize go. She tightened her grip and then kissed his forehead gently. "I'll be back."

"Yes. You will. Now go, before Jasmine gets too mad," Giselle said. She reached out a hand and squeezed Cassandra's shoulder.

"Take care of him tonight," Cassandra pleaded as sadness turned her trickle of tears into a flood of emotion. Her face swelled with anger as she stood and took a step toward Jasmine.

Giselle could only imagine the heartache. She'd only just met her father; Cassandra had been carrying the torch for so long. If it had been up to her, she'd have let Cassandra stay all night and they could bask in the glow of their newly healed family. But Cassandra's angry cries, though heartbreaking, were nothing compared to the threatening look on Jasmine's face. She had to go. Now before the wicked witch surfaced, and that was something no one wanted to see.

Giselle exchanged places with Cassandra supporting the near-unconscious Orion in her lap.

"I will not ask again." Jasmine's voice trailed down the hall.

"Go!" Giselle shouted to Cassandra.

Cassandra wiped the tears from her face and sucked in a stuttering breath as if those might help her put on a convincing mask of neutrality. They wouldn't, but at least the effort had been made. Shoulders squared to the world, Cassandra turned to leave the room without looking back at Giselle or Orion.

36

Moments went by in silence as Giselle sat staring down at her father. Her mind was abuzz with questions she wanted to ask, things she needed to tell him, and general awe of the fact that he was here. She'd spent so long dreaming of a family, feeling unwanted. And in so short a time she had been given the world and more.

He too looked up at her as if not truly believing what he was seeing.

Giselle had imagined this moment, dreamed of it even, but now the she was with him, words failed her. She wanted to tell him of her life, and learn every last detail of his, but where to begin?

Orion groaned, pushing his straining muscles in a sorry attempt to sit up.

Giselle too felt the echoes of unwilling muscles that had been pushed past their limits. They'd both been through a lot this evening, and with untested magic, there was no telling how injured they both had been in the process.

"Easy now." Giselle helped support his weight as he came up off the ground. "Take it slow," she cautioned.

Orion pressed his hands to the ground to stabilize himself, and with Giselle giving a little push, he came up on his knees. "Moving seems a bit harder than I remember," he joked in his raspy voice. Inch by inch he pushed up to his knees and then used the bed sheets to help pull himself up further.

"We have all the time in the world. And you've been a vegetable for the last seventeen years. Remember that," Giselle answered back.

"Lesson one, my little wolf, never let them see you weak. I'll get myself up to standing now, or it will never happen," Orion responded. His voice regaining some strength and depth. "And as soon as I do, I'm getting myself that glass of water on the side table."

"I can get it." Giselle tried to push herself off the ground and found her muscles completely unwilling; like jello, they maintained their shape, but when pressed held no form.

"You just sit right there and let me do this." Orion's strength of will was a reason he'd been Alpha, and already Giselle saw the stubbornness that drove everyone mad. She'd have laughed if it didn't hurt to do so. There was no doubt whose daughter she was.

Good as his word, Orion stood by his own power and took two very slow and wobbly steps to the side table to retrieve his water. The glass shook in his hand as he moved it, and Giselle could swear she was experiencing the same tremors in her own limbs.

He drank deeply once the cup touched his lips and then allowed himself to sit on the edge of the bed as reward for all his hard work.

That was how an Alpha handled business, and after seeing his struggle despite his destroyed muscles, Giselle could not complain about her own tired ones. She'd scrape herself off the ground and sit in a chair like a lady if only to prove it.

"You say you are my child?" His voice had gained some strength, but his words were still breathy and labored.

"I am. I was lost for many years." Mimicking his show of determination, she dug deep to pull herself up and into the chair she'd been strapped to earlier. "My name is Giselle."

"That's a good name."

"Well, I'm glad you like it," she chuckled nervously, not really knowing what else to say.

Orion scrutinized her face. His eyes moved back and forth across her features like the fingers of a blind person reading braille, slowly deciphering the meaning of each dot. "I am sorry for not being a father." His voice uncertain, as if he were still coming to grips with it all.

As weird as it all was for her, Giselle could only imagine how surreal it must be for him – to wake up one day and find your baby had grown up. "What do you remember?" Giselle hoped she hadn't been too blunt with the question.

"We had a baby. A beautiful girl. And then she was gone…" Pain etched across Orion's face. He attempted to hide by taking a sip of his water, but she saw past the ruse. "I was trapped; unable to save her. It's hard to explain."

That part she knew. His loss was hers, too. "Have you been awake all this time?" Giselle asked, desperate for more information.

"I wouldn't say I was fully awake." Orion's eyes left her face briefly for a quick look around the room, but they were back before he could get in a full breath. "Aware of the passage of time, yes, but not fully invested in this world. This place, for instance. I knew we moved from the other home, but the memory of it all is like a dream that leaves you wondering if it really happened."

It sounded more like a nightmare to Giselle. "Do you remember David and his wife taking care of you?"

"Are they here?" His eyes lit up eagerly.

"No. David… is gone." Giselle sighed. That was a conversation she'd not wanted to bring up right at the start. Better that they talk of happier things; but now that they'd traveled down the dark path, there was no coming back.

Orion's initial excitement crashed into despair upon hearing his own brother had died. "How?"

"It all happened so quickly." Bluntness would not serve well here, but Giselle didn't have the tact needed to deliver such a painful explanation. "He was executed by Richard for breaking supernatural law."

The great Alpha hung his head, catching himself in his hands. "Why?" His voice cracked.

Giselle gulped down a knot in her throat. The first thing her father heard when he woke from eternal slumber was that his brother was gone. And the reason it all happened would be a knife in the back. She couldn't hide the truth from him, but she wished someone else could be the bearer of this bad news. Anyone but her. If Cassandra had not left, she'd have called her mother back in and made her do it.

In the silence between them, Orion lifted his head back out of his hands and locked eyes with Giselle. "Why?" he asked again.

"He tried to have Cassandra killed after she was deemed innocent of your affliction," she blurted out, ripping the bandage off of this revelation as quickly as she could, hoping it might avoid further pain for her father.

Orion's jaw clenched. His eyes grew dark, the irises nearly enveloping the color of his eyes. "He would dare?"

"He seemed mad with grief over you, if that helps."

"My brother was a good man," Orion said through gritted teeth. "What of his wife?"

"She doesn't like me very much," Giselle said, with a snort.

"What has she done?" Orion asked in no mood for levity. His wolf peeked out from behind his green eyes: deadly, dangerous, and ready for a fight.

Giselle nearly choked on her words, feeling the power of her father's anger. "With David dead, the position of Alpha is up for grabs."

"And she wants it?" Orion asked. "She was always a bit power hungry."

"I thought so, but it seems she's vying for her sons to get it."

"She has children?" Confusion stole his anger for a fraction of a second before Orion regained it. "Yes. Of course. The twin boys."

"Ace and Jay. I met them all when I was sent up to Washington to go before the Council."

"Why did they bring you up?" Orion asked.

"Because as your child, I was considered in line."

Orion's eyebrow lifted with curiosity. "And are you?"

"No." Giselle shook her head. Another conversation she would rather not have. "I am not worthy. The Council called for trial by combat to pick a new Alpha."

"You are more than worthy!" Orion sounded hurt more than angry that his own daughter had been passed over.

"I appreciate that, but I don't need the title. I'm happy having my family back." She hoped to guide the conversation back to more cheerful things. Having her father and mother together and alive was more than she'd ever wanted in her entire life. They deserved to enjoy it and be happy. Let the wolves fight for leaders; she couldn't care less.

"You were deemed unworthy?" Orion remained stuck on that point. "In the five minutes I have known you, I can see you are more than capable of the task."

Giselle smile beamed from ear to ear. "Thank you, Father."

"I wish to know more. My memory is sparse. The time I spent in this state has left me with great holes in time and place. Where are we?"

"Vegas."

"Why so far south? Our territory is to the north."

"I was sent south because the foster system had a hard time placing me with a family who could handle a wolf—"

"You mean you were not raised in the pack?" He cut her off. "But Vivian knew about you. Why did she not come to your aid?"

"She knew about me? I'd have never guessed that when we met in Washington. She seemed annoyed to be in the same room as me." Giselle thought on that for a moment, wondering if her anger had been misplaced.

Vivian could have been angry that Giselle had been found, hoping that if she'd been lost this long, she wouldn't ever resurface. Or she could have been angry that the reason for Orion's affliction was standing in front of her. Mind reading would be a handy superpower. Why hadn't Giselle been graced with that? She had been born through magic, after all.

Orion's face wrinkled with confusion. He spent moments in silence, as if trying to reach through the memories one by one to find what he needed. "Vivian was part of our magical pact. She was one of the few to know our secret. She had personally arranged for the wolf to be our surrogate."

That sounded nothing like the Vivian Giselle had come to know, the conniving power-hungry wolf who'd do anything to discredit her. She'd helped arrange for her birth? No way in hell!

"Did David know?" Giselle asked.

"No." Orion dropped his head shamefully. "He was against it. He knew I'd have to abdicate my position, and he didn't want to take over. His wife, however, helped arrange it and was held to the code of secrecy."

None of it made sense to her. But then, magic was such an odd subject, with more rules than it was worth, in Giselle's opinion. "But even after you were taken in as a… well, a vegetable, she didn't say anything. I met David. He never let on he knew the situation. He was so angry at Cassandra, blaming her for what happened."

"She might have believed there would be some kind of reprisal on her for sharing the secret even then. Who knows?" Orion looked just as confused as Giselle about the whole thing.

"She's not a nice lady, if you ask me."

"She's family," Orion cautioned. "Beyond that, she's *pack*."

Was he actually defending her? Giselle took a moment to try to process what she was hearing. "You'll have to excuse me for not understanding. I did not grow up with wolves."

"There is a lot that has been kept from us both, I fear. And that is something we'll address. I need to speak with Vivian myself."

"She's here at the trials, with her oldest son Ace scheduled to fight."

Shock or fear or maybe both crossed Orion's face upon hearing those words. "When are these trials?" he asked.

"Now. My whole adoptive pack is there, overseeing them with the rest of the Alpha Council.

"Then you will take me there... now," Orion demanded.

37

"You can't go!" Giselle protested. Just one look at him was reason enough. "What did you just say was lesson one? These trials are being presided over by the Council of Alphas."

"Which is exactly why I must be there. I am by rights still the Alpha."

"Okay, not to be disrespectful and all, but you don't look it. And you could barely get up. How are you going to go before all those wolves like that?" Giselle hoped he'd listen to her. She had just gotten her father back. If something happened to him now, she'd never forgive herself.

"Your worry is endearing. But I owe it to my people, as well as you, to do this. Do you know how many foolish deaths come from trials such as these?" Orion asked. "And another of my family is about to be put into the fray… no! I cannot stand for this."

"But you've been a vegetable for seventeen years. Surely you…" Giselle's words trailed off as she watched her father rise without hesitation.

She herself felt the strain of muscles as if she were the one fighting to stand, though she hadn't gotten up from her seat.

Only the slightest hint of strain showed on Orion's face as he rose proudly to his full height.

The moment passed, and the pain in Giselle's muscles subsided.

"I have woken from a long rest. My wolf and I have shirked our duty for too long. It's time I put things right and ensured the safety of my pack."

Being on the other side of that stubborn streak gave Giselle a new perspective on what it must be like for others to deal with her. When she got a bug up her ass to get something done, there was no stopping her, and understanding this about herself confirmed that her protests would have no effect on Orion.

But still she had to try. "Please don't. Let it go. We're a family: you, me, and Cassandra. Don't risk that by trying to stop these trials."

Orion bent down and caressed Giselle's face. "We are a family. We will always be a family. But the pack needs leadership. More than just my life is at stake."

It was like the years of him sleeping through things had not mattered. Or maybe he still hadn't grasped the amount of time he'd been gone from the world and its politics. "Others are volunteering to fight for Alpha." Giselle hoped reason might sink in where her pleading had not. "They're risking their lives knowing what's at stake."

"The battle for Alpha is supposed to be one of dignity and courage. I have no doubt the wolves who volunteer are hoping to show that. However, trial by combat is only a last resort, when an appropriate heir is not found."

"That's what they said when I was brought up before the Council."

"Both you and Ace should have been worthy candidates. Why, then, were both of you passed over?"

"Ace was a second son. And he's fighting for his right to the title. I was allowed a champion, but I declined."

"Neither of you should have been." Orion growled with frustration. "By rights you are my heir, and Ace is David's. There was no need for a third option unless… Ace is not worthy?"

"Ace is!" Giselle hadn't known him long enough to have full faith in that statement, but what she'd seen of him was more than admirable. And she had wanted him to have the position, too. At least then it would stay in the family.

"Then there was no need for a spectacle like this." Orion's wolf peeked out from behind his eyes, filled with anger but not aimed at her.

Giselle remembered how Jay had tried to warn her. How friendly Brady had been. Both of them acting, at least to her, unusual. Both of them sticking close to her but not enough to make it seem out of sorts. Were they protecting her?

"You think the fights are rigged?" She hadn't reasoned why but maybe they knew more than they were letting on. Jay had specifically told her to stay as far away as possible.

"I wouldn't' put it past some of the Alphas."

"But why? We're fighting for our territory, not theirs." Giselle hadn't put the puzzle pieces together, but in her mind a hazy picture was beginning to form.

"Territories were formed through alliances and wars. If, for example a weak Alpha was installed, they might be pressured to alter borders of their territories." Orion slowly hobbled over to the dresser and selected some suitable clothing. To a bystander, he might have looked as if he were tired and had just woken up. But Giselle knew he was re-learning how to move and use his body after so long. Her body ached, too, echoing his pain. The residual effects of the magic had left her feeling as if she were the one whose muscles had atrophied and then been forced back into service.

"I would hate to think my fellow Regional Alphas have any influence on the outcome of the trials, but if so, it is my duty to be present and claim my right as Alpha." Orion's determination got him moving as if he were unaffected. If not for the warning bells going off, she'd be so impressed with the man she called father.

"If they are rigged, then all the more reason to stay away." Giselle sighed, wishing she had something better to say.

Orion turned around with surprising quickness and asked, "You'd let others die?"

She almost said yes, but stopped herself just in time, realizing how horrible it sounded. Yes, they'd all volunteered to fight for the title of Alpha, but assuming a fair fight. The alternative was just lambs to the slaughter.

"But what can you do? Show up, and then they'll stop the trials?" she asked.

Orion's shoulders slumped and he let out a long breath. "That would be ideal. But in case that doesn't happen, I'm prepared to fight the current leader."

That was exactly what she did not want to hear. Especially in his current state. He might be a great leader, but the man who stood in front of her needed time to heal from what had been done to him. Maybe in a month he'd have regained his strength and speed, but not tonight.

"And if you lose? What then? Goodbye, Father... again." Giselle hadn't meant to sound so selfish, but at the heart of her she felt it so strongly. She'd lose her father as well as possibly herself, since their connection was still new and untested, and she wasn't completely certain how closely their souls were intertwined.

"Have more faith in me, child," Orion said, stretching as if he were preparing to fight that very moment. He winced ever so slightly as he pulled his muscles tight. Clearly he was a man of determination, but that alone could not guarantee success.

Giselle again felt her own muscles tingling. Not aching as much as they were earlier, but still, there was some slight discomfort to the sensation. "I'm going with you, then." Giselle resigned herself to the possibility of defeat, and if that were the case, she'd at least be there with him in his last moments.

"Of course. Especially since I have no clue where I'm going." Orion carried himself with confidence, but below the surface Giselle could see the weakness he hid. And now that they were linked, she felt it.

Giselle sighed and walked to the door. "We'll stop for some food and painkillers first, okay?"

"Good plan." Orion followed behind her, and each step he took echoed in Giselle's muscles.

38

This was the worst idea ever, Giselle mumbled to herself the entire trip into the desert. After getting some food and raiding her adoptive parents' medicine cabinet for the strongest painkillers she could find, Giselle could stall him no longer, and Orion demanded they head out.

If she'd been a smarter wolf, she'd have driven them straight down the 15 freeway and kept on going until they reached the ocean. At least then they'd have been far away from the battles taking place. But unable to defy her father's wishes, she turned down the unlit dirt road that led to the arena and the rest of the wolves.

Giselle pulled the car to the end of the road and stopped. "Good luck," she offered solemnly, and exited the car followed by Orion.

She still felt a tug on her muscles as he moved, but the pain had since subsided, so either the painkillers were working or he was regaining his own strength. Either option had her wondering what the future held for them, especially with the uncertainty of this night.

She took a sobering breath and led Orion toward the arena they'd erected earlier in the week.

Screams and cheers preceded their approach, as well as the scent of freshly spilled blood.

Giselle's wolf awoke with agitation as the scent clung in her nose. Danger. Death. Each step was leading them closer to their doom, for sure. Her wolf clawed just below the surface, begging to come out in her defense.

If Orion was bothered by it, he gave no indication. His steps quickened, nearly surpassing Giselle's as they hit the edge of the awaiting crowd.

Eyes settled on them, and murmurs of recognition began to replace the cheers for those still fighting in the arena.

Orion overtook her and led the way into the center, yelling at the top of his lungs, "This trial is over!"

Silence fell on the crowd.

Giselle caught up to Orion and instinctively reached for his hand.

Vivian stood from her spot in the seats nearest the bar. "How is this possible? Orion?" Fear was etched across her face as her voice trembled from the shock of seeing him awake. "You've been...." She choked on the words, and Orion filled the silence with his.

"Vivian, wonderful. You have positively identified me as Orion Silverman." Owning the crowd with his presence and the power of his voice, Orion's eyes found their target at a collection of seats filled with well-dressed wolves: the Council of Alphas. "I am the Alpha of the Pacific region, returned to claim my position."

None of them looked happy to see him.

Giselle watched he faces of others with rapt attention as they took in the sight of their once-proud Alpha.

"You *were* Alpha once." Misha stood from where she'd been sitting. Neither fear nor joy filled her face as she stared back at Orion. "You've been away for too long."

Orion met her stare as if it were a challenge. "And now I have returned."

Misha chuckled and let her gaze fall on the Council members around her, but her words were still directed at him. "You left your pack. Your people. All for what? A witch."

Murmurs both of outrage and acceptance caught in Giselle's ear. It seemed that more than a few people felt angrier that he left the pack than they did about why. She filed that note away under *remember later*.

Charles Marsden of the Rufus Reds stood and gave a respectful nod to Orion before speaking. "You'll have to excuse us if we do not readily jump to the claim of someone who abandoned their pack for another creature."

"Is that what we're calling the witches these days? I've always known them to be our allies," Orion shot back at him, keeping his tone loud enough for all to hear without sounding as if he were shouting.

"Allies, of course. Always our allies, as are many other of the supernatural races – but we do not breed with them." Charles's smiled turned wicked as his eyes moved from Orion to Giselle.

Before Giselle could even open her mouth, Orion squeezed her hand as if he knew she'd be unable to hold back.

"It is you, then, who denied my daughter's claim?" Orion asked Charles.

"She was given opportunity to be included in these trials," he responded.

"There was no need for a trial by combat." Orion's eyes darted over to Vivian, who had remained standing where she was. Biting her lip as if she were scared to death of what was to come, she looked as if she might be sentenced to death. "If not my daughter, then why not her son Aeson? Is he not a Silverman too?"

Misha appeared to be enjoying the spectacle of seeing Orion center stage and the fear his presence had on certain members of his former pack. "Aeson might have been acceptable, had his father not been sentenced to death for breaking wolf law. Even Alphas must be held accountable for their actions – don't you agree, Orion?"

Giselle hadn't seen it before, but Misha was one devious wolf. With only words, she was setting the pieces in play to cause others to battle while she watched. Giselle turned to the crowd and hunted for familiar faces, looking to see how those she knew were receiving this information.

"Alphas, yes, but children have never been made to pay for their father's sins," Orion responded.

"Fathers teach their sons," Misha answered back with sugary sweetness. "We cannot have the flouting of our laws passed down the lines, even if the reason is noble."

"You feel my brother's death was a noble one?" Orion asked.

Giselle saw the trap Misha was laying. How had Orion not? She squeezed his hand, hoping to stop him from being led into this conversation.

"Your bother was avenging his own. We knew of the spell you were under, and we were all saddened when it happened." Misha maintained her sweet tone as she played to the audience with her words of false condolence. "But!" She paused for effect, and the whole crowd looked at her. "The witch was not found to be guilty by trial, and he attempted to carry out sentencing anyway – in front of his son, who would hope to succeed him."

"And learned what happens to wolves who break the law. Yes, I know how he died. Where is my enforcer? Richard, come forward," Orion commanded.

The assembled crowd mumbled among themselves as they waited for him to come out. Giselle finally spotted Jay, who was not sitting with his mother, surprisingly. Vivian's second son had taken a place with a group of wolves about his same age. None of them looked familiar, nor did they look friendly. As she locked eyes with Jay, his face darkened. He shook his head *no* and mouthed the words, "Go. Leave now. Not safe."

It was beginning to make sense to her, though the details were hazy. She hadn't been denied the title because she was unfit; she'd been sabotaged. Someone really did not want her to have the title. Her bet was still on Vivian, but Misha was a close second. Hiding behind the law and her own position of power, she could do a lot without actually having to get her paws dirty.

And as her eyes flitted over to Vivian, trembling in the lower stands, the former Alpha's mate seemed less likely to be the mastermind of such espionage.

Richard pushed his way through the crowd. "Orion. Good to see you, sir."

Her father smiled genuinely at the old wolf. "You still kicking around, then?" he asked.

"My place has always been as the guard for the Silverman pack," Richard replied.

Orion released Giselle's hand and extended his to shake Richard's. "I heard you took special care of my daughter recently."

"To the extent that I could, yes. But she's got the Silverman stubbornness in her." Richard gave Giselle a cursory glance, but Orion clearly had his attention. The old wolf smiled as genuinely as anyone could seeing Orion standing alive and well in front of him. His allegiance had never been called into question, nor would it after seeing the true admiration he had for his leader. "Would have served her well."

"And that's why I'm here." Orion turned his attention to the crowd. "Richard, did you pass sentence on David Silverman?"

Richard's smile faded. "Yes. And carried it out myself, sir."

"And did his sons attempt to stop you?" Orion asked, making sure his voice was loud enough to be heard by all.

"No. Neither of the Silverman boys acted or spoke against it." Richard replied.

Orion patted him on the back. "You see here? His sons gave no reason to question their understanding of wolf law. Their claim should have been honored, along with my own daughter's claim."

The crowd again began to mumble amongst themselves. Giselle let out a breath, feeling as if her worry had been unfounded. Orion had so far managed to avoid a fight, and his arguments were valid enough that any rational wolves should accept them. She might not be Alpha, but if they honored Ace's claim, it would be good enough for her.

"You of course present a very compelling argument, Orion Silverman. And it is a credit to your time as Alpha that you are so well versed in our laws; however, we do not all agree that either child should rightfully hold this claim."

"Who denies my daughter her right? Speak your grievances to me. A child does not pay for the crimes of their father, yet you'd punish my own flesh and blood and risk the lives of others in trial by combat."

Charles cleared his throat. "It is not only the broader actions that have given us cause to question these wolves. There are things that are better discussed in a private Council than aired like dirty laundry to the assembled wolves here."

"Seeing as how the trials are being held now, there is precious little time for Council meetings. State your grievances here and now, so we can address them."

"As you wish, sir." Charles turned his eyes toward Vivian. "Mrs. Silverman, the former Alpha's mate, has aggressively painted a negative campaign against your beloved daughter. She has, rightfully so, pointed out the circumstances surrounding the birth of your daughter. We must carefully consider all claims, of course, before making a decision that will affect the whole of your region. Being only half true wolf and raised human, she did not seem equal to the task. It was put to a vote."

"And she was denied the claim." Orion finished his statement with a growl at the edge of his voice.

"Yes." Charles smirked at Orion then turned to Vivian. A near-silent conversation passed between them, whispers too low for Giselle to hear from her vantage point, but she understood that they were not happy words. When Charles again met Orion's gaze, there was nothing but disgust in his voice. "Also, in seeing the fervor with which Mrs. Silverman attempted to smear your poor girl's name, and taking into account the way her husband met his end, we also voted against her son. The Silverman pack has, of late, lost the confidence of the Council."

Orion looked again to the crowd. "And all of you feel this way?"

Voices slowly began to argue, some for, some against, but with no one really wanting to be the voice of the people.

"The Council can only deny a claim if the Alpha's position is under contestation. I have been named. I have been witnessed. I am Orion Silverman. Former Alpha of the Long Teeth, and as I have clearly returned, who dares to oppose me reclaiming my title?" Orion asked.

Giselle hoped that this would be it, seeing how many people were visibly agitated by his presence. Some even displayed fear at the challenge he posed.

Orion's presence was power, pure and simple. He was a true born Alpha and there could be no doubt of that fact. No hesitation. No quivering in his voice. He gave no indication of worry. Only Giselle knew the truth of how weak he had been. She hadn't felt a tingle or twitch echoed from his injuries for a while, though. Food had helped him regain his strength, and painkillers had covered the weakness in his limbs. But would that be enough?

Misha snorted. "Your claim to the title ended when you passed it to your brother. Rules are rules."

Orion nodded as if he'd expected her to say something like that.

Giselle's heart nearly stopped, knowing what was going to happen next.

"Shall I prove why I am the Alpha here? Do I need to enter this arena?" Orion glanced to the arena they'd erected. Blood clumped patches of the sand below. Two opponents stood, having shifted back to their human forms, panting and covered in a dripping layer of sweat. "I will gladly step inside to show these children what a true Alpha can do. But their blood will be on your hands, not mine."

Giselle looked to the two men, hardly children, in the arena. Easily both over six feet tall and skilled in the art of combat. She'd piss herself if she had to go in there and fight them. But Orion still looked as calm as ever. If anything, she could see his wolf peeking out from behind his eyes.

She reached out and took hold of Richard's arm. "You said you would be my champion."

Richard sighed. "I'm afraid Misha is correct. As the trials have already begun, he cannot just claim the title. He must join the trials. I cannot be his champion, nor can I now be yours. Only one member of the pack may join the fight."

Giselle choked on her words in panic to get them out fast enough. "I make the challenge. Not my father. Richard, please be my champion. Fight for me. Not Orion."

Orion turned on his daughter in anger. "You will not!"

"I can and I will. I was in line. It is my challenge to make." She feared for the life of her father more than his anger.

Richard, caught between the two Silvermans, looked as if he feared the retribution of both, but he chose his master as he took hold of Giselle's arm and started to drag her away. "Little wolf, you will not defy your father, especially not here in front of the Alphas."

"You don't understand," Giselle wailed as she was pulled against her will. "He can't..." She nearly let her secret out, but caught herself before it was too late. She could not reveal what had happened to wake her father, nor the fact he was not as strong as he pretended to be. Not even to Richard.

Orion turned away from his daughter and addressed the Alphas. "So be it, then. I do not take pleasure in the slaughter of innocent wolves. No disgrace will come to any who wish to withdraw their challenge." Orion tore off his shirt and walked to the arena gate, pulling it open before stepping inside.

Giselle buried her head into Richard's chest. "Why?" she sobbed.

Richard wrapped his arms around her. "It will be all right, little wolf. Have faith."

Jasmine had warned her the debt had not been paid. She'd warned her that her secret was not one to be shared – not on pain of retribution from the cosmos, but from her own kind. It was clear they would take any advantage they could, and a weak Alpha was more than reason enough to stack the odds against Orion.

The crowd collectively took a breath and Giselle, fearing the worst, pulled her head from Richard's chest long enough to see why.

Orion stepped up to the two men who'd already had their battle halted. "Which of you two am I to fight?"

Both men looked to each other, then cast glances to the crowd and back before answering.

The taller of the two, blond, held up his hands. "I concede."

The other, younger, bald-headed and tattooed, cracked his neck and dropped into a fighting stance. "I do not."

Orion stepped aside to let the blond pass him by, and as soon as the gate closed, he turned on the bald man. "We fight as wolves."

The bald man nodded and shifted down into a large gray wolf.

Orion followed, shifting down into his own dusty wolf.

Giselle had never felt pain in a shift, but when Orion shifted down into his wolf, a sudden spike, like an icepick through her chest, nearly stole her breath.

Richard was there to catch her as she crumpled to her knees.

"Are you all right?" Richard asked.

Giselle tried to catch her breath, but just as the pain subsided, she could feel teeth in her arm. She looked up to see the fight had begun.

"I'll be... *ouch!*... fine." If she'd had any doubts before about their link, it was plainly obvious now, though she couldn't let on to anyone else. "Just pulled a muscle."

Richard helped her to a seat near the arena, and to her dismay, he plopped her down right next to Vivian.

Panting through the pain as she felt teeth biting and claws raking her skin, she tried to focus on the fight, hoping that the wounds being inflicted on Orion were less than those to his opponent.

"You don't look too good." Vivian spoke cautiously.

"Just concerned for that poor wolf," Giselle said, summoning up all the strength she could to hold back the pain. She would not let Vivian get the upper hand with her again.

"You shouldn't be here." Vivian's tone was hard to decipher. With her arrogance gone, it almost sounded as if she cared, but that didn't seem right either. Self-serving as she'd been the entire time Giselle had known her, she doubted Vivian cared for anything aside from her children.

"Well, I am. And so is my father," Giselle replied, pain making her words harsher than she'd intended. Her eyes were locked on the battle in front of her. So much dust flying up in the air made it hard to see clearly, but the smell of blood caught in her nose.

The two wolves were a blur of motion, but the pain she felt needling every inch of her body said there was nothing poetic or beautiful about their dance.

"What did you do to wake him?" Vivian asked.

"Who said I did anything?" Giselle refused to allow her any more ammunition. She'd already run a perfectly good smear campaign with the information she'd had, and that had earned both Giselle and Ace a black mark on the Council.

Meanwhile, in the arena, a final yelp of pain signaled the end of the fight. When the dust settled, both wolves were lying on their sides. Giselle felt the wound – a nasty tearing sensation in her ribs that nearly took her breath away – but knowing they were linked, feeling the pain gave her hope that it was her father who was victorious.

"It's obvious, dear. You have a terrible poker face," Vivian laughed.

Giselle tried to ignore her, but she seemed to enjoy seeing any reaction, even if it was just faux disinterest.

The crowd waited for one of the two fallen wolves to move.

Giselle too. Her eyes locked on the dusty brown wolf that was her father.

His tail shifted. Just a fraction of an inch, it seemed, but it was enough to prove he was alive, and the winner.

Giselle breathed through the pain of what had to be broken ribs and looked up with a smile to Vivian.

If looks could kill! But thankfully, they couldn't; and though Vivian looked murderous, she would not dare touch her. Not with all these witnesses.

Orion slowly shifted and reached for his fallen clothes. He dressed and stood, lifting a victorious hand in the air. "Who denies me now?"

39

The crowd had hushed, no one daring to utter a peep after Orion had set the challenge.

In that moment, Giselle felt as if she were able to breathe. Orion's wounds were bad, though he didn't show it. Giselle felt their sting and did her best to hide the pain.

Those who weren't paying true attention to her might not have seen how she'd doubled over in pain during Orion's battle, but Vivian had been right next to her. No way had she missed it. A cursory glance sideways revealed the horrorstruck face of her devious aunt, though thankfully she hadn't opened her mouth yet to start another fight.

Lesson one: Never let them see your weakness. The words echoed in her mind, and Giselle gritted her teeth and forced herself to sit upright, despite the angry protest of her muscles.

"You need your mother." Richard bent over, and whispered in Giselle's ear, "I'm going to get Martina."

His words nearly sent her into a full-on panic attack. As much as she feared her father's fate, she knew she was as good as a dead girl when Martina was done with her. The list of things she'd done recently to break rules was a mile long. Had she not been a child, there was no doubt in her mind she'd have been exiled from her pack. But scared as she was of her adoptive mother's retribution, she had more worry being seated next to the woman who'd been key in the masterminding of this whole spectacle.

Her voice would betray the pain she felt, and that would reveal her weakness. Rather than allow Vivian the pleasure of confirming how bad she was, Giselle only nodded in response to Richard's question.

He backed away into the crowd and Giselle hugged her chest, pressing against her sore ribs as if needing to hold them in place. If she was this bad, how was her father?

In the arena, Orion stood as if waiting for the next challenger, while two of Nathaniel Thrace's sons dragged out the fallen wolf and wrapped his body.

"I'm waiting," Orion said boastfully. Small wounds on his body oozed blood, but no other indications of his injuries were apparent, not even in the way he carried himself: walking around the arena, tall and proud, meeting the eyes of the spectators as he passed them. He looked youthful, virile, and confident in his own power.

As an Alpha should. In his day, he had to have been one of the best. Pride flooded though Giselle, watching how comfortable her father was in that role. He had been meant for it. She had barely felt comfortable in her own skin, even after learning that it was okay to be a wolf. But Orion was wolf through and through.

Fallon and her mate Aiden stood, and from her vantage point, it looked to Giselle as if they were saluting him as he walked up to the seats where the Council of Alphas had been assigned.

"Well fought," Aiden said. "The Olde Town stands behind you, Orion Silverman." He took Fallon's hand in his own and she bowed her head respectfully, confirming her mate's words of praise and support.

Seeing the Boston wolves throwing their support behind Orion had many in the crowd rising to their feet and cheering.

Hope blossomed within Giselle. Maybe this would end quickly. She doubted her father could handle another brawl. He might look okay, but she still felt as if she'd been hit by a truck.

Misha too stood in her place, hushing the crowd with a wave of her hand. "We need to clarify, Silverman – are you fighting for your claim, or your daughter's?"

"Does it matter? We are family," Orion stated.

His words must have struck a chord with Misha. By all appearances she looked pleased by what Orion had said, but like a predator who'd watched its prey come into view, the smile parting her lips had a hungry edge. Still, though, when she spoke, her voice was laced with saccharine and betrayed nothing obviously devious. "It does. The Silverman reign ended when we voted out both your daughter and Aeson Silverman in Council."

"I am Alpha by birth and lineage," Orion retorted.

"You *were* Alpha," Misha said pointedly. "Why was that again?"

Silence fell upon the crowd again. Her question, though leading, was valid, and even Giselle knew it had to be answered.

"Are you calling my leadership into question, or my personal life?" Orion asked.

"Are they not tied together?" Misha responded.

"I would ask the same of you – an Alpha with no rightful heir. Some might question your personal choices, though I do not. We do not control whom we love. What we do control is how we govern our people. And my record stands clean on that respect." Orion stared down at Misha, daring her with his eyes to continue her line of questioning.

"My ability to produce an heir is not on trial here." Misha's eyes quickly darted to her mate, Brianna, and back to Orion. "However, your leadership is. Abandoning your position does mar that perfect record of your Alphaship."

"Do you think the wise Alphas of the Council here have not seen through your weak attempts to discredit me and my family?" Orion's eyes narrowed as his lip curled into a sneer, revealing teeth still stained with blood of his fallen enemy. "What does that say of you as a leader that you resort to such childish tactics when something so important is at stake? You'd risk the lives of many a good wolf in trial by combat rather than allow a valid claim to be upheld?"

Charles rose to his feet, standing next to Misha. "There appears to be a grievance between the two of you, so let me be clear when I say that we take this matter quite seriously. We would never risk the lives our own on something frivolous."

"And yet, here you are," Orion shot back at him.

"Orion, you did abandon your post. There is no denying that. And because of this we cannot, in good conscious, uphold your claim. What if you chose to do it again?"

Charles' words struck a chord with the crowd, and murmurs of agreement rose up to meet their ears.

Anger bubbled within Giselle, seeing firsthand the deviousness this Council was capable of. And worse, the Council had revealed who the leaders opposing them were and how flimsy their reasons had been, but no one in the crowd appeared to grasp the concept. Orion had been forced to step down because he loved a witch. An Alpha is required to produce an heir – that much she remembered from the hundreds of little talks Richard had given her about wolf politics – and yet Misha had no heir and was allowed to keep her post. Fallon had said as much when she'd told her about why she had to choose to go wolf to be with Aiden. And with the facts staring them in the face, both Misha and Charles were working as hard as possible to discredit her father for stepping aside to follow the letter of the law and allow his brother, who had already had two male heirs, to take the lead.

Names like *deserter* and *renegade* were being flung from the crowd at Orion like rotten tomatoes.

"Can't they see that Misha and Charles are twisting things to make him look bad?" Giselle mumbled to herself.

Vivian, of all people, answered back: "The mob has no reason,"

"Since it's clear you mean to discredit me, I fight for Giselle Silverman, my daughter and rightful heir." Orion glanced over to Giselle. "Her claim is still valid by your rules, so I will be her champion."

She held her chest tightly as if it would spill open from the wounds, but as his gaze hit her, she sucked in a breath and rose to her full height to acknowledge him.

"So be it," Misha said. "You are named her champion." Sweet as ever, her tone had the bitter aftertaste of deceit. For someone who had not wanted Giselle to be part of this, hearing that Orion would be her champion lit Misha's eyes with something akin to pleasure.

The crowd was divided again among those who seemed to support Orion and others calling for his death in the arena.

Giselle watched Misha for a moment. She whispered something to her mate, Brianna. On the surface it looked as if they were excited to resume the fight, but once Misha's eyes returned to the arena and Orion, her smile turned dark.

Charles retook his seat on the opposite side of Misha. Her ally, Giselle made the mental note. The two of them had been against her, but she did not sense the same deviousness in his reasons. Charles struck her as being by the book.

Behind Misha, Fallon and Aiden were still standing, looking even more pleased to see Orion taking the role as champion for Giselle, but unlike Misha, their pleasure was genuine.

She knew beyond a shadow of a doubt they were firmly on her side. So who else in the Alpha Council had chosen sides?

Giselle studied the others. Tito looked bored where he sat in the stands. His wife too. Yanira held on to their youngest pup, her attention on the child rather than Orion or Giselle. When she'd spoken to the Lobos in Washington, they'd been keen to create an alliance by marriage. She doubted they had sided with Misha either.

That left the Canadian packs, their neighbors to the north, as the other voters: Leif and his mate, Nikita. In

Washington, Leif and Nikita had been neutral and had not voiced an active opinion. Watching them sit idly in their seats gave Giselle no indication of where their minds were.

Misha was the only one who had obviously opposed her. She had the look of a predator watching its prey slowly walk into a trap.

But why? What could she gain by this? Giselle wondered.

After speaking with Brianna and the other Alphas around her, Misha stood again and addressed the crowd. "We will break for ten minutes before the next battle." Misha turned her predatory gaze on Orion. "Go and clean yourself up. Speak with your daughter and confirm whether she actually wants you to fight for her. When last we spoke, the little werewolf had wished to follow in her father's footsteps and abdicate her claim to the title."

Misha's words had the crowd rumbling again with their dissension. She was playing a keen game, and Giselle hated seeing how the crowd ate up the sweet sound of her words like candy.

40

Martina came up behind Giselle, and before she said anything, Giselle felt claws in her right shoulder.

She'd expected her adoptive mother to be mad. She had deceived her. She had stolen her phone. She'd gotten away with it had been because she'd masterminded all this while Martina had been so busy trying to impress the Alphas. And the only reason she was not having her head bitten off that very moment was that her claim to being one of those Alphas was still in contention.

"Before you scream, I'm sorry," Giselle started to say as she turned to face her adoptive mother, but pain stole her breath before she could finish the sentence.

Mothers must be gifted with a keen sense to know the pain in their children without having to feel it. Martina's anger changed sharply into worry the moment she saw the strain in her daughter's face.

Giselle did the best she could to hide her pain and be the little Alpha she was expected to be.

"What did you do?" Martina knelt down and pulled Giselle into a hug.

Feeling as if her ribs might shatter, she breathed through the pain. "I can't say."

"Magic," Martina said knowingly. The realization of what that meant increased her fear.

"Yes," Giselle answered truthfully.

"How am I supposed to protect you from yourself?" Martina asked in frustration.

There was no answer to that, but one look at her father confirmed it was a Silverman trait.

Orion joined them, wiping the sweat from his brow.

Richard grabbed him a water to drink and another to wash the blood from his skin.

"You are?" Orion asked looking directly at Martina.

Martina stood and met him eye to eye, with the ferocity of a momma ready to fight for her pup. "I am the one who cares for your daughter."

Alpha as he was, Orion was not a mother. He might exude the power of leadership, but Martina was the deadlier creature at that moment.

Orion must have realized it. The smile that crossed his face wiped away the fierceness and replaced it with admiration. "You have my thanks for that, and I will forever be in your debt."

"I'll hold you to that. She's no easy charge to maintain," Martina laughed, relaxing her protective stance.

"She's a Silverman. I'd expect no less." Orion winked at Giselle, but once his eyes met hers the humor left him. "What happened to you, child?"

Before Giselle could answer, Vivian interrupted. "Your daughter, just like her father before her, has dabbled in dangerous magic."

"I've not yet dealt with you." Orion turned his anger on Vivian.

"Deal with me when you can, but deal with her first," Vivian said, with a nod toward Giselle.

"I'm fine." Giselle sucked in a breath and, mimicking her father's resolve, put on the best face she could and stood tall. "Besides, if you're here worrying about me, you can't deal with what's happening out there."

"I'll defeat any wolf stupid enough to challenge me," Orion said, too self-assured for his own good.

"But Misha won't make an open challenge," Giselle responded.

"Good girl. You were paying attention," Orion praised his daughter.

"What are you two talking about?" Martina asked, as if she'd been left out of a very important conversation.

"There was no reason for them to deny both my and Ace's claim to the position," Giselle answered her adoptive mother. "Even with Vivian's smear campaign."

Vivian opened her mouth, but Orion silenced her with a hand over her mouth. "You've spoken enough," he growled at her.

"Even with her badmouthing, there was no reason to pass Aeson up for the title. The Regional Alphas are attempting to control who is brought to power, and they don't want a Silverman in play," Orion said bluntly.

"Where is Ace?" Giselle asked, suddenly afraid he might have already been taken out of play.

Vivian mumbled something, and Orion removed his hand. "He's with the others awaiting their turn, behind the Council's seats."

"Why there?" Giselle asked.

"Those who are to fight are kept out of view, so they don't risk losing their nerve." Vivian's voice lacked all arrogance now. Fear had taken hold after hearing Giselle and Orion's suspicion.

"Can we get him out of there?" Orion asked Richard.

Richard looked up to the Alpha Council and back at Orion. "I will do my best."

"Go, then," Orion ordered. "His safety is paramount."

Richard bowed his way out and disappeared again into the crowd.

"What of *our* daughter?" Martina asked, placing her hands on Giselle's shoulders.

Giselle had not a care for her own life; her link with Orion had entwined their fates, and only his ability to stay alive mattered at that point.

"You are her guardian by law. I have no fear you will shirk that responsibility now," Orion said to Martina. "I will do my part to fight for her honor in the arena, while you keep watch over her here."

Misha's voice bellowed over the din of conversations going on around the arena. "It is time. Our next trial begins now."

"That was a short ten minutes." Orion dumped half his bottle of water on his head and drank the rest before turning to go back.

"What do you want me to do?" Vivian asked.

"Nothing," Orion said. "You've done more than enough."

Unable to stop him or tell anyone why, Giselle whimpered helplessly as he strolled back toward the gate of the arena. Even if she could tell him, he was a Silverman. Stubbornness was in their genes. He'd still fight as long as there was a sliver of a chance he'd win. Giselle braced herself as her father walked back into the arena. If he had any fear at all, it didn't show. That he could hide; but his pain was still there. Ribs had begun to heal, and the ache had lessened significantly. His neck had been tweaked; Giselle felt it as she turned her head left – a pinch that almost forced her to avoid that direction entirely. It could pose a problem if a wolf attacked from that side.

Before she could let that fear sink in, another challenger presented himself – a deceptively thin male who had to have stood nearly six feet tall. He stepped freely into the arena to the sound of cheers, clearly a favorite despite his lanky stature.

Giselle, Martina, and Vivian all retook their seats with the rest of the crowd.

The crowd roared for blood, only falling silent when the cage door closed and both wolves had shifted.

Snarls and teeth and more dust. All battles looked the same, with wolves both dark and light going head to head.

The long tan wolf swiped a claw, connecting with the darker brown of Orion, and Giselle's head tilted sideways with the blow.

From the corner of her eye, she saw Vivian gasp at her reaction to Orion's wound. She might have been able to hide it if Orion had been doing better in this battle.

"Whatever magic you used to bring him back, it will get you both killed," Vivian whispered under her breath.

"That should make you happy," Giselle responded in kind. She scanned the crowd again, searching for familiar faces. Jay she spotted immediately, though he was not in the same spot he'd been in last. It looked to her as if he were strategically seated. His vantage point placed him in direct line of sight of his mother as well as the Alphas at the end of the arena. Whether it was for Vivian's benefit or his brother's, she didn't know, but if he was able to see the Alphas, she was willing to bet he was trying to keep an eye on Ace behind them.

Asher, however, was nowhere to be found, and neither were her sisters. For that matter, Gavin and Christina were out of view too. "Where is our family?" Giselle whispered to Martina.

"We were given special seats there." Martina pointed to a place just next to where the Council were sitting. The arena and all of its dust as the two wolves battled made it nearly impossible to see them.

If they were in danger, she would have no way to reach her family. A knot formed in Giselle's throat. Their only saving grace was Fallon. Giselle knew her new friend was not part of any plot. She, Giselle trusted. But as she looked at Fallon and her mate, she noticed another wolf was missing – Brady.

He should have been with his brother. Where had he gone and why?

The uncertainty of everything turned her anxiety up to eleven, and there was nothing she could do to bring it back down.

Dust kicked up in the arena as the two wolves had begun to circle each other, but it wasn't until a sharp pain in her leg snatched her attention that she dared to look and see what was happening.

The crowd was cheering at the snarling and growling, but neither wolf had really connected their attack until the tan wolf lunged low, snapping at Orion's tail, and Giselle shot upwards from her seat with a yelp.

She didn't want to watch. It was bad enough that she'd feel every wound, but knowing how much hinged on these fights made it that much worse.

"Are you okay?" Martina asked, with all the care and concern of a mother. She might have been annoyed by what Giselle had done, but in that moment, it didn't matter.

"I don't know," Giselle answered honestly. Her hand moved instinctively to the pouch around her neck. The small stone that seemed so insignificant the first time she'd laid eyes on it had quickly become the most important thing in her life. Keeping the title of Alpha didn't matter to her as much as it mattered to her father, but his life was tied to it all, and that was what was at stake.

"I didn't not want this," Vivian said to Giselle, not looking in her direction. "I never wanted it to come to this. You need to know this."

Giselle rolled her eyes, but didn't respond. Vivian was a snake. She'd shown her hand early on. No amount of kind words would change that now.

A sharp pain in her side made Giselle yelp in her seat. She jumped up, feeling the bite, but this time not from teeth; she turned to find not another man standing behind her, knife at the ready, dripping with her blood.

41

Derek, the butler who'd served in Vivian's home and waited on the Council meeting in Washington, snarled, "For the Long Teeth," as he swung his blade at Giselle.

It all happened so fast, she could hardly make sense of it, but she jumped back, narrowly escaping wide swing of his knife. Another pain sent her knees buckling. Orion had been injured in the arena. A shrill yelp from a wolf confirmed it, but as she crumpled to the ground, there was no way for her to look back and see if he was all right.

Had she been alone, Derek might have overtaken her and plunged his knife straight into her chest, but Vivian and Martina had her covered, taking the bastard down before he could make another attempt.

"What is going on there?" Misha cried, as she called the trials to halt.

Vivian hauled up her butler and put his knife to his throat. "Who put you up to this?" She shouted angrily.

"Don't play games, Vivian. We know who it was," Martina sniped at her.

"Tell us," Vivian said, pressing the blade harder into his skin. A small cut opened and blood began to bubble at the knife's edge.

"Death," Derek said proudly.

Vivian gritted her teeth and looked as if she might slit his throat, but before she moved, Martina had the butler by the balls. She squeezed them tight, and the butler's eyes bulged as if they might pop from their sockets. A vein pulsed at his temple and his face all but turned purple under the strain.

"Talk. Or before your death comes, I will dismantle you piece by piece for messing with my child. Do you understand me?" Martina had never looked as scary as she did that moment.

"They'll do me worse," Derek whimpered, but his eyes revealed the truth before it escaped his lips. Nervous glances up to the Alpha Council seat all but pointed out the guilty parties.

"Oh, I highly doubt that," Martina said. She leaned in close and whispered something Giselle could not hear into Derek's ear.

Whatever it was, it worked. He broke down in tears and whispered a name in response: "Misha's mate, Brianna."

All three sets of eyes – Martina's, Vivian's, and Giselle's – looked toward the Alpha Council to the spot where Brianna had sat. But she was gone.

Panting and out of breath, Jay appeared at his mother's back as if he'd run top speed around the arena the moment the scuffle had started.

Before he could do or say anything else, Vivian whacked Derek in the head with the handle of the dagger and knocked him out. "We'll need his testimony later, but first, find Brianna."

Jay nodded and headed back into the crowd on the hunt.

"You think this proves your innocence?" Giselle asked Vivian, still trying to find the link between her and Misha.

"I know you think it so, but I am not your enemy. I am sworn to secrecy by the same magic that brought you into this world, or else I could explain more, but this you must know: I had nothing to do with what happened to your father." Vivian spoke truth. There was no hint of a lie there, but her half-truth still cloaked in mystery gave her no added trust.

"I ask again. What is happening over there?" Misha called out across the now-silent arena.

The crowd and the two wolves in the arena awaited the answer. All eyes were on Giselle, still crumpled on the ground.

"This man assaulted my daughter," Martina called up to the Alpha Council.

"Don't you mean Orion's daughter?" Misha corrected.

"Don't twist words with me when one of your henchman attacked my girl," Martina said.

"You would dare to accuse me?" Misha rose up to stand and addressed Martina directly.

Orion shifted back to his human form. "Who dared to attack my child?"

Martina looked to Vivian. "You want to prove yourself? Keep her safe while I deal with this."

"No," Giselle protested. Weak and bleeding, she did not want to be left in the hands of her enemy.

Vivian heaved a deep sigh. "It's all right. I am family, remember? If nothing else, trust in that."

Giselle turned away, not wanting to answer, and watched as her adoptive mother headed toward the Alpha Council.

"This paragon of the central territories has conspired against your family to disrupt the balance of power," Martina said as she walked. "And when we find her accomplice, they will both meet with my justice."

Orion exited the arena and began to follow in Martina's wake.

Martina continued, "Her assassin has named Brianna as the guilty party, but we all know that the word came down from you, Misha Noels."

"Accusations are easy. But will you put your life on the line to hold them up?" Misha looked as menacing as any Alpha, but Martina had the fierceness of a mother protecting her pup.

Orion looked just as murderous, and as the two of them walked, it became a race to see who would be first to strike.

"It's a fight you want, then?" Misha hardened her eyes, looking at Martina.

"I will cut you down where you stand," Martina said.

"Not before I do," Orion snarled.

"One to one fighting is our way. You may both bring your challenge, in turn, but not together." Misha looked as if she welcomed a fight.

She should have looked scared, with Martina and Orion both vying for the opportunity to cut her down. But their anger only added to the pleasure in Misha's eyes. And the fact Misha looked so confident was unnerving.

"Of course you know I cannot be asked to fight. I am a Regional Alpha, and should I fall, my absence would be noted. I name…"

"No naming. You are accused. You will stand in the arena and fight for your honor," Orion said.

"What do you know of honor?" Misha asked. "You who deserted your people for a witch."

"At least I don't conspire to kill children. Now come down off your high seat and fight, or I and Martina will both drag you down by your hair."

Misha heaved a sigh and looked to her fellow Alphas. "Will you allow this insult to my honor to stand?"

Charles immediately came to her aid, rising to his feet in support. "An Alpha cannot be called to fight."

"She is no Alpha – dishonoring herself by hiring someone to kill my daughter," Orion said. "An Alpha must be willing to spill blood if that is the sentence they pass on a lesser wolf. They do not cower behind the acts of others."

"Where is your proof that Misha Noels conspired to kill your child?" Charles asked.

Orion stopped in his tracks, but Martina continued to prowl ever closer to the Alpha Council seats, only stopping when she heard a woman struggling behind her. "I have the word of the would-be assassin."

"The word of a killer," Charles scoffed. "Is that what you expect me to believe over an Alpha of this Council?"

Jay pushed his way through the crowd with Brianna struggling in his grip. "Here's your proof."

Anger burned in Misha's eyes as she watched her mate being pulled up through the crowd.

Brianna had not the poise of an Alpha nor the strength to fight. She held her head in submission as Jay roughly walked her up front.

"Release her!" Misha demanded, and looked as if she might make a move to free her mate herself, but after that slight twitch of muscles, she remained where she stood.

Giselle pushed herself up to stand, fighting against the protests of her angry wound. "She was named by Derek as the one who ordered the attack on me. If Misha is innocent of this, then toss Brianna into the arena and let her prove her innocence through trial by combat."

"That is not our way," Misha snarled.

Her posturing only gave strength to Giselle's defiant tone. She met the eyes of her enemy, with her wolf begging to be called into the fight. "And cowardly attacking me when my back is turned is?"

Words chosen carefully had the most power, and though Giselle's words had been rashly thrown out in anger, they were scooped up by the surrounding crowd. Rumbles of anger toward Misha combined with outrage at someone attacking a pup began to rise up. And when they hit the ears of the Alphas, the anger in Misha's eyes faded into fear. Brianna would be sentenced to fight in the arena by the will of the packs, not the Alphas, and she knew it.

Brianna stood silent, her eyes darting between Giselle and her beloved Misha.

For the briefest of moments Giselle felt pity for her. Brianna didn't look like a formidable wolf; her posture alone screamed beta. She might have been guilty of the crime of ordering Giselle's death, but by all appearances, it had been done on the command of her love and leader.

"An Alpha must set an example. Fight for their honor. Or else they are not an Alpha worth following." Aiden rose and spoke to the crowd. "Someone must be held accountable. Either Misha or Brianna should face the arena."

Fallon nodded, and so did Tito from the southern territory.

Misha looked as if she'd been betrayed by her people. Shock widened her eyes so much that even her wolf peeking out from behind them cowered against the might of the packs' will. Slowly inching backwards as if to make an escape, she scooted from her seat, but Brady came up behind her like a ghost. He grabbed hold of her arms and forced her forward toward the arena.

"Make your choice. Either the woman you claim to love, or yourself. One of you will enter that arena." Brady, the great big teddy bear of a wolf, was anything but at that moment. A second son to be proud of, he had the strength of muscle and might working in his favor, and as he pushed Misha toward the arena, it was clear she was no match for him.

Misha looked back to Charles, as if he were supposed to help her, but the Alpha who'd been her ally sat back down and turned his head away.

Giselle found her strength, pressing her hand against the wound in her side to stem the flow of blood, and started to walk toward the arena herself.

Vivian tried to protest, but Giselle would not be stopped. She walked proudly toward her father and adoptive mother. She might be injured, but as her father had taught her, she'd not let anyone see. Exuding strength and determination, she walked, gritting her teeth against the pain while keeping her mouth a hard line and her eyes locked with deadly intent on Misha.

Misha screamed insults and tried to struggle free of Brady's grip, but he held her firm. Before he walked her to the arena, he stopped in front of Jay. Her verbal assault ended the moment she came face to face with Brianna.

The lesser wolf whimpered, "I'm sorry," and reached a shaking hand up to gently kiss the cheek of her love.

Anger broke into tears as Misha took hold of her mate's hand. She pulled it forward and held it to her beating heart. "You have nothing to be sorry for. I absolve you of my crimes." Misha looked to Brady, and her resolve came back for a fraction of an instant. "Let her go," Misha pleaded.

Brady's hard jaw tightened. "Only after justice has been done."

Misha gave one last squeeze to Brianna's hand before letting it drop.

Whether she had accepted her fate or not was uncertain. She might have held power, but it was gone the moment the packs unified against her and her mate. Even more telling, Misha put up little resistance, despite her struggling against Brady. How had she risen to power when she was clearly not a fighter?

Giselle was certain of Misha's weakness as she met Martina and Orion at the gate to the Arena. And the knowledge that this would not be a true battle gave her the strength she needed to end the fighting.

"Father," she said calmly, and took his hand. "Let Martina do this."

Orion looked angry at her for suggesting someone other than he finish this, but after the moment passed, he saw that her injuries had gone beyond the wound at her side. "Is this what you want?" he asked.

"It's what needs to happen." Giselle struggled to find the right words to explain why but came up short. "You and I cannot fight anymore battles." Her free hand rose to the soft pouch at her neck, and she clutched the stone inside. "I struck a bargain to bring you back. I do not regret it at all, but we both have to step aside and allow others to take the lead now."

The look on Orion's face shifted between confusion and understanding, and once he grasped the gravity of what she'd said, the stony mask of his Alpha took over.

"Martina is to be your champion, then," he said, with a heavy breath.

Giselle looked at Martina. "You have more cause than most to tear down this false Alpha, after all the trouble she's put us through."

Martina smiled at her. "You honor me with this gesture, but I know it won't be the end of all troubles."

"I have to keep life interesting," Giselle grinned. A small part of her wanted to ask if Martina was sure she could do this. Her father's life had been a risk she was forced to take because of his stubbornness, but Martina's was not. Of course, asking her that would have been an insult. And the look on her adoptive mother's face said quite clearly that she was ready for battle.

Momma wolf had her claws sharpened and ready as she entered the arena with Misha and prepared to fight.

Orion walked back to the seat with Giselle. "I won't ask, because I understand all too well how magical contracts work, but I will say this: I wish you had warned me before I went into the arena to begin with."

"Would it have really stopped you?" Giselle asked.

Orion did not justify her question with an answer, but his grin confirmed it without words. Silverman wolves were a special kind of stubborn.

Richard walked up, with Ace safely behind him. "We're all here, then?" Richard asked.

"I'm not really sure what's going on," Ace said, looking confused and in shock at what had gone down in the last few minutes. "Are you okay, Giselle?"

"I am now. That's all you need to know," she responded.

Ace looked past her to his mother, standing on the sidelines as if awaiting judgment. "And my mother?"

Orion cleared his throat. "We'll discuss her later. For now we need to stay here and keep our eyes open for any other trouble."

In the arena, Martina shifted down and stood before Misha, awaiting her opponent's shift.

Brady backed away but did not leave the arena. He nodded to the gate, and the wolf on guard shut it. "Will you not shift and fight?" Brady asked Misha.

The defeated Alpha turned back one last time to look at the Council of Alphas. No one stood for her. No one made a sound. Her eyes shifted to Jay holding Brianna by the arm. She too stood silent; her eyes, though, told a story of sadness and loss. For all her plotting and deception, she'd found no one to absolve her. She hung her head low, the final confirmation of her guilt.

"Your answer, please, Misha," Brady said again.

"Just do it," Misha whispered, as she closed her eyes, ready for death.

Martina struck quickly.

Giselle turned away, not wanting to see more bloodshed.

The crowds surrounding the arena, rather than cheer as they had done for previous battles, fell silent.

42

The only sound to pierce the quiet that had fallen in the arena was the soft crunch of feet in the desert sand as Martina donned her fallen clothes and walked slowly to the gate.

Orion patted her knee before standing to address the crowd. "Are we done with this spectacle?" he called out.

All eyes fell on the Alphas, waiting for one to deliver judgment. That had been Misha's responsibility, but in her absence, it appeared that no one wanted to be the voice on the Council.

Orion walked to the gate and opened it, allowing Martina to walk out, and took her place in the center.

"Who denies my family's claim now?"

Charles stood; he'd been the other dissenting member who'd swayed the vote. Giselle knew what he'd say, and she dreaded any continuation of useless bloodshed.

"*Your* claim is denied based on your abdication of the position, Orion," he started, and Giselle felt the anger rising up within her. "However, we will honor your family's claim to the title."

Giselle hadn't expected that, and if not for the wound at her side, she would have jumped up with joy upon hearing it.

Orion looked to Giselle. His expression hardened for the briefest of moments before he blinked and turned his eyes to Ace, who was standing beside her.

Giselle whispered to Ace, "You think you can handle it?"

Confusion spread across his face. "Don't you want to claim your right?"

If she rolled her eyes any harder, they'd have popped out and hit the dirt. "I'm not cut out for this. We both know it. I'm too wild." Giselle had said it from the beginning: the position demanded more of her than she was willing and able to give. And especially now, with her precarious tie to her father, she could afford no battles in the future that might put either of their lives on the line.

"You'd have made things interesting, that's for sure." Ace winked at her. "But as a Silverman, you deserve a place in our pack, should you ever want it."

She might not have known her cousin very long, but Giselle got the feeling he'd be a good leader. He'd do right by the territories and maybe even breathe some fresh air into all the stuffy wolf politics. "I'll remember that when you have me up on charges of mischief in the future," Giselle laughed.

"Already planning to test my leniency?" Ace glared at her menacingly, though it was no more intimidating than his smile.

"You know how I operate." Giselle winked.

"You're a Silverman, no doubt about that," Ace said.

Giselle nudged him forward. "Then get in there and claim your title."

Ace walked into the arena and joined Orion's side.

Vivian whispered, "Thank you," to Giselle, but she had no desire to acknowledge it. Vivian had done all she could to make Giselle look bad. For what reason, she could not begin to fathom, but the fact she'd done it had ruined her reputation forever. Her only saving grace was that she was family. For that reason alone, Giselle would not seek retribution.

Orion took Ace's hand and held it up. "I name Aeson, son of my brother David Silverman, former Alpha of the Long Teeth and holder of the Regency over the Pacific territories, as my rightful heir to the title. Will you all honor this choice?"

Giselle, along with every other wolf in attendance, looked to the Council of Alphas for their response.

Fallon met Giselle's eyes with sadness. She hated to disappoint her new friend, and hoped it wouldn't ruin the relationship they'd just begun. Besides, being free of the Regency meant she'd be able to travel, and might someday get to meet Alyssa and the vampires that Fallon was friends with.

Aiden stood and voiced his vote, confirming Aeson as Alpha.

The rest slowly came to agreement, standing in unison to proclaim him the new Alpha and end the trials.

43

"I am Aeson Silverman, eldest son of the Alpha David Silverman, and I claim the Pacific territories as my father did before me. If anyone would bring challenge to my right, let him do so now."

Silence answered his question as one by one, wolves in attendance took a knee, an awe-inspiring sight that brought tears to Giselle's eyes as she too bent a knee to her new Regional Alpha.

He had been bred for this. He had the knowledge and understanding of their ways, as well as the backing of the proud Silverman name to bolster his reign. There was no doubt in her mind she'd done the right thing in passing the role to her cousin.

She'd made out better in the deal, anyway.

Her father slowly exited the arena, allowing Ace his time in the spotlight, and came to stand next to Giselle.

"Don't think for a second that this is over," he laughed.

"For me it is." Giselle's chest relaxed as she breathed out the tension she hadn't realized she'd been holding onto. She stood, wincing a little with strain. She'd need to give herself time to heal completely, but at least she had that time.

"You're a Silverman. Part of a powerful family. You'll be an Alpha someday, of that I have no doubt, but even beyond that, you'll have a duty to act for your family's interest."

"I won't have to move north, will I?" Giselle asked.

"No. But you are like royalty. Even if you're not the king, you still have to put on a good face and play your part for the good of the family." Orion cast a sideways glance at her, as if expecting the fit she wanted to throw.

"Can't I just be a normal wolf?" Giselle whined.

"Nope. You're my little wolf." Orion hugged her a little too tight, and when she whimpered again, he released her quickly. "How much can you tell me about this?" He pointed to the small velvet pouch around her neck.

"Just that we appear to be linked. So I feel your pain," Giselle said.

"That could be problematic in ways you probably haven't considered yet," Orion said.

"Why?" Giselle asked nervously.

"Wolves are crafty. For example, someone wanted to take down the entire Silverman family. They placed spies in Vivian's home; they made sure to discredit you and Ace. Why is that, do you think?"

"They didn't want us in power," Giselle answered quickly.

"Because?" Orion asked.

"Well, we've been in power a long time," Giselle said hesitantly.

"Right, and they would have brought in new and un-tested leadership if they'd succeeded. Leaders that might be more malleable."

"So Misha could swoop in and take control?" Giselle offered.

"Our territory is too big to be held by one other Re-gional leader. And Misha was too obvious in her dissent against our family."

"Charles, then?" Giselle asked.

"No. I believe his reasons were true. He wasn't com-fortable with you as a leader. And his pack is too far away from our borders to benefit from encroaching on our territory."

"You think someone else was silently plotting against us, and let Misha take the fall?" Giselle asked.

"That's certainly what I aim to find out; but if our condition places both our lives on the line, I may have to enlist some help," Orion said

"Just when I was starting to relax," Giselle sighed.

"Nothing dangerous will happen right now. I doubt anyone would make a move here and now, but I don't want you to let your guard down. And I'll make sure someone keeps an eye on you when I'm gone."

"Gone? Where are you going?" Giselle's heart began to pound. "I just got you back."

"I'm just forewarning you. If there's a threat remain-ing out there to our family, I will ferret it out. And that will require some movement on my part."

"But what about Cassandra?" Giselle hoped the men-tion of his wife would snap him out of this crazy talk of leaving to hunt down rogue wolves.

Orion stood thoughtfully before responding. "I hope she'll come with me. Now that we can be together, I hope we can build a new family together."

As long as he doesn't go get anyone killed with all his traveling. She'd dreamt of coming home after school to her father and mother, telling them about her day over supper, and fighting with them over curfews and boys. Even now, those dreams seemed so far-fetched. She looked to Martina and the picture skewed a bit. She had a home now. A family. A mother and a father who loved and cared for her. Pretending after all this time that a nuclear family with her birth father was anything more than a dream was laughable. They were family in love and blood, but her ties of home and hearth would always be with Martina and Gavin.

She reached out and took hold of Martina's hand. "You don't have to worry about me, Father, I have the best protection money cannot buy – the love of a mother." She looked to her mother, knowing she was grounded for life for all she'd done over the last few weeks, but also confident in the fact that the bond of love they'd developed over the last year was solid. She was to Martina a daughter, blood or not. And now that she knew her blood relations, she felt the strength of her bond to Martina just as powerfully.

Tears welled in her mother's eyes as she looked to Giselle. "If I'd have known what I was getting into when I adopted you…" She sniffled. "I'd have done it a hundred times over."

Giselle's eyes stung with fresh tears too.

Martina sniffled again. "But don't for a second think that you're getting out of trouble for all of this." She waved a hand out at the arena. "Because let me tell you, sweetie, your ass is mine until your eighteenth birthday, and you will be working off all the trouble you've caused."

"Fair enough." Giselle attempted to look bashful and hide the smile creeping across her face.

"And while we're on the subject…" Martina's eyes narrowed. "Where is my phone?"

Giselle almost wished she were the Alpha now, under the gaze of the dangerous momma wolf. "Sorry."

Orion snickered. "I have no doubt you'll be in the best of care with Martina."

"Oh, she'll be lucky if she sees the light of day when I'm through with her," Martina responded.

"Good! We Silverman wolves need a firm hand." Orion met Giselle's eyes. "As for us, little wolf… I know you want us to be a family. And we will be. But part of being in a family is looking out for each other. I think you understand that concept well; I'm proof of that. But it also means looking out for the pack. And Aeson will need that at the start." His eyes darted quickly to Vivian and back. "There are too many question marks hanging around."

Giselle looked over her shoulder. Vivian stood like someone waiting for their turn at the gallows. No doubt she'd heard their suspicion. She'd been privy to their family talk. And still she said nothing. Guilty people often made excuses and were the first to offer explanations. As much as Giselle wanted to point a finger at her, the signs weren't all there to back it up.

Orion cleared his throat, bringing her focus back to him. "Are you going to be okay with that?"

"I have no choice." Giselle shrugged, acting as if it didn't bother her, when deep down her heart was breaking. She'd sacrificed everything to have her father around. She'd endured so much pain for him. And duty was to call him away before she could enjoy the spoils of her efforts.

"I won't endanger myself or you in my dealings. Richard has been my right hand since I was Alpha. He has served our family well as an enforcer, and he will be my right hand again."

Giselle opened her mouth to protest, but Orion continued. "And Jay, as the second son, must take his rightful place now as the pack enforcer too. He's quite capable, as you've seen. So please, do not worry for my safety. I'll come back to you."

His words had no effect on her mood, but she smiled anyway, as if he'd comforted her. "Okay, Father."

Orion winked. "You can't fool a Silverman, little wolf."

"Then don't ask me to," she responded.

On that they could agree, and Orion turned away with a sigh and headed toward the Alphas. His path took him straight past Jay, who held a crying Briana in his arms.

"What will happen to her?" Giselle asked, already knowing the answer.

Vivian rather than Martina responded. "She'll be questioned for information and then…"

"Tortured?" Giselle asked.

"No, dear. That is not our way. A wolf can smell a lie, remember?" Vivian's voice had regained some of its strength.

"But she'll die either way?" Giselle turned to face Vivian, still uncertain about what she should feel for the old wolf. She'd gotten her way – Ace was the Alpha – but at what cost? Had she been in on the conspiracy from the start, or merely a pawn? A wolf could smell a lie, but Vivian bathed in so much perfume it was hard to pick out a single scent among the others burning her nostrils.

"She conspired to assassinate a member of the Silverman family, and one in line for the Alphaship." Vivian all but shrugged with the deadpan delivery of that sentence.

"But Misha already paid for that with her life, didn't she?" Giselle asked.

"Misha paid for her *own* crimes. Brianna had a choice. She made the wrong one."

The reality of wolf law had never been laid at her feet so bluntly before, but for the moment, Giselle understood the rigidity of it.

"And your crimes?" Giselle asked, spearing Vivian with a questioning gaze.

"Your life came at a price. There were many people involved in your birth, as well as your years of being hidden from our world. Magical contracts affect each person they are tied to. Some of the others involved in your birth broke the contract, and they paid the price. But those who were involved in protecting your true identity remained strong in their promise for as long as it was applicable. Your whereabouts were a closely guarded secret to protect you from enemies who might seek to use or abuse a child born of magic."

Her revelation shocked Giselle. She understood the tale from her mother and father's point of view, but that only went as far as the point she'd been lost to the system.

Vivian sighed, as if she worried about the effects of what she was revealing. "Did you know that before I married David Silverman, my maiden name was Rich-ards?"

Giselle nearly choked on her breath.

"You couldn't be raised by family, of course. It would be the first place anyone looked. But have you ever wondered why your true nature was swept under the carpet each time you were forced to move to a new home?"

Magic. Of course. She hadn't considered that at all. Usually when she was dumped back into the system, she was in such a deep state of depression she hardly paid attention to what was happening.

"The truth about who you were was never supposed to be revealed. But when you were transferred to Las Vegas, everyone involved in keeping you safe lost the ability to cloak you. The truth of a child born of magic and wolf would have all manner of enemies lining up. That's why I had to fight so hard to discredit you. You couldn't come to power. You had to remain on the fringes, where anonymity could be re-established."

There was no lie to smell. And the pain in her words confirmed it. This woman who'd worked so hard to make her life hell had been the one responsible for the hell that was her life. And Giselle wanted to be angry at her, for all the years of feeling unloved. All the years of feeling unwanted. All the years of being a freak.

But it had been done to protect her.

"And now my secret is out." Giselle whispered the revelation, feeling the sudden need to look over her shoulder.

"Yes. But now you have a strong family backing you. Both here" – she nodded to Martina – "and in the north, with me and my boys."

"Good to know, I guess." Giselle struggled to find words. Her head was spinning from all the new information and new worries that came with it. She looked to Martina, as if her mother might have an answer or at least something to say to break up the silence now hanging between them.

Her mother squeezed her hand, a silent confirmation of strength; it was something, but not nearly as comforting as she'd hoped.

"I'm sorry if my words or deeds have added to your misery. Family comes first. That is the number one rule among our kind. We always protect our own. In the best way we can," Vivian said. "I did what I could. I failed. I can only hope you're in a position now to deflect any new dangers that might come from the knowledge of who you truly are."

What could Giselle say to that? Part of her wanted to claw the woman's eyes out for ruining her childhood, while the other part of her wondered how much worse it might have been had Vivian not done what she did to keep her secret.

"Is it safe for me to go find my sisters?" Giselle asked Martina. "I'm a little in over my head with all this."

Martina looked as if she wanted to say no, but then sighed and nodded. "Go now. But when we get home, it will be a whole new world for you. Understand?"

"I know. I know. Grounded for life."

"And for your own protection," Martina added, as Giselle walked away.

44

"You okay, girl?" Taylor found her before she had even taken three steps. Instantly putting an arm around Giselle's shoulders, she walked in step with her toward the seats where the others were. "I don't even know where to begin. What did you do to bring back your dad? Wait. Don't answer that… magical contract, right? How's your side? Are you still bleeding?"

Wolfy healing had scabbed her wound over already, and though it still ached, she knew she'd heal from it with no complications. "I'm fine. I just need some…" Words escaped her. So much drama had been set in her lap over the last few months, and now learning the truth of why she'd been raised a loner had her head spinning. "I need to be a teenager for a minute."

Taylor laughed. "What?"

"I need some drama-free, act-my-age time."

"I don't get it." Her sister shrugged.

"Take my mind off of things. Tell me about your outfit. Have you seen any cute boys? What's the latest gossip?"

"That bad, huh?" Taylor faux-pouted. "You poor thing. Okay, so Di is mega-crushing on Jay right about now. She saw him..." Taylor trailed off seeing Giselle wince at the mention of Jay.

Who was about to have Brianna put to death.

"Okay, so, Asher was asking about you." Taylor changed the subject as they came into view of the big bad wolf himself.

"You're really not good at this, are you?" Giselle tried to laugh through the tears brimming in her eyes.

"Hard to not talk about wolf stuff when we're surrounded by them."

She couldn't argue with that logic, though she desperately needed to think of anything but wolves and politics.

Di jumped up the minute she saw Giselle, but as she opened her mouth to speak, Taylor silenced her with a look.

"I'm cool. I just wanted to hang with my sisters... oh, and Ash. Hey, buddy." She nodded to him.

He popped up from his seat and offered it to Giselle. "Glad it's over?"

It was anything but over for Giselle, but she smiled at his attempt to make small talk. "So I guess that means back to school tomorrow. Harper is going to seem like a pussycat after all this mess." She attempted a laugh.

Asher joined her with a chuckle. "I don't know. He's one tough old guy. My advice? Lie low and get your work in on time."

"At least now I should have time to do it. Silver linings and all."

Di chewed her lips, looking as if she were bursting with questions, but either knew better than to ask or couldn't decide which she should ask first.

Giselle met her eyes. "I'll tell you everything. Just not today. Not here. Can we just enjoy the peace for the rest of tonight? Make stupid jokes. Small talk. Sneak a beer when no one is looking?"

That got a rise out of Di. "Don't you dare! You're already in deep shit with Martina."

"Oh, I know." Giselle genuinely laughed that time. "Martina owns me... like until I graduate college."

"If she lets you out of her sight long enough to go to college. I'll be surprised if she doesn't homeschool your ass starting tomorrow." Di's words had a serious tone that made Giselle wonder if Martina might actually try.

"Speaking of being let out of someone's sight..." Fallon stepped down from her seat and joined them. "If you ever do get let out on good behavior, you have to come and visit me back east."

Giselle perked up, standing to greet her new Alpha friend. "Really?"

"Definitely." Fallon winked at her. "When you get off the leash. And If Alyssa is back, you can meet her and the Peregrinus clan too."

"For that, I'd do just about anything to earn my freedom." Already imagining her first face to face with a vampire had her smiling like an idiot.

"Though I have to say I'm sorry you didn't take your rightful place, I'm glad you made it through and brought your father with you. I'm sure there's a story there." Fallon looked as if she wanted details and Giselle would have loved nothing more than to recount her one success, bringing Dad back, but Jasmine's warning weighed heavy on her mind, especially now that she'd learned why she had been kept secret all this time. Giselle had no doubt in her trust of Fallon, the one wolf who'd led the fight to help her when all other members of the Council wanted to push her aside. They were kindred spirits, both being half wolf in their own right and both needing the magic of another to exist. But there were too many ears here, and her story was too important to be told so openly.

"Story for another day," Giselle said politely.

Fallon seemed to understand, though the disappointment showed clearly on her face. "When you come to Boston, then."

"That sounds fair!" she agreed

"Until then, I want you to know you have allies with me and my mate in Boston. If ever you need anything, don't hesitate to call on us." Fallon handed Giselle a card with her phone number scrawled across it. "I mean it. Anything."

Giselle took the card and threw her arms around Fallon in a great big hug. "Thank you," she whispered. "You don't even know how much this means to me."

Fallon pulled back from the hug and met Giselle's eyes. "Oh, I think I do." Behind Fallon, Brady appeared like a guard watching over his charge. "It's not easy being different. We girls have to stick together."

"I'm glad I've got you and the brothers in my corner," she said to Fallon, but nodded to Brady as well.

He cracked the smallest of smiles, but it was the wink that really confirmed it. If there had been any doubt at all in the true friendship of the Olde Town pack and its leaders, it melted away at that moment.

The road ahead should have been clear, after all the muck she'd trudged through in recent months, but life saw fit to place a few more potholes and puddles in her way the minute her boots hit dry land. Murphy's Law was her life, but at least she knew whom she could rely on as she attempted to walk down the path of uncertainty.

Her family, her pack, and her allies would be at the ready the next time shit hit the fan.

Other Books By Katie Salidas

The Chronicles of the Uprising
Dystopian thriller with a Paranormal Twist!

Book 1: Dissension

2015 RONE award Winner for best Paranormal

In the new world order, being supernatural is a crime.

Vampires once thought to be mythical, have been discovered, assimilated, and enslaved. Used for blood sport in the gladiatorial arena, their immortal lives are allowed to continue only for the entertainment of the human masses.

Book 2: Complication

The myth of Sanctuary was all that kept Mira strong during the endless years of slavery in the Iron Gate arena. When she finally finds it, the truth of what lay behind those well-protected borders threatens to destroy the last shred of her humanity.

Book 3: Revolution

Peace is an illusion. Blood, violence, and death follow Mira like shadows.

Battle lines have been drawn between human and Otherkin, and a bloody war is on the horizon: one that will end in either a shift in the world's balance of power...or ultimate destruction.

Book 4: Transition

Peace is just a breath between battles for Mira, and during this brief respite Mira is gifted one of her greatest weapons. If she can use this to her advantage, she'll have a new ally in the next battle to come.

Book 5: Retribution

Former gladiator turned freedom fighter, Mira has carved a trail from New Haven to Caldera Grove and back, freeing her people, the vampires, from enslavement by the humans. But with victory almost within reach, a new and powerful enemy emerges. One who'll be satisfied with nothing less than complete subjugation--or destruction--of all supernatural beings.

Book 6: Annihilation

2017 RONE award Finalist

Still clinging rabidly to power, the Elites spin lies of prejudice and hatred, stoking the flames of war between humanity and otherkin. Mira, had sacrificed everything. But it will take

more than even she can give to end this war or face annihilation.

The Immortalis Series

"Becoming a vampire is easy. Living with the condition, that's the hard part."

Book 1: Carpe Noctem

Bloodlust, fanatical vampire hunters, thousand-year old vendettas, and a pair of sharp, new fangs. Newly-turned vampire, Alyssa got a lot more than she bargained for when Lysander gave her the dark gift of immortality.

Book 2: Hunters & Prey

Rule number one: humans and vampires don't co-exist. One is the hunter and one is the prey. Simple, right? Not for newly-turned vampire Alyssa.

Book 3: Pandora's Box

When the box is opened, the sinister creature within is released, and only supernatural blood will satiate its thirst. Alyssa and the Peregrinus clan soon learns how it feels when the hunter becomes the hunted.

If you like Shifters

Both the Olde Town Pack (Adult) and the Little Werewolf (Young Adult) series belong in the Immortalis Series world.

The Olde Town Pack
Book 1: Moonlight

Good girls don't wear fur, fight over men, or run around naked, howling at the moon. Good thing no-one ever called Fallon a good girl.

Book 2: Mated

All the man-candy you can take, with none of the calories, because this one's off limits. The ultimate forbidden fruit. Confirmed bachelor, serial womanizer, and self-proclaimed sex god.

Boyfriend or mate... No way! He'd never let a woman tie him down... like that.

But Rachel Marsden might give him a reason to change his ways.

Book 3: Being Alpha

Newly minted Regional Alpha, Aeson Silverman hit the jackpot. Power, prestige, and wealth, he's got everything a wolf-shifter could ask for.

Except love.

About the Author

Katie Salidas is a best-selling author known for her unique genre-blending style.

Host of the Indie Youtube Talkshow, Spilling Ink, nerd, Doctor Who fangirl, Las Vegas Native, and SuperMom to three awesome kids, Katie gives new meaning to the term sleep-deprived.

Since 2010 she's penned four bestselling book series: the Immortalis, Olde Town Pack, Little Werewolf, and the RONE award-winning Chronicles of the Uprising. And as her not-so-secret alter ego, Rozlyn Sparks, she is a USA Today bestselling author of romance with a naughty side.

Facebook
http://www.facebook.com/pages/Katie-Salidas-Author/214780936916

Web
http://www.katiesalidas.com/

Twitter
http://twitter.com/QuixoticKatie

Email
KatieSalidas@gmail.com

SpillingInk
https://www.youtube.com/c/spillinginkshow

Join the Paranormal Posse
Readers and get exclusive updates and connect directly with Katie Salidas!
https://www.facebook.com/groups/ParanormalPosse/

Please Review

Your opinion matters! When people first look at a book, beyond the description and the cover, they pay close attention to what others **like you** have to say.

If the book is getting overwhelmingly good or bad reviews, it can weigh heavily on that readers decision whether or not to click that purchase button.

It does not have to be a book report.
It does not have to be 5 stars. *I would never ask for any special favoritism.*

A book review is simply sharing what you thought of the book. It answers two very simple questions:

Did you like it?
Would you recommend it to someone else?

That's it. Your opinion matters. Most importantly to me, because I want to ensure you are enjoying the books I write. But beyond my hope for your satisfaction, the review you write caries great weight in the publishing realm as well. It can quite literally make or break a book.

So, here I am, groveling at your feet.
If you have read one (or more) of my books, would you do me the greatest of honors and leave a review?

Want some FREE reads?
Join the VIP Reader Group!
http://www.katiesalidas.com/p/newsletter.html